*Kar*

A N

*Document of Flames*

# Kannani

AND

# Document of Flames

TWO JAPANESE COLONIAL NOVELS

Yuasa Katsuei

*translated and with an introduction and*

*critical afterword by Mark Driscoll*

Duke University Press   Durham and London

2005

Printed in the United States of America on

acid-free paper ⊗

Designed by CH Westmoreland

Typeset in Scala by Tseng Information

Systems, Inc.

Library of Congress Cataloging-in-

Publication Data appear on

the last printed page of this book.

*Kannani* was originally published in 1934.

*Document of Flames* was originally

published in 1935.

Supported by the Japan Foundation

2nd printing, 2007

In memory

of my own "Kakashama"

Ann Theresa Sullivan Driscoll

(1929–2001)

# Contents

# Acknowledgments

I have come to think of translation in ways similar to Sigmund Freud's rendering of heterosexual sex: although it appears that there are only two people involved, there are actually doubles and sometimes triples of each person. So I want to be perfectly "straight" and Freudian about the translations here; even though it might seem as if it's only me coupled erotically with Yuasa Katsuei's texts, there were always several people in the room Among those people were Tôyama Sakura, who helped me dash through the first three chapters of *Document of Flames* over the winter holiday break of 1998; Douglas Lanam, one of my Ph.D. students at UC Berkeley in 1999, who provided a rough draft of chapters 4 and 5 of *Kannani*; and Nagano Fumika, who helped me transform chapters 1 and 2 of *Document of Flames* in Tokyo in November 2003. More ghostly still was the input from an anonymous reviewer at Cornell University Press in 2000, who clarified two passages in *Document of Flames* that had resisted interpretation from non-Japanese scholars of Japanese literature and several native speakers of Japanese. Many other people helped out less formally, including Kim Taejun at Kimi Ryokan, Professor Nakagawa Shigemi of Ritsumeikan University, and countless others who were queried at lunch or in the lounges at the National Diet Library in Tokyo.

The introduction benefited from my participation in study groups on Japanese imperialism in Tokyo in 1996 at Waseda University and in 2003 on Overcoming Modernity and Japanese Colonialism, organized by Professor Yonetani Masafumi at Tokyo Foreign Language University. While a visiting professor at the University of Michigan in 1998–1999 I had the chance to introduce Yuasa and read *Document* in Japanese with an energetic and fun group of Ph.D. students there, including Jan Anderson, Alex Bates, Ema Jitsukawa, Hoyt Long, Robert Rama, and Shawn Walker. The next year, while a visiting professor at UC Berkeley, I read through and discussed parts of *Kannani* in a graduate seminar on Japanese imperialism with Douglas Lanam and Odagiri Takushi. The final form of the introduction was conceived after discussions with Professor Ikeda Hiroshi in Kyoto in July 2002; an earlier version owed much to a team-taught course on Colonialism and Culture with the fabulous Nakahara Michiko at Waseda University in winter 2000.

The conclusion benefited from comments and criticisms received after presentations at Duke University, Waseda University, the University of Calgary, and the University of Alberta. It also was enhanced by conversations with my Duke University–University of North Carolina colleagues, arguably the best group of junior scholars in Japanese studies in North America: Leo Ching, Christopher Nelson, and Tomiko Yoda. The form of the conclusion shifted dramatically over the past three years or so, and my reviewers for Duke University Press in 2002 inspired me to confront head-on the modes of exclusion specific to the power/knowledge regime of Japanese studies in North America. The resultant broad-based attack on modernization theory in the conclusion would have been impossible without the wise lessons I received, often stubbornly, from my main teachers in Japanese studies over the past decade: Brett de Bary, Harry Harootunian, Victor Koschmann, and Naoki Sakai. The whole manuscript was completely rewritten in Shibuya, Tokyo, thanks to a six-month fellowship grant from the Japan Foundation from July to December 2003. Special thanks go to Sharon Hayashi for being an energetic interlocutor during that stay in Japan.

Penultimately, I was fortunate that my readers at Duke University Press—Professors Michael Bourdaghs and Miriam Silverberg of UCLA—helped me realize the disciplinary and political importance of this project and were willing to go way beyond the standard interpellation of professional duty in offering translation suggestions and corrections, as well as crucial comments on the introduction and conclusion. Michael Bourdaghs is my new best friend; he read through both novels and, while consulting the Japanese original, offered on virtually every page sound suggestions for amendments, corrections, and deletions. I dare not imagine what the outcome of this project would have been without his ethical, superhuman commitment to it. Thanks also to Ken Wissoker and Courtney Berger at Duke University Press for magnanimous editorial support and to Kate Lothman for her work on the manuscript in its late stages.

Finally, my thanks go to Professor Ikeda Hiroshi, whose groundbreaking work on Yuasa provided the original stimulus for this project. Moreover, he graciously agreed to meet with me (but only after being assured of my leftist credentials when he heard that I had attended the counterglobalization protests against the annual G-8 meetings in Kananaskis, Alberta, the month before!) twice in Kyoto in July 2002 to discuss various aspects of the project and to facilitate the copyright issues with Yuasa's family.

Affectionate thanks go to the Nelsons: Lois for proofreading the novels before they were sent off to Duke University Press and Diane for being the most generous lover and *compañera* a work obsessed Japanese studies scholar could ever dream of.

This book is offered to the memory of my mother, Ann Theresa Sullivan Driscoll.

# Introduction

Yuasa Katsuei's 1940 novel *Aoi Chokori* (Blue jumper) begins with
a Japanese landscape painter named Masuda Miyoshi boarding a
railway car.[1] He is taking the imperial Japanese Manchuria Rail
Company (Mantetsu) line in the city of Dalian, China, which,
along with the whole of the Liaotung peninsula, has been under
Japanese lease and colonial control since 1905. Several of the other
passengers are Japanese soldiers worried about rumors of attacks
by Chinese *bazoku*, mounted bandits resisting Japan's imperial
takeover. The train moves through a large swath of Manchuria
in northeast China, also under Japanese occupation since 1932,
when it was renamed Manchukuo, or Manzhouguo in Chinese.
The destination of the trip is Beijing, which, like all the large cities
in China during the Japanese-Chinese War of 1937–1945, is under
Japanese military occupation.

Masuda strikes up a conversation with a sergeant sitting across
from him. One of over a million Japanese immigrants to Manchuria, the soldier tells Masuda how wonderful his little "development village" (*kaitakumura*) is in northern Manchuria.[2] Showing the painter photographs of his village, he confides that after
Japan eventually wins the war, "All I want to do is retire from
the army and go back there to work the fields" (6). As the soldier lapses into reveries of his "hometown," Masuda notices a
"Korean" and Japanese couple on the train arguing, and he remarks that this is surely proof of their "tough, passionate love"

(*araarashii aijō*).[3] These mixed marriages and the projection of harmonious progress achieved through the collective efforts of Japanese, Chinese, Russians, and Koreans in northern Manchuria are the celebratory signs of Pan-Asianism, depicted in this Japanese colonial discourse. However, as the train moves through development village after development village, Masuda brags internally, "This train is moving through fields that we Japanese developed ourselves" (6). Upon viewing for himself the impressive effects of Japan's development/invasion of northeast China, Masuda exclaims to the Japanese sergeant, "If one has power and force, there's nothing that can't be accomplished" (11).

Similar to the author himself, the novel's protagonist was raised from infancy in a well-to-do, ancient town thirty kilometers from Keijō (Seoul) in colonial Korea, called Suwon (but renamed Mizuhara in Japanese). Also like the author, at eighteen he went off to university in Tokyo.[4] At this point in the novel, he has just concluded a short visit with his family and is heading off to Beijing to meet two Japanese friends. They plan to enjoy the particular pleasures of imperial consumption available for Japanese men: Chinese sex workers, Chinese food (incomparably [*muteki*] delicious in Beijing), cheap liquor, and the exquisite landscape of the old Chinese capital, where he hopes to paint a portrait or two. After his two friends, Uchigawa and Takaura, greet him at the Beijing station, they leave immediately for a bar and a brothel, en route ogling all the "gorgeous women that you find here in Beijing." Takaura elaborates, "It's impossible to describe their sex appeal! When they massage your shoulders and massage your . . ." (27). While checking out with approval the Chinese women sex workers in their modern, European-style clothes, Masuda remembers his other "occupation" as professional painter and offers up more aestheticized images of Beijing: "The trees lined the wide roads impeccably. The fall here is truly amazing; Beijing seems like something out of this world [*yo no mono to ha chigau*]" (14). Uchigawa notices Masuda's surprise at how peaceful Beijing is and explains, "If you don't stray outside the metropolitan perimeter, you would never know that this city is under wartime occupation; it's as safe and sound as Tokyo" (19). Masuda seems incapable of maintaining his aestheticism at too ethereal a level, however, and his attention quickly shifts to two Chinese sex workers the men have chosen from a larger group. "As we waited for them here in the bedroom, their bodies looked as fresh as college students under the light of the lamp" (20).

The novel shuttles back and forth between Beijing, Seoul/Suwon, and Tokyo, where Masuda has an art studio. As it does so, the reader is introduced to Masuda's other friends from Korea and Tokyo, all of whom appear to mix equally well with Koreans and Japanese. Twenty-somethings, they seem clueless about the impending Pacific War, the intensification of the China War, and the total mobilization in Korea, Taiwan, and Japan that was needed to sustain the full-scale war in China. Their preoccupations appear to be centered on romance, tourism (sexual and otherwise), and transcendent notions of art and beauty. Accordingly, Masuda spends his time in Tokyo painting and deciding if he is in love with his "hometown" (remember, he was born and raised in colonial Korea) Japanese sweetheart Keiko or if he is developing a crush on a Korean woman named Kang Ǔn-sǒng who is in Japan. Kang is also from his Korean hometown but has moved to Tokyo with her brother to further her studies after graduating from an elite technical school for women in colonial Korea.

Back in Korea, as Keiko waits for Masuda to move back and propose, she and her friends live a life of colonial splendor. Colonized Korea and Seoul are captured by the same aestheticized language as occupied Beijing, as they go on hikes, hang out in cafés, and plan their vacations around the change of seasons in the entirety of Japan's empire. "Cuz we hate winter so much, when it gets cold here in north Korea, we'll go first to south Korea, then Kyūshū, then Taiwan, and finally to the South Pacific [Nanyō]. . . . Then when summer gets too hot there, we'll cool off in Hokkaido, Sakhalin, and Mongolia" (210–211). At some point, Kang returns to Korea but does not go to see any of her old friends (even though she tells Masuda that all her friends in Suwon and Seoul are Japanese [naichijin]; 198), apparently because she has become jealous of Keiko, Masuda's Japanese love interest. When her Japanese friends realize that Kang has returned to Korea without visiting them, rumors start to circulate that she and Masuda are involved romantically (enbun) in Tokyo.

When Masuda himself realizes that he is developing a crush on Kang, he invites her to Manchuria and Beijing for a holiday. But on the way there from Tokyo, Kang sees Keiko waiting for them at the Seoul station and assumes he has betrayed her by previously alerting Keiko. She panics and sneaks off the train without informing Masuda, and disappears into the darkness. She ends up near a brothel surrounded by soldiers (263–265). As the novel ends here, readers are left to wonder if this is the naturalized fate awaiting the colonized Korean woman: denying the Korean-Japanese love affair and dooming Kang to sexually serve Japanese men within the violent hierarchy of the "comfort" system of military-imposed sexual slavery.

Two years later, in 1942, Yuasa published a popular novel titled *Ōryokkō* (Yalu River). It appeared in ten monthly installments in the Manchukuo propaganda organ *Kaitaku* (Colonial development) and was issued as a book a year later in February 1943.[5] *Yalu River* is set in northern Korea at the border of Manchuria and narrates the successful construction of the famous dam and hydroelectric power facilities begun in 1934. After World War II, Japanese apologists frequently invoked this project and the nearby Suiho Dam, the second largest in the world at that time, to show how Japan's colonization of Korea and northeastern China contributed dramatically to economic development there.[6] These and other hydroelectric projects in northern Korea and Manchuria were designed to showcase Japanese agricultural and industrial development in Manchuria and to lure Japanese, colonized Korean, Okinawan, Taiwanese, and White Russian immigrants into the resource-rich area.[7] This development intensified after the Depression of 1929. Japan tried simultaneously to ease economic hardships in its countryside and in impoverished areas in the colonies and to populate Manchuria by encouraging Japanese-speaking settlements there (most colonized Koreans, Okinawans, and Taiwanese would have had some proficiency in Japanese).

Although Yuasa is the most well-known novelist of colonial daily life who wrote in Japanese, he is also considered the central figure of the *kaitakubungaku*, or "colonial 'development' literature."[8] The other representative texts of this genre include Wada Den's 1939 novel *Dainimukemura* (A Manchurian village turns toward imperial Japan) and Fukuda Seijin's 1940 novel *Nichirinheisha* (Sun on the military barracks). The genre of Japanese colonial development literature normally featured heroic Japanese settlers and soldiers developing Manchuria. Like most colonial-imperial settler discourse, these books tend to ignore that it was already a heavily populated area and that it was the home territory of the Manchu rulers of the Ch'ing Dynasty. Instead, they depict the area as "empty" and an "open frontier." At first glance, Yuasa's *Yalu River* seems to avoid this trap of pure colonial propaganda. In place of heroic Japanese, the novel is centered on *Korean* settlers in Manchuria, settlers that volunteer to assist with the construction of the huge dam and bridge project at Yalu River.

The main character's given name is Yang Tae-gi, but he has changed his name to the Japanese Ōyama Eiji; throughout the novel the references to him and his family are as Ōyama.[9] We find this out early on when a Korean woman whom Ōyama encounters at Yalu River notices another Korean wearing a Japanese army uniform and says to him, "Hey, that's Kang. Mr. Kang's here! Go take a look; isn't it him, Yang?" Ōyama answers peevishly, "Yeah, I saw him. But my name's not Yang. I officially changed it [*sōshi shite*] and I'm now Ōyama Eiji" (31). Soon to become his fiancée, the young Korean woman proceeds to address him for the rest of the novel as Ōyama

Like many colonized Korean and Japanese farming families, Ōyama's immigrated to Manchuria from the southern part of Korea in the late 1920s and Ōyama was raised there. The novel is spatially centered around these three topoi: the northern Manchuria development village Ōyama calls home; the huge development projects at Yalu River and the surrounding areas in northern Korea; and the small village in southern Korea where Ōyama was born and where parts of his extended family still reside. As Yuasa himself suggests in his afterword to the novel, these three spaces correspond to *temporal* coordinates on the developmental schema of Japanese colonial imperialism. The small southern Korean village corresponds with the early period of Japan's annexation of Korea in 1905; the deterritorialization of Manchuria by colonial-developmental villages links to the late 1920s–early 1930s; and the huge bridge and dam projects in northern Korea and Manchuria form the temporal coordinate for the *daitōakyōeiken* (Great East Asia Co-Prosperity Sphere), *kōminka*, and total mobilization of the late 1930s and early 1940s.[10] As Ōyama moves through these three space-time coordinates and eventually contributes to the successful construction of the Yalu River project, one quality works to link the three in a seamless colonial-imperial narrative: Ōyama's complete and absolute Japanization. The partly volitional *kaimei* (shift from Korean to Japanese names) represents only the beginning.[11] With the sole exception of a short scene featuring an interaction between Ōyama and an old Korean man from his family's hometown in southern Korea, Ōyama speaks exclusively Japanese with the many Korean characters in the novel. The elderly man he reminisces with about old times in southern Korea goes so far as to complain that the Korean language is used so infrequently by native Korean speakers these days that it has become difficult to understand (90). Moreover, Ōyama speaks Japanese even in private conversation with his mother and father in Manchuria, interspersed with the sole Korean word *adori* (son; 270).

This complete displacement and overcoding of the Korean language by Japanese establishes Ōyama as a perfect vehicle for imperialism. He functions as a mouthpiece for all the ideological program codes of Japan's colonial imperialism: the unification of Japan and Korea (*naisen ittai*), the superiority of Japanese spirit, impartiality and equal favor for all imperial subjects (*isshi dōjin*), the Great East Asia Co-Prosperity Sphere, and so on. Moreover, he is also physically guided and instructed by Japanese throughout the novel. After a scene of pure colonial mimesis where he parrots the phrases of a Japanese group leader (80–81), while he is in Manchuria and at the Yalu River construction project Ōyama is under the constant guidance of Japanese superiors. Although this subservience is clearly inscribed in the text, because of his absolute Japanization the direct leadership of Japanese is gratuitous. As he himself claims, "With the annexation of Korea by Japan in 1910 Koreans became Japanese, which was good for both Japan and Korea" (52). The Koreans in the novel are so thoroughly pacified and so noiselessly assimilated that there does not even seem to be any *unconscious* negativity toward Japan and the Japanese colonizers. Colonial ideologues everywhere could not have dreamed up a more effective scenario for control.

Taken as a whole, these novels from 1940 and 1943 appear to be the work of a writer completely faithful to and ventriloquizing colonial imperial ideology. In *Blue Jumper*, Yuasa Katsuei depicts a consumerist fantasy for colonizer males, where Chinese women and Japanese-occupied landscapes in Asia are emptied of history, stripped of any resistance to Japanese control and consumption, and offered up as reified commodities for imperial masculinity. The violent deterritorialization and imperial takeover of Manchuria by Japan's military-industrial machine is mystified by the aesthete colonizer Masuda Miyoshi as "development," and this same Masuda (with whom, it should be pointed out, all the Chinese, Japanese, and Korean women in the novel seem to be infatuated) is self-congratulating throughout the novel, stating twice in reference to Manchuria and Korea that "we Japanese developed this." In *Yalu River*, the mouthpiece for Japanese imperialism is a colonized Korean subject who insists on speaking exclusively in Japanese and who thinks and acts exactly like a nonrepentant Japanese colonizer. Insisting that Koreans are much better off having been forced to become Japanese, Ōyama Eiji functions as a clone for colonial imperialism and seems to offer no space for resistance to Japan's imperial project of cultural, territorial, and historical engineering.

## *Kannani* and *Document of Flames*

At first glance, the two novels translated here seem to provide a dramatically different account of Japan's colonial imperialism. The first, *Kannani*, won the special prize for a first novel from the left-wing magazine *Kaizō* (Reconstruction) in February 1934. Apparently too dangerous to publish in that journal, it appeared first in a greatly abridged version in the mainstream *Asahi Gurafu* (Asahi graph) entitled *Sesō* (Sign of the times) in April 1935 and a month later as a novella in the liberal journal *Bungaku Hyōron* (Literary review).[12] Even after significant revisions, the *Literary Review* version was full of Xs and Os marking sections too incendiary to publish. In a short parenthetical afterword, the editor of *Literary Review* acknowledged that the entire second half of the original had been "deleted" (*sakujo*). The editor explained: "*Kannani* is a work that the author left with us about six months ago, but we knew it was going to be difficult to publish in the form it was in then. Even in the poor shape it's in now, the whole novel has been weakened further by our editorial recommendation that the entire last section—that takes up the theme of the March 1st, 1919, demonstrations for Korean independence against Japanese colonial rule [*banzai jihen*]—be left out.[13] Because the author has informed us of his intention to rewrite this second half, I think readers will soon get another chance to lay eyes on the complete text."

"Even in the poor shape it's in now," the scene where the Japanese schoolboys rape the young Korean woman with a stick (chapter 5 in the English version here) was included with only two or three sentences expurgated. The discussion of the colonial classroom for Korean children (chapter 3 here) was censored slightly but still provided contemporary readers of Japanese with a rare fictional sketch of the scene of colonial education and assimilation (*dōka*).

The highly censored *Literary Review* version enjoyed a considerable circulation in Japan. The translation of *Kannani* here is about three times as long as that version, as I worked from a post–World War II novel that Yuasa restored from his notes when he was repatriated to Japan in September 1945 with his family, after thirty years of living in Korea. The reader will notice a number of cuts in the English translation. Even in the restored version a great deal of material was excised, this time not owing to censorship restrictions but because Yuasa could not remember what was in the original; the full version was lost years before. In offering to English-language readers what Yuasa felt to be closest to his original version of *Kannani* I wanted to demonstrate some of the textual production of a liberal—not communist or radical—critic of Japanese colonialism.[14] The parts that were censored in the 1934 and 1935 original included the section in chapter 10 referencing U.S. President Woodrow Wilson's insistence on self-determination for all peoples in his Fourteen Points, promulgated at the opening of the League of Nations.[15] Not only had Japan withdrawn from the League in 1933 because of the dispute over its occupation of Manchuria, but the reference to the self-determination of Koreans would have been construed as an explicit attack on Japan's colonial domination of Korea. Nevertheless, lots of interesting things did make it into the versions published in 1934 and 1935.

*Kannani* stands alone among Japanese colonial literature in its rich, ethnographic depictions of the daily life of colonized Koreans.[16] The scene of the Korean marketplace in chapter 4 offers several realist, daily life sketches: eating different foods from small shacks in the open air with friends; the theatricality of Korean-style fighting; Koreans purchasing basic kitchenware. What to my mind is the most intriguing scene takes place in chapter 1, which describes several Korean children's games. Inherently interesting, this scene leads further to the twelve-year-old Japanese boy Ryūji desiring the same toys and the same kinds of clothes as his Korean neighbors. Although assimilation (dōka) is almost always configured as unidirectional, where the colonized is expected to become *like* or *mimic* the colonizer, the scene here inverts this model. In what must have logically occurred time and time again, given the historical fact that a minority Japanese colonizer population lived among a vast majority of Korean, Chinese, and Taiwanese colonized, the Japanese child Ryūji attempts to mimic the Koreans. In desiring what the Korean children desire, Ryūji wishes to become Korean.

Clearly, this is in part the desire or investment of *Kannani* as a novel. Accordingly, readers are offered evocative scenes of Korean and Japanese children interacting in ways the novel wants to represent as natural and happening before the corrupt ideology of ethnic superiority (Japanese over Korean) had completely overwritten this natural purity. In this case, the genre determination of *Kannani* (liberal melodrama) insists that an innocent, nonracist humanity preexists the ethnoracial hierarchies imposed by any particular society. The subsequent imposition and reversal of this childlike innocence by adult colonial ideology leads to the tragic death of the young Korean woman Kannani and the obliteration of youthful innocence. But the anticolonial message of *Kannani* rings clear: Let's all try to follow the lead of these children and transcend ethnoracial discrimination, leaving behind what Freud called the "narcissism of minor differences."

Nevertheless, despite the depiction of innocent, youthful humanity, the novel does not shy away from depicting the antagonism that must have existed just as ubiquitously alongside its innocent counterpart.[17] The traces of sexual violence that remain in the censored version of the rape scene and the incessant taunting of Kannani and Ryūji's first love are just two examples of the youthful violence that was often the flip side of childish innocence in the sites of colonial domination. Moreover, *Kannani* offers several scenes in which the abject poverty of the colonized Koreans is represented in its immediacy. The most salient example of this is when the young Korean children drown trying to retrieve melons lost in the seasonal floods that uprooted many impoverished Korean homes. Upon witnessing this at a riverbank, Ryūji is dumbfounded as to why anyone would risk his or her life for what seems to him to be a fairly tasteless fruit. Gradually, he comes to realize that eating the sweet melon temporarily mollified the brutal hunger and hopelessness of colonized Koreans.

Finally, *Kannani* also acutely depicts the life of new Japanese immigrants to colonial Korea. The novel tells us how much easier it was for uneducated Japanese men like Ryūji's father, Matabe, to become upwardly mobile in Korea, where he relocates to join the burgeoning ranks of the Japanese colonial police.[18] It also communicates through its formal realism how terrifyingly uncertain the move to Korea must have been for peasant and working-class Japanese families.

*Homura no Kiroku* (Document of flames), the second Yuasa novel translated here, thematizes the issue of class even more explicitly and refracts it through a feminist lens. Nuiko and her mother, Tokiko, are displaced from their home in southern Japan to colonial Korea; the move to the colonies is represented as the only option left them. Here Yuasa sketches in bold the situation of desperate Japanese women, victimized by Japanese patriarchy at home and by the sexism of commodity capitalism in Korea.

*Document of Flames* was published in *Kaizō* in April 1935 as it appears here, also suffering from cuts and ellipses.[19] Unlike his work on *Kannani*, Yuasa did not rewrite the novel after repatriating to Japan in 1945, and this is the only known version of it. Some of the sections in the Japanese text, especially the description of the underground left-wing political group in chapter 9, are so chopped up by deletions that they are difficult to read. I might beg the reader's forgiveness here by interjecting that this condition made them doubly difficult to translate. It is not known whether the author, publisher, or Japanese government officials censored the expurgated sections. However, because *Kaizō* was a well-known leftist monthly, the probability is that its editorial staff made the deletions directly from Yuasa's manuscript.[20] Nevertheless, the fact that *Document of Flames* was published at all should make scholars and students of Japan pause before reading the fascism of 1940 and 1941 back into the period before 1936, clearly a less chilly time for publishing works that were critical of Japan's imperialism.

The novel begins in a small town in Kyūshū, Japan, where a woman named Tokiko has adopted a child, Nuiko. Unable to conceive herself, her husband becomes increasingly angry at this assumed failure of femininity and eventually arranges to have a sex worker move into the house to live and sleep with him. Tokiko openly resists this, and after several instances of domestic violence she leaves the house and is immediately divorced by him. Several weeks later, she returns in disguise to rescue Nuiko. Having returned to her family home in the interim, Tokiko was confronted by the patriarchal gender bias saturating the legal and cultural rights of divorced and single women in Japan at the time. She contemplates suicide, but decides to give existence one last shot, concluding that the only future for a divorced woman with an adopted daughter lies in the colonies.

Beginning with an explicit critique of the gender ideology of Japan in the early twentieth century, *Document of Flames* extends that critique as mother and daughter arrive in colonial Korea sometime in the 1910s. After a brief honeymoon period hustling brown rice bread in Pusan—where sales are driven by Tokiko's attractiveness as a single Japanese woman in her twenties roaming the streets of the colonial city—their first Korean winter finds them surviving mainly thanks to the kindness of various Korean neighbors. They are forced to give up bread selling the next year as Tokiko finds a job as a longshoreman, working alongside Japanese and Korean men. It gradually becomes clear that she is supplementing her income by occasional sex work. Tokiko finds herself enmeshed in Japan's colonial discourse and commodity capitalism wherein Japanese women were eroticized as the paragons of "Eastern beauty," allowing her to extricate herself from one form of wage labor exploitation only to find herself disempowered by a different form of gender and labor oppression.

Moving from town to town as an itinerant sex worker, Tokiko

gains a small degree of autonomy, enough to be able to refuse most forms of physical contact with men. Eventually settling in a beautiful, ancient town twenty-five miles from Seoul named Suwon (where the author grew up), Tokiko gets romantically involved with a powerful and corrupt Japanese landlord. After he dies suddenly, she inherits his huge estate. Tokiko slowly develops the farms and forests into a huge export business and is able to send Nuiko to a boarding school for women, where she is groomed into a bourgeois colonizer young lady. During school vacations Nuiko starts to function almost as a geisha and courtesan for her mother, who orders her to wear beautiful kimono and lavish makeup around the house and to play traditional Japanese music for her. The daughter is slowly transformed into the female entertainer that her mother had been when she met the man who willed the property to her. When Tokiko eventually comes on to her daughter sexually after a night out drinking, the morality of the novel codes this lesbian encounter as the logical outcome of the mother's masculinization, a process that is described as a physically cellular one. Through her work on the farm overseeing the Korean workers and developing and exploiting her Korean laborers and land, Tokiko comes to smell, sound, and desire like a straight man.

When it becomes clear that Tokiko is paying for the sexual services of a Korean gigolo, the inversion of the natural that the novel assumes (homophobically, in the scene where Tokiko initiates an erotic encounter with her daughter) to follow logically from colonial domination comes full circle. As it was in *Kannani*, colonialism is depicted in *Document of Flames* as a violent inversion of the organic state of political nature. Tokiko has now reversed the cycle of oppression installed by patriarchal power; the barren woman at the bottom rung of the social hierarchy in Japan has become a rich landowner and oppressor of colonized Koreans. The novel then assumes, in ways similar to those in *Kannani*, that the equally natural response to colonial domination is to overthrow this same order politically, and the last quarter of *Document of Flames* depicts with a surprising explicitness Nuiko's radical political awakening. Moreover, this section articulates yet another naturalized connection between the struggle against patriarchal capitalism in Japan and the struggle against colonial domination in Korea.

It is indisputable that both of these novels represent clear oppositional positions to various elements of Japan's colonial imperialism. However, it is important to point out that Yuasa Katsuei's adolescence was spent in Korea during a time when Japan's official colonial policy there shifted dramatically after the March 1, 1919, independence uprisings. This policy shift from the iron fist of military rule (*budan seiji*, 1905–1919) to the velvet glove of a more open, liberal policy of cultural politics (*bunka seiji*, 1919–1931) instituted by Saitō Makoto (and in a similar way by the civilian governor-general of colonial Taiwan, Den Kenjirō) granted colonized Koreans more political freedom and even allowed for limited critiques of the legitimacy of colonialism itself, critiques that were gaining more force inside Japan at this time as well.[21] Under the sign of what the historian of Japanese colonial imperialism Komagome Takeshi calls "neocolonialism" during the cultural politics period, Japan's colonial authorities actively encouraged interest in Korean history, language, and culture, as well as approving mixed marriages between Japanese and Koreans in the 1921 law.[22] In other words, the critique of the brutality of Japan's colonial domination during the 1910s featured in *Kannani* differed in degree but not in kind from the substance of official Japanese explanations given for the reforms of the cultural politics period. This period was so materially different from the military rule of the 1910s that many Korean intellectuals and political leaders assumed that it would lead eventually to decolonization.

## A Second-generation Japanese Growing Up in Korea

Yuasa Katsuei was born in Japan in February 1910; before his second birthday, his father moved to the colonies, bringing his son and wife there permanently four years later. He was raised and educated in Korea. His father worked for the Japanese colonial governor-general in a police position, very much like Ryūji's father in *Kannani*. In 1929 he went off to Tokyo to attend Waseda University and stayed there off and on for six years, usually returning to his family residence in Korea for summer holidays. After his first year at Waseda he became involved in proletarian literature circles in and around Tokyo, including one group whose members featured the prominent Korean writer Im Hwa. Im had also gone to Tokyo in 1929, where he quickly became a leader among Korean students there interested in proletarianism and radical modernism.[23] Yuasa's presence as a speaker of conversational Korean must have intrigued the Korean writers and intellectuals hungry for ideas in Tokyo. What can be said with less speculation is that intellectuals close to proletarian cultural circles at the time adapted to the intensified crackdown by the State on the communist and socialist left by shifting their internationalist emphasis away from proletarian revolution to issues regarding Japan's colonies, and Yuasa's background retrofitted with this shift. In early 1936 he decided to return to Korea for good after his first wife died suddenly in Japan. Although born in Japan, he always described himself as a Japanese *nisei*, or second-generation Japanese resident of Korea, and heavily identified as such his whole life. Some of his last literary efforts empathetically depicted the lives of second-generation Japanese in Brazil and Peru.[24]

Ikeda Hiroshi, who has done groundbreaking work on Japanese colonial-imperial cultural production, warns off potential poststructural analyses of Yuasa's texts, asserting, "Yuasa's characters are so limited because of the fact that he based almost all his fiction on his own life experiences."[25] A Korea-based scholar of Japanese colonial literature, Nam Pujin, argues something similar in his four-page introduction to the Japanese reprint of *Yalu River*.[26] To aver that autobiographical contents are transmitted directly into texts has been a bone of contention for some fifty years in the fields of cultural and literary criticism. Not wishing to go over those debates here and begging the forgiveness of readers inclined more to deconstructive and poststructural reading protocols (protocols holding that texts are irreducible to the biography of the author), I do want to follow Ikeda's and Nam's recommendations and argue that the novels contain numerous referents for Yuasa's experience growing up in colonial Korea and subsequent university education in Japan. However, some of my reasons for following Nam and Ikeda on this point have to do more with my insistence that Yuasa's novels were constrained by genre determinations." Accordingly, I situate these two novels in the genres of proletarian realism and the "I-novel" (*shishōsetsu*) that dominated literary and journalistic circles in Japan and its imperial territories during the 1920s and 1930s. Both of these literary genres demanded that textual production be based in either the author's lived experience (I-novel) or in an ostensibly scientific and objective configuring of social reality (proletarian realism).

This much is to say that there are obvious doubles of the author Yuasa in the young boy Ryūji, in the aesthete Masuda, and in the paternalistic Japanese project leaders who guide the Japanized Korean Ōyama Eiji through various development projects in Korea and Manchuria. Nevertheless, it is highly doubtful that Nuiko's underground political activities depicted in the penultimate part of *Document of Flames* were based on Yuasa's own experiences. In all likelihood this information was related to Yuasa by left-wing acquaintances. Nevertheless, examining the extent of Yuasa's political activities is crucial in attempting to adjudicate the dramatic turn (*tenkō*) to outright support for Japanese imperialism and fascism he and his writing took between the time he wrote *Kannani* (1934) and *Document of Flames* (1935), and the period beginning around the start of the Chinese-Japanese War of 1937, when he authored only texts that advocated Japan's colonial imperialism, such as the 1940 novel *Blue Jumper* and the 1943 novel *Yalu River*. Can we explain this political reversal by assuming that Yuasa was pressured by the Japanese police to recant his anticolonial beliefs? Or are there elements encrypted in the early works and in the form of Yuasa's political liberalism itself that would explain his sharp turn to the political right and support for Japan's colonial-imperial expansion in Asia?

The much discussed process of a turn to the political right is called *tenkō* in Japanese and was of central importance for the specificity of fascism and imperialism in East Asia of the late 1930s and 1940s. Merely rendering this term into English has been difficult, as the signifier is translated variously as "apostasy," "political conversion to support for the Japanese emperor," "collaborator," and "turncoat." The two Sino-Japanese characters that make up the word in Japanese can be rendered simply as "fall/turn toward the direction of." Attempts to historically explain this process have been fraught with accusations and counteraccusations over how and why almost all liberal and left-wing Japanese converted from varying degrees of political resistance to outright support for Japan's imperialism and fascism. Still, there is general agreement that a large number of socialists and communists were forced (through different mixes of physical and psychological intimidation) into signing an official document rejecting leftism and supporting the Japanese emperor and imperial polity.[27] However, what happened in the case of liberals remains much murkier. Within the protocols of critical social and political theory, the political conversion (tenkō) of liberals to open support for fascism and imperialism in Japan in the 1930s and 1940s is often explained as their inability to overcome nationalism.[28] Against this, most communists and socialists would have held then, as many hold now, antinational and transnational positions.

Yuasa was connected to proletarian literature and research circles in Japan during the six or so years before he returned permanently to Korea, mainly through his connection to the literary journal *Jinmin Bunkō* (People's library). During a short stay in Tokyo in October 1936, while he was attending a Meiji (1868–1912) literature study group with acquaintances from *People's Library*, the participants were rounded up by the police and brought in for questioning. Yuasa and one other member spent a night in jail and were released the next day. Apparently, the police had mistaken the "soft proletarians" and liberals in the *People's Library* group for an underground resistance group and the mistake became clear as soon as they began questioning the two. In writing about the incident in 1951 in the popular culture monthly *King*, Yuasa made light of the whole incident, flippantly calling it the "*People's Library* incident [*Jinmin Bunkō jihen*]."[29] Professor Ikeda Hiroshi, for one, does not find any indications that this was a situation involving coerced tenkō, and Yuasa's son, Yuasa Katsuhiko, related to me that he understood the brief detention to be a botched case of mistaken identity.

In other words, except for the censorship of the novels translated here and this sole, almost farcical incident, Yuasa never had any direct run-ins with the authorities over his early, overtly anticolonial writings.[30] From what I can deduce from his son's account and Yuasa's own narration of the event, I agree with Ikeda Hiroshi's interpretation that Yuasa's dramatic turn to the political right in support of Japanese imperialism and fascism cannot be explained by political pressure and intimidation, at least for the most part. Therefore, we are left to search for clues elsewhere.

It would be stating the obvious to say that the process of tenkō operated differently for second-generation Japanese who grew up in the colonies. As paradoxical as this might sound at first, one way to begin to configure the problem historically is by *not* translating tenkō into English. This would allow us to categorize the different modalities of tenkō depending on what sociopolitical positions the converted people held before the process of tenkō. I have found it useful to construe figures like Edogawa Rampo and other "erotic-grotesque-nonsense" writers as intellectuals who underwent a kind of tenkō from a position advocating erotic liberation of various types.[31] As the modes of erotic liberation called for by these erotic-grotesque writers were referred to by the signifier *hentai* (nonnormative) in the 1920s and 1930s, we might think about the specificity of political conversion for these figures as "hentai tenkō." Similarly, following Ikeda Hiroshi's suggestion, the specificity of Yuasa Katsuei's turn to overt support for Japan's imperialism and fascism might be clarified by adding the adjective "colonial" to tenkō to differentiate it from the political conversion that was characteristic of tenkō inside Japan.

In other words, although the phenomenon of tenkō in Japan dealt mainly with conversion from different forms of left-wing internationalism to support for Japanese nationalism, the emperor system, and fascism, colonial tenkō featured a conversion from support for Korean, Taiwanese, and Chinese independence movements to an endorsement of a Japan-led Pan-Asianism and to support for varying degrees of the assimilation of Asians to Japanese linguistic, cultural, developmental, and governmental forms. Considered the founder of the modern Korean novel (*Heartless* [*Mujong*] was written in 1916–1917 while he was a student at Waseda University in Tokyo), Yi Kwang-su coauthored the March 1, 1919, Declaration of Korean Independence that was stridently proclaimed at Pagoda Park in Seoul, kicking off a week of intense, countrywide protests. A little more than a decade later, he became one of the first Koreans to officially change his name to a Japanese name (Kayama Mitsurō), and by the mid-1930s he was wearing exclusively Japanese clothes, bowing in the direction of the Japanese emperor's palace every morning, and urging Koreans to eradicate the Korean language; Japanese, Yi insisted, was a universal language of progress and modernity.[32]

The conversion in Yuasa's texts from the explicit anticolonialism in *Kannani* and *Document of Flames* to the equally explicit endorsement of imperialization/Japanization (*kōminka*), compulsory assimilation to Japanization (dōka), the unification of Japan and Korea (naisen ittai), the East Asian Cooperative Polity (*tōakyō-dōtai*), and the Great East Asia Co-Prosperity Sphere (*daitōakyōei-ken*) a mere five years later in *Blue Jumper* and *Yalu River* is homologous with Yi's trajectory. Although there are salient elements of proletarian literature in Yuasa's early work and he was intellectually close to the proletarian culture movement inside Japan, rather than configuring Yuasa's tenkō through the standard category of leftist tenkō, it seems to me to have more in common with instances of tenkō among colonized Korean leftists who converted from involvement in anti-Japanese activities to varying degrees of support for Japanese imperialism up to and including thorough Japanization. Along with the colonial tenkō of Yi Kwang-su and Yuasa's acquaintance Im Hwa, the important Korean leftist intellectuals Hyun Yong-sŏp and In Chŏn-sik tenkōed to support the policies of Great East Asia Cooperation and the unification of Japan and Korea.[33]

Although I find it useful to place Yuasa's case together with those of the colonized leftist Koreans, I should point out the clear differences. In Yuasa's case, the tenkō moves from support for equality between Koreans and Japanese, which for him meant more "hybridity" and interactivity (erotic, linguistic, and political) between Japanese and Koreans, to a position of clear Japanese superiority. For the most part, the colonized leftist Koreans move, like Yuasa, from support for Korean independence and equality between Koreans and Japanese to an endorsement of Japanese superiority in the policy of the unification of Japan and Korea, again similar to Yuasa. Nevertheless, along with supporting the unification policy (which meant partial cultural eradication and Japanization), colonized leftists supported the policy of the East Asian Cooperative Polity because they thought it would lead to a type of decolonization and partial sovereignty for Korea. In other words, important colonized Korean leftists hoped that cooperation would turn into something that happened between at least two distinct entities (Korea and Japan), and that participating with Japan *as assimilated Japanese* in the total mobilization effort for World War II beginning in 1938 would, paradoxically, contribute to Korean independence some time in the near future.[34]

## Later Works and the Issue of Tenkō

Karl Marx's famous introduction on methodology in the *Grundrisse* provides a way to move the argument forward from here. While criticizing mainstream, bourgeois economists for reducing the complexity of any historical material situation to "ever more simple concepts,"[35] he recommends that the only method qualified to respect the richness of the concrete world is one that moves from the specific, material thing back to human philosophical thinking—what Stuart Hall called the "detour through theory"—and finally back again to the material thing, multiplying the determinations along the way. "The concrete is concrete because it is the concentration of many determinations, hence unity of the diverse. It appears in the process of thinking, therefore, as a process of concentration, as a result, not as a point of departure" (101). Although it is beyond the scope of this introduction to produce an adequate concentration of the many determinations that constituted Yuasa's specific situation, we need to take a brief detour through postcolonial and psychoanalytic theory to try to concretize more fully how and why intellectual, critical thinkers like Yuasa, Im, Hyan and In tenkōd in the colonies to support the Japanese state's imperial project. First, it is important to remind readers that, among many other factors that should be included in a determinately abstract analysis, Japanese imperialism promised to banish the Euro-American colonial powers from Asia. Euro-American capitalist expansion and imperial penetration was not only successful in establishing colonial regimes in India, Malaysia, Burma, Indonesia, Vietnam, Hong Kong, Singapore, and the Philippines, but it threatened every other area in Asia as well. It is worth noting this because the brute geopolitical fact of Euro-American colonial imperialism is occasionally elided in academic accounts and often completely absent from journalism on the period. By mentioning it here, my intention is to resist the expectations for scholars based outside of East Asia (for scholars and students based in East Asia the problematic shares similar issues, but appears to be more overdetermined with regard to the degree of one's support or not for contemporary nationalisms) to treat instances of colonial tenkō and leftist tenkō alike as victims of false consciousness—as individuals who were duped by the dissimulating, conniving slogans of Japanese imperialism.

Similar to the ways I was taught to interrogate these issues as an undergraduate in the United States, it is not unusual for East Asian studies scholars and students to pose such questions as: How could people like Yuasa and Yi have been so naïve as to fall for Japan's trap? Couldn't they see through the veil of propaganda and figure out that what the glossy phrases "Asia for Asians" and "Great East Asia Co-Prosperity" *really meant* was simply Japanese racial superiority and domination? In other words, it is frequently assumed that Euro-American–based scholars in particular enjoy a privileged access to the "truth": what those treacherous Japanese imperial ideologues *truly* meant when they deliberately disguised and masked this truth with mere lies about Pan-Asianism and liberating Asia from Euro-American colonialism.[36] It should be said, though, that almost all Korean and Japanese intellectuals (as well as other astute political figures such as the future leader of Indonesian independence, Sukarno Achmed) believed enough of Japan's imperial ideology not to openly resist it. Perhaps, just perhaps, this is similar to the way the vast majority of us believe enough of the rhetoric of the G-8's "war on terror" not to openly contest *it*. Reframing the question like this shifts the lines of interrogation away from underlying assumptions in Euro-American scholarly work that sometimes border on a racialized rendering of the inscrutability of Japanese power and the inability of nonwhite, "underdeveloped," and easily manipulated East Asians to criticize and resist this inscrutability.

Before I go on to fulfill the genre requirements of a critical introduction, I want to add one last level of abstraction to the one introduced above. Like the first, this one is meant mainly for readers who may still be perplexed as to why people like Yuasa and Yi did not openly resist Japan's imperialism and fascism. What were the alternatives? Joining the political resistance in Japan meant almost certain torture and imprisonment and probable death. Resistance for Koreans meant a long-term commitment to a life of unimaginable hardship in anti-Japanese guerrilla areas liberated by Chinese and other East Asian communists—*and* almost certain death.[37] With regard to a third option, students in my classes on colonialism and postcolonialism in East Asia understandably wonder why more people did not escape and defect to the West. The answer to this question is simply that for many intellectuals throughout Asia (Tagore in South Asia, the great Chinese communist writer Lu Xun, Yi Kwang-su and almost all intellectuals in Korea and Taiwan), *Japan was the West.*[38] In other words, Japan was where many intellectuals in Asia went to become modern and immerse themselves in the most up-to-date trends in medicine, technology, and modern art, whether physically, like Lu Xun and Yi Kwang-su, or virtually, through books. It was thought by many that Japan's impressive level of development was equivalent to levels in Europe and the United States. Moreover, despite the stubborn ethnoracial hierarchies that continued to exist alongside more idealistic and democratic beliefs that Asia should be for Asians, Japan was much more welcoming than other places competing for titleholder of "the West," such as the United States, where anti-immigration laws against East Asians formalized decades of brutally racist Yellow Peril discourse and practice. Furthermore, as I mentioned above, Japan's official colonial policy in Korea shifted significantly after the March 1, 1919, independence demonstration to the more liberal policy of cultural politics. When all these issues are added to the sense held by prominent intellectuals in Asia and elsewhere that the barbaric carnage of World War I in Western Europe was a logical outcome of Euro-American technophilia and capitalist materialism run amok, it should not seem at all strange that people living within the confines of Japan's imperial territories did not consider *that* West to be a viable alternative.

Yuasa and Postcoloniality and Its Reversal in East Asia

The historical process referred to as "postcoloniality" takes on multiple shadings and significations and encompasses an array of political and poetic positions. Nevertheless, a consensus of sorts has developed that narrates a fairly linear movement advancing from a state where entities are purified ethnoracially and monoculturally, to a transcultural, transnational condition of increased hybridization, mixing, and mélanging. Although postcoloniality is often used today as a code for "multiculturalism" and even "globalization," the relentless historical process of transculturation and hybridization is usually understood to have begun locally under regimes of colonialism. The standard claim is that transculturation and hybridization break out of their local confines after decolonization and expand to include the generalized global contents of postcoloniality proper. Although this master narrative of postcoloniality is barely withstanding the critiques imposed on it,[39] through the trajectory of tenkō in Yuasa's texts I want to introduce an analysis here (that will be fleshed out in the conclusion) of the ways postcoloniality in East Asia has been displaced and, in many cases, reversed.

Though it might seem anachronistic to say so given that postcoloniality is deployed more and more often to refer to our contemporary globalized condition, Japan's official multiethnic colonial imperialism operated before 1940 in ways that would be called postcolonial today.[40] Japan's colonial-imperial policy of encouraging mixed relations and marriages between Japanese, Koreans, and Chinese, the policy of increased transculturation in the empire during the 1920s, and the multiethnic, multilingual transnationalization ideologized and practiced in Japanese-controlled Manchuria for a decade all arguably qualify as postcolonial.[41] Furthermore, and to reiterate, although I have identified *Kannani* and *Document of Flames* as works mainly critical of Japan's colonial imperialism, some of their elements that might seem now to have contravened official colonial policy (the staging of the puppy love between young Koreans and Japanese; nonracist, Korean-speaking Japanese) were actually direct expressions of Japan's colonial policy. This colonial policy went so far as to install laws against ethnoracial discrimination and advocate for and legalize mixed marriages between colonizer and colonized.

In what should be "provincialized" now as something not universal,[42] but a mere European story inapplicable to several regions of the world, today's Euro-Americancentric postcoloniality assumes and celebrates a linear historical trajectory of ethnoracially homogeneous coloniality → decolonization → global, multicultural postcoloniality. To a great extent, this Eurocentric trajectory moves backward and is reversed in the case of Japan's empire in East Asia; the historical trajectory in East Asia can be said to *begin with multicultural postcoloniality* in the period of Japan's colonial-imperial rule and *end with an ethnoracially homogenized cultural nationalism*. In other words, antithetical to the supposed exuberant expansion of multicultural postcoloniality in our (still stubbornly Eurocentric) contemporary world, historical conditions have dictated an opposed tendency in Japan and East Asia toward intensified homogenization, dehybridization, and monoculturalization—postcoloniality in reverse.

Even though many of the postcolonial themes in *Kannani* and *Document of Flames* are reflections of Japan's official colonial policy and therefore tainted by it, does this mean that they are worthless for us today as potential seeds for a more enlightened, transnational postcolonial future? I don't think so. The scenes of Ryūji's reverse assimilation into wanting to be Korean, his bilingual friendship with the young woman Kannani, and the creolized erotic exchanges between Tokiko and male Korean sex workers and hosts provide a fertile terrain where crossing and mixing could have pointed the way toward a more democratic and ethically negotiated postcoloniality. But for this more democratic postcoloniality to have taken place in East Asia, the process of decolonization would have required a dramatically different script from the one that was written mainly by the United States following Japan's surrender in August 1945. Nevertheless, those of us concerned with a radically democratic, transnational future can still find uses for those postcolonial moments in *Kannani* and *Document of Flames*. Reconfigured as such, the defeat of postcoloniality in East Asia by the ethnoracial homogeneity and monoculturization of the various nationalisms (Japaneseness, Koreanness, Chineseness) need not be construed as irreversible, but only deferred and still full of potential for a more enlightened future to come.

The process of postcoloniality in reverse in East Asia can be said provisionally to have been consolidated with the shift in Japan's imperial ideology of mobilization for total war in 1940, a shift that can be registered directly in the texts of Yuasa Katsuei. Just three years after the publication of *Document of Flames* the deletion and reversal of the postcolonial potentialities in that text and in *Kannani* began. As I suggested in my discussion of Yuasa's *Blue Jumper* and *Yalu River*, after 1938 there was no longer any sense of antagonism between colonizer and colonized, no more creolization (or the frequent deployment of the Korean language both in the text and appended in the Japanese *katakana* next to Sino-Japanese characters he used in the earlier novels), and no more instances of political awakening of colonizer Japanese like Ryūji in *Kannani* and Nuiko in *Document of Flames* to the violence of Japan's colonial imperialism. Instead, we have Koreans like Yang Tae-gi, who, considering that so many Korean men like Yang were conscripted into the Japanese Army, are "dying" to become Japanese, and Japanese men like Masuda whose masculine allure "naturally" incites the desires of Chinese, Japanese, and Korean women alike. Moreover, although many of Yuasa's novellas and short stories of 1934–1937 feature erotic relations between Koreans and Japanese, in the period after 1938, those relations are denied or marginalized; recall that the text prevents the love affair between Masuda and Kang in *Blue Jumper*. A fortiori, the political conversion and reversal in Yuasa's texts from the 1934–1935 period to the 1940 period reveals the elimination of colonialism as a problem tout court. Colonialism not only ceases to be a problem for Japanese liberals like Yuasa, but becomes reconfigured as a positive vehicle for the development and modernization of Korea and northeastern China. Because of this forgetting and disavowal of colonial violence and antagonism, when World War II ends and Japan's empire is dissolved in Asia, ethnoracial tensions and economic violence carrying over into the periods after colonialism can neither be coded problematically nor expressed discursively.

The politics and poetics of postcoloniality often work toward a more enlightened future through trying to come to terms with the colonial past. However, when this difficult and painful assessing of the colonial past does not take place, as it did not take place in Japan, the effect is to redouble the smug paternalism and ethnocentrism (instanced in Masuda Miyoshi's arrogation that "we Japanese developed Manchuria") that was latent in the colonial-imperial project in the first place. It is all too easy to see how this operates in liberal and conservative neonationalism in Japan today, where politicians like the governor of Tokyo, Ishihara Shintarō, sound exactly like Masuda in their self-congratulating opinions of the superiority of Japan's colonial imperialism, and, similar again to Masuda, contemporary neonationalists like Kobayashi Yoshinori imagine that East Asian women are erotically drawn to Japanese men like themselves.

Yuasa Katsuei never apologized for his significant contributions to imperialism and fascism. More disturbing, it was inconceivable to him that there was anything at all problematic in the texts he wrote after 1938 explicitly advocating Japan's colonial-imperial policies. In this representative case of postcoloniality in reverse, Yuasa utterly failed to register the shift to the political right (colonial tenkō) in his texts after the publication of his early work, such as *Kannani* and *Document of Flames*. Furthermore, as he did during the 1920s and 1930s, after he returned to Japan for good after World War II he continued to refer to Korea as home and to the Korean town he grew up in with the emotionally laden Japanese signifier for home, *furusato*.

His most important post–World War II novel, *Mihei Monogatari* (Mihei's story), published in November 1948, is a barely fictional memoir of the events in decolonized Korea in the weeks following Japan's surrender on August 15, 1945.[43] It represents the only significant attempt by Yuasa to come to terms with Japan's colonial-imperial past and his own central role as a popular propagandist and one of the public faces of naisen ittai, the unification of Korea and Japan. Nevertheless, there is almost no registration in this long novel of what happened in Korea from the mid-1930s to August 1945: the near elimination of several Korean cultural practices, the marginalization of the Korean language, the laws that forced Koreans to Japanize their names, the Korean men forced to die for the emperor in the Japanese military, and that 80 percent of the estimated 150,000 to 200,000 "comfort" women— sex slaves—who were forced to serve the Japanese military during the fifteen-year war were Korean. In its place, readers are offered only nostalgia and homesickness for Korea as the Yuasa double Mihei organizes his family's departure from their estate in Suwon during the week after Japan's surrender, which also meant the liberation of Korea from thirty-five years of domination. Along with some nine hundred thousand other colonizer Japanese forced to repatriate, in the rush to organize and sell most of the family's belongings, Mihei/Yuasa recollects fondly the thirty years he has called colonized Korea home.

Continuous with Yuasa's colonial tenkō, his fictional avatar Mihei's recollections are bereft of colonial antagonism and imperial violence. Symptomatic is the fact that the recollections in *Mihei's Story* of his early, anticolonial novels, including *Kannani*, are also devoid of any agonistic friction between colonizer and colonized (10–11). His description of the period around the March 1, 1919, Korean independence movement is euphemistic when compared to the account in *Kannani*. Not only does he not remember any of the tensions of coloniality, but he does not even *remember when he remembered* these tensions and violences. Therefore, it is predictable when we learn on page 6 that Mihei/Yuasa "felt confused and angered at all the Korean flags replacing the Japanese flags." He is also perplexed at why the "Korean police seemed to be enjoying their new-found power and authority." Later, he is "angry at all the cheers for Korean independence" (44). In other words, because Yuasa's framing of Japan's colonial imperialism after his colonial tenkō denies the antagonism embedded within it—to the contrary, this same colonial imperialism "developed" Korea and Manchuria and provided the ground for sweet memories of his relaxed and luxurious life there—Mihei/Yuasa is at times incredulous as to why Koreans would be ecstatically celebrating Japan's surrender. Even though there were rumors of summary executions of Japanese military and colonial officials and Mihei's father had worked as a policeman in the colonial government, when they hear of rioting in Seoul, Mihei reassures his family that "because we always loved Korea so much, nobody is going to harm us" (30). Ikeda Hiroshi relates that after Japan's surrender Yuasa actually considered staying on in Korea with his elderly parents, child, and young wife. Only after friends talked some sense into him and convinced him that his father could be killed for his activities with the colonial police force did he reluctantly decide to repatriate to Japan.

Here again, Yuasa massively disavowed the antagonism between colonizer and colonized and assumed that because he had always demonstrated his adoration for Korea, he and his extended family would not be harmed by his beloved Koreans. At this historical conjuncture during the period immediately following Japan's surrender and Korean liberation we might expect to find some kind of historical accounting from the author of the critical *Kannani*. However, in *Mihei's Story* and in his other post–World War II writings Yuasa consistently refused to accept responsibility in any sense, and instead allowed nostalgia to take over and re-press the antagonisms of coloniality. There is an important scene at the beginning of *Mihei's Story* where Mihei/Yuasa is remembering an incident from his youth when he, his mother, and his sister were invited to the important Korean aristocrat Yi Kunt'aek's huge mansion sometime after the March 1, 1919, demonstration for Korean independence. As Yi spoke no Japanese, the ten-year-old Mihei/Yuasa is left to keep up the conversation in his bad Korean. After the dinner, Yi and Mihei/Yuasa retire to the Korean count's study, where he shows the young Japanese child curios. Then, according to Mihei/Yuasa, Yi "pulled out a Korean flag and started waving it around, yelling in Korean 'Three Cheers for Korean Independence!'" (19). Mihei/Yuasa is startled and cannot believe how animated the old prince becomes as he mimes how he and most other Koreans comported themselves during the week of the March 1 independence uprisings. The scene closes with Yi begging the child not to tell his mother or policeman father about his theatrical reenactment with the outlawed Korean flag (20).

At this point in the text it would have been easy for Mihei/Yuasa to connect this strong desire on the part of Koreans to be free from Japanese domination in March 1919 with the August 1945 present, but the text does not seem capable of linking the memory of the joy of the 1919 uprisings with the explosion into the contemporary context of liberation from colonial rule. It freezes up and refuses the possibility of joining the earlier moment of aborted independence to the moment of real independence happening in Suwon and bursting out with joy in the streets of Seoul in August 1945. Similar to the way colonial antagonisms and violence had been repressed and disavowed in Yuasa's texts from 1938, the antagonism is again repressed after liberation, as in several sections of *Mihei's Story* Mihei/Yuasa assumes that if he just continues to love Korea, *actually existing Koreans* (who had largely disappeared from his texts after 1938, except when they appeared as gratefully and completely Japanized) will not begrudge him his memories and happy past as a colonizer. In 1948 the nonrepentant liberal colonizer reconsolidates his advocacy of postcoloniality in reverse even as real decolonization is happening in Korea. The erasure of the "truth" of coloniality (a "truth" readers will in part discover and produce for themselves in the two novels here) prevents the negotiations of what could have contributed to a more enlightened postcolonial future in post–World War II East Asia. In its place, we are handed a condition of postcoloniality in reverse that stubbornly persists today despite capitalism's transnational propensities and global exigencies. The protocols of postcoloniality in reverse in East Asia and elsewhere reductively define people exclusively by their assumed identification with their "own" nation-state and their assigned obedience to dehybridized monoculturalism in all its forms.

## Notes

*Unless otherwise specified, all translations from Japanese and Korean are mine.*

1 *Aoi Chokori* (Blue jumper) (Shōwa Shobō, 1940); all citations in text.

2 Although Japanese migration to the area began in the 1880s, Japanese and Korean settlers flooded into Manchuria after Japan's victory in the Russo-Japanese War in 1905, and then again after Japan's military invasion of Manchuria in 1931, when they were joined by colonized Okinawans and Taiwanese.

3 I put scare quotes around "Korean" to flag the fact that it was not yet a nation-state, but only became one through the process of colonialism and decolonization. The same should be done for "Japan," because the "Japanese" nation-state did not preexist imperial extension that began in the 1870s in Okinawa (then went on to take "Taiwan" as a colony in 1895 and then "Korea" as a colony in 1910), but was an after-effect generated in and through the process of colonial imperialism itself. Moreover, to avoid the essentialist trap of assuming that nation-states preexist the ways they are determined both in the system of global capitalism and in the discursive regimes that produce and reproduce the meanings that circulate about this or that country, *all names of countries* are best

placed in quotation marks. Similarly, quotes should be placed around adjectives that determine people solely on terms of their presupposed cultural-national identification: "Korean," "Japanese," "American," Chinese." I urge readers to mentally make this correction to my text.

As one element in a pluralist imperial program that included the insistence that Japanese biological ancestry was a hybrid mix of at least Korean and Chinese parts, from February 1921 official policy actively *encouraged* mixed marriages between colonizer Japanese and Koreans and Chinese, although it was unofficially encouraged from the first years of Japan's colonization. See "Naisenjin no kekkonga minpōjō mitomera-reru!" (Mariages between Koreans and Japanese will be recognized by civil law!), *Keijō Nippō* (Seoul daily report), February 2, 1921, 5. The first issues of the central colonial monthly *Chōsen Kōron* (Korea digest) in 1912 and 1913 had regular columns celebrating these intermarriages with pictures and interviews, which on occasion also mentioned unmarried mixed couples living together. In the colonial monthly magazine *Chōsen oyobi Manshū* (Korea and Manchuria) there was a regular feature article that ran for eight issues from April 1912 called "Japanese-Korean Tales of Romance between the Sexes" ("Nissen danjo tsuya monogatari") that described couples consisting of Japanese women and Korean men in Seoul along with their courtship and extended families. All the Korean men seem to be middle and upper class, whereas the Japanese women are predominantly peasant or working class, which is the pattern that will hold later on in much of the Japanese empire.

4 Ikeda Hiroshi's fifty-page commentary (*kaisetsu*) to his edited collection of Yuasa's novellas, Yuasa Katsuei, *Kannani: Yuasa Katsuei sho-kuminchi shōsetsushū* (Kannani: A collection of Yuasa Katsuei's colonial novels), ed. Ikeda Hiroshi (Inpacuto Shuppan, 1995), is a concise intellectual biography of Yuasa that provided the framework from which my introduction builds. I am in debt to him for both that and for his support and assistance with this project.

5 Yuasa Katsuei, *Ōryokkō* (Seinansha, 1943). All citations are in the text.

6 See Ishihara Shintarō and Morita Akio, *"No" to ieru nihon* (The Japan that can say "No"!) (Kobunsha, 1989), 157–58. Ishihara is currently the very powerful governor of Tokyo who has become increasingly vocal about how positive Japanese colonialism was for East Asia. For example, on October 29, 2003, he proclaimed that Koreans "wanted to be colonized by Japan." *Japan Times*, October 30, 2003, 2. After a huge outcry, two days later he appended that "Koreans decided between China, Japan and Russia and they picked Japan, which was the right choice. No colonial power except Japan installed a modern, educational system."

7 Before they became memorialized as a preferred undergraduate alcoholic beverage, the "White" Russian was differentiated from the

"Red" and meant royalist and conservative anticommunist. The Japanese government's acute anticommunism meant that Imperial Japan, along with its colonies and territories, welcomed White Russian defectors and escapees from the victorious Red October Revolution in 1917.

8  "Development" is almost always understood on one side of a political equation for something that is often *experienced* as "plunder" and "imperialist expropriation" on the other side of the equation. This was the case in Manchuria during World War II, and it is still the case differentially today with the World Bank and IMF having the power to impose a developmental agenda onto many places in the global South. It is no accident that this agenda enriches the multinational agents of this "development" based in the North.

9  The 1939 colonial policy of *kaimei* legally required all Koreans to take on Japanese names, but some Koreans adopted the practice earlier.

10  I do not have the room here to adequately address the shift in Japan's imperial policy from *dōka*, or assimilation, to *kōminka*, or imperialization. However, kōminka is usually understood as an intensification of the process of Japanization and an extension of it to all colonized subjects of Japan's imperialism.

11  The Japanese colonial authorities, under the program of *naisen ittai* (the unification of Japan and Korea), pursued a policy of forced assimilation from 1934: eliminating the use of the Korean language in school instruction (1934), requiring attendance at Shinto ceremonies (1935), and the kaimei or forced adoption of Japanese surnames (1939). These edicts intended to assimilate colonized Koreans to the Japanese language would not have been applied with quite the same force in Manchuria, where Ōyama grew up. For example, none of the other colonized Korean residents of Manchuria in *Blue Jumper* appear to have changed to Japanese names. It is worth pointing out that despite these edicts, the Korean vernacular language continued to be used in newspapers and in other mass media right up until the end of World War II.

12  *Bungaku Hyōron* (May 1935): 32–61. I searched in vain for two years for a rumored English translation of this abridged version. After I finished a second complete draft of this translation, Ikeda Hiroshi finally showed me a copy of the long sought-after translation when he graciously met with me to discuss this project in Kyoto in July 2002. About one-third the length of the fuller version here, it appeared in the Bombay *Orient Digest* in May 1954.

13  On the March 1, 1919, Korea-wide demonstrations against Japanese colonial rule, see Moriyama Shigenori, *Nikkan Heigō* (The merger of Japan and Korea) (Yoshigawa Kōbunkan, 1992); Iwanami Koza, ed., *Kindai Nihon to Shokuminchi*, vol. 6, *Teikō to Kutsujū* (Resistance and submission) (Iwanami Shoten, 1992); and Kang Chae-on and Iinuma Jirō, eds., *Shokuminchiki Chōsen no shakai to teikō* (Society and resistance

in Korea under Japanese colonial rule) (Miraisha, 1982). In English, see Gregory Henderson, *Korea: The Politics of Vortex* (Cambridge, Mass.: Harvard University Press, 1968) and Andrew Nahm, ed., *Korea under Japanese Colonial Rule: Studies of the Policy and Techniques of Japanese Colonialism* (Kalamazoo: Western Michigan University Press, 1973).

The English-language archive of work on Japan's colonial imperialism includes Peter Duus, Ramon Myers, and Mark Peattie, *The Japanese Informal Empire in China, 1895–1937* (Princeton: Princeton University Press, 1989); Ramon Myers and Mark Peattie, *The Japanese Colonial Empire* (Princeton: Princeton University Press, 1984); Peter Duus, *The Abacus and the Sword* (Berkeley: University of California Press, 1995); Hilary Conroy, *The Japanese Seizure of Korea, 1868–1919* (Philadelphia: University of Pennsylvania Press, 1960); Louise Young, *Japan's Total Empire* (Berkeley: University of California Press, 1996); and Gi-Wook Shin and Michael Robinson, eds., *Colonial Modernity in Korea* (Cambridge, Mass.: Harvard University Asia Center, 1999). Leo Ching's excellent recent work on colonial Taiwan, *Becoming Japanese: Colonial Taiwan and the Politics of Identity Formation* (Berkeley: University of California Press, 2000), has initialized a rash of new cultural work in English on Japanese colonialism; in addition to this book, Faye Yuan Kleeman's *Under an Imperial Sun: Japanese Colonial Literature of Taiwan and the South* (Honolulu: University of Hawai'i Press, 2003) is an invaluable addition to the English-language scholarship on Japanese colonial culture, as will be John Whittier Treat's forthcoming work on Korean writers under Japanese colonialism. Some of the new work in Japanese and English is indebted to Oguma Eiji's *Tanitsu minzoku shinwa no kigen* (The origin of the myth of the homogeneous nation) (Shinyōsha, 1995). The study by colonial historian Komagome Takeshi, *Shokuminchiteikoku Nihon no bunkatōgō* (The cultural integration of colonial-imperial Japan) (Iwanami Shoten, 1996), has also impacted new work in English and Japanese.

14 Yuasa Katsuei, *Kannani: Yuasa Katsuei shokuminchi shōsetsushu*, ed. Ikeda Hiroshi (Inpacuto Shuppan, 1995).

15 Censorship operated in at least two ways at the time. Before they submitted a copy of something for public distribution, publishers, sometimes working with authors and sometimes not, would signify with ellipses, Xs, and Os that a particular passage had violated the censorship codes. Different from self-censorship, the censorship section of Japan's Interior Ministry (Naimushō) naturally had the authority to ban the public sale of magazines or books (*hakkin*) or limit their distribution (*genteiban*) to a certain number. Publishers were normally free to resubmit texts that had not been approved for distribution after making the appropriate changes. Although distribution was controlled, it was almost impossible for the authorities to entirely prevent the printing of

a text. Some books that were in clear violation of the codes (for the most part, Article 175 of the Criminal Code prohibiting "obscene" texts and texts that upset public order) were still able to circulate if they were designated as intended for private, subscription sale. Leftist publications were routinely excluded from this exception, especially after 1928 and then more stringently after 1933. See Yonezawa Yasuhiro's introduction to his *Hakkinbon* (Heibonsha, 1998).

16　One has to go into the archive of colonial monthlies published in Korea and northeast China for comparable descriptions. Japanese readers can check out the column that appeared in the colonial monthly *Chōsen Kōron* (Korea digest), "Kiki kaikai hengen shutsubotsusen" (Strange, uncanny things that appear and disappear) from September 1913 until 1918. The author, Ishimori Sei'ichi (one of several monikers for the same writer), was the gossip and society columnist and often wrote exposés of urban colonial life.

17　This staging of colonial antagonism also has the effect of naturalizing the countrywide uprising against the Japanese colonizers of the March 1, 1919, independence movements, reverently referred to as Sam'il Undong in Korean. The depiction of this uprising is central to the last part of *Kannani*.

18　The Japanese system of military and civilian control changed significantly over the thirty-five years of colonial rule. The first period of the annexation of Korea was characterized by a repressive, militarized colonizer presence that consolidated after 1910. After the massive Korean demonstrations for independence beginning on March 1, 1919, the Japanese military responded brutally and tens of thousands of Koreans were killed and arrested in March and April alone. Responding to international, Korean, and domestic Japanese criticism of the heavy-handed crackdown, the colonial government initiated a system of demilitarization and civilian police ( *junsa*) that replaced soldiers and military police (*kempei*) in the streets of the cities. The Japanese government-general police chief Takeyama Ryūtarō referred to this as a dramatic shift away from the overly aggressive military policy of "security police" (*chian keisatsu*) to the new, more sensitive civilian policy called "cultural policing" (*bunka keisatsu*) that would require more anthropological and historical knowledge of Korea for colonial civil servants. On this change, see "Chian keisatsu yori, bunka keisatsu e" (From military-security police to culture police), *Keijō Nippō* (Seoul daily report), April 2, 1921, 1. See also *Gaimushō no Hyakunen* (One hundred years of the Foreign Ministry) (Hara Shobō, 1969), 2: 1370–1403.

19　I have worked from the reprint of the novel published in 1995 in the collection of Yuasa's novels called *Kannani: Yuasa Katsuei shokuminchishōsetsushū*.

20　In addition to n. 9 above, Japanese readers should consult Ikeda

Hiroshi's fine book *Kaigai shinshutsu bungaku* (Literature of the invasion of Asia) (Inpacuto Shuppan, 1997), both for the discussion of censorship in Chapter 1 and for the discussion of Yuasa in the second chapter. In addition to Ikeda's book, readers of Japanese can consult several of Kawamura Minatō's works on Japanese colonial literary and cultural production. Tarumi Chie has pioneered Japanese-language criticism on colonial production in Taiwan in her *Taiwan no nihongo bungaku* (Taiwan's Japanese-language literature) (Goryu Shōin, 1995). In English, Leo Ching's groundbreaking work *Becoming Japanese: Colonial Taiwan and the Politics of Identity Formation* (Berkeley: University of California Press, 2000) is the first book-length treatment in English of the process of subjectivization initialized by Japanese colonialism. Tani Barlow's edited *The Formation of Colonial Modernity in East Asia* (Durham, N.C.: Duke University Press, 1996) is an indispensable volume containing important essays on Japan's colonial imperialism along with an excellent overview of the erasure of colonialism from the purview of the area studies of East Asia by the editor.

21　For Oguma Eiji this policy culminated in what he calls the "politics of compromise," whereby elements of Taiwan and Korea were "subsumed and included" (*hōsetsu sareta*) and other elements vehemently "excluded" (*haijo sareta*) from the confines of Japan's colonial imperialism. See his *"Nihonjin" no kyōkai: Okinawa Ainu Taiwain Chōsen shokuminchi shihai kara fukki undō made* (The boundaries of "The Japanese": Okinawa, Ainu, Taiwan, and Korea from colonial rule to the movement for reversion) (Shin'yōsha, 1998), 168.

22　See n. 3 and Komagome's *Shokuminchiteikoku Nihon no bunkatōgō* (1996), 214–219. Among several discussions of this in English, I recommend Henry H. Em's *"Minjok* as a Modern and Democratic Construct: Sin Ch'aeho's Historiography," in Gi-Wook Shin and Michael Robinson, eds., *Colonial Modernity in Korea* (Cambridge, Mass.: Harvard University Asia Center, 1999), 336–61.

23　Nin Tenkei, *Nihon ni okeru Chōsenjin no bungaku no rekishi: 1945-nen made* (A history of literature written by Koreans in Japan until 1945) (Hōsei Daigaku Shuppankyoku, 1994).

24　See Yuasa Katsuei's 1957 *Amazon Imin* (Japanese immigrants in the Brazilian Amazon; Shūkan Shōsetsu); and his 1958 *Latin Amerika e no shōtai* (An invitation to Latin America; Nihon Shūhō Shakan).

25　Ikeda Hiroshi, "Kaisetsu" (Commentary), in *Kannani: Yuasa Katsuei shokuminchi shōsetsushū*, 601.

26　Nam Pujin, "Kaisetsu," in *Ōryokkō* (Yamani Shobō, 1997).

27　For the best new discussion of the problem, see Hasegawa Kei, ed., *Tenkō no Meian* (The light and shadow of political conversion) (Inpacuto Shuppan, 1999).

28　For students in North America at least, some central channels of the mass media might lead one to think that "liberals" are dangerous subversives. However, political and cultural theorists on the left often construe political liberalism as one of the main ideological supports for nationalism, despite the fact that liberals often taken progressive stances on cultural, social, and human rights issues.

29  Yuasa Katsuei, "*Bishōkushō monogatari*" (Tales of smiles and smirks), *King* (March 1951).

30  Yuasa himself referred to the incident as "farcical" and the other sources seem to concur with this description. Nevertheless, we should be careful not to downplay the factor of intimidation and torture that was fairly standard for these incidents with the police.

31  The so-called *ero-guro-nansensu* (erotic-grotesque-nonsense) dominated mass culture in Japan from around 1927 until 1936. Although examples of it appeared in sexology, anthropology, and psychiatry, its main genres were the detective novel, the tabloid newspaper, and mass culture monthly magazines. The detective and horror writer Edogawa Rampo is considered the most important face of the erotic-grotesque-nonsense. Miriam Silverburg's forthcoming work will deepen significantly the understanding we have of it as a historical phenomenon.

32  Kim Sōkpom, *Tenkō to shinnichiha* (Tenkō and Koreans who sold out to Japan) (Iwanami Shoten, 1993). My reading of Yi has benefited from a presentation by John Treat given at Duke University on October 18, 2001. New scholarship on the tenkō of colonized Korean leftists is dramatically displacing the older binary paradigm of "traitor/patriot" and "complicity/resistance." See the essays by Cho Kwangja, "Shinnichi nashyonarizumu no keisei to hatan: 'Yi Kwang-su = minzoku hangyaku-sha' to iu bankyū o koete," in *Gendai Shisō* (December 2001), and Hyŏn Haedong "Shokuminchininshiki no 'gure- zo-n': Niteika no 'kōkyōsei' to kiritsukenryoku," in *Gendai Shisō* (May 2002).

33  On this, see the book by Miyada Setsuko, *Chōsen minshū to "kōminka" seisaku* (The colonized Korean people and the policy of "imperialization") (Miraisha, 1985) and the more recent essay by Matsumoto Takenoru, "Shokuminchishita no Chōsenjinha ikani tōjisaretaka?," *Jōkyō* (December 1997). Hyun, In, Im, and Yi (along with many others) are referred to in Korean as *ch'inil*, which means something like "close to Japan," but has the sense of being a traitor to Korea.

34  For this point I draw on the superb essay by Ch'oe Chongsuk, "Pak Chuh ni okeru bōryoku no yokan," *Gendai Shisō* (March 2003).

35  Karl Marx, *Grundrisse*, trans. Martin Nicolaus (New York: Viking, 1973), 101.

36  It is no accident that popular texts in English-language Japanese studies (e.g., Ian Buruma's *Behind the Mask* [New York: Meridian, 1984]) have often featured a dynamic where white Euro-American men have

abrogated unique authority to "remove," "unveil," and "strip" the mask and dress to reveal the "truth about Japan."

37 Readers should be reminded that the People's Democratic Republic of Korea (North Korea) was established after World War II by several hundred of these brave, heroic guerrillas who fought the good fight against Japanese imperial fascism.

38 Naoki Sakai's wise sermons have been instrumental in my thinking on this issue. See his "You Asians: On the Historical Role of the West and Asia Binary," in *Millennial Japan*, ed. Tomiko Yoda and Harry Harootunian (Durham, N.C.: Duke University Press, 2001).

39 For the best discussion of recent issues surrounding postcoloniality, see Stuart Hall, "When Was the 'Post-colonial'? Thinking at the Limit," in *The Post-Colonial Question: Common Skies, Divided Horizons*, ed. Iain Chambers and Lidia Curti (London: Routledge, 1999).

40 Oguma Eiji, *Tanitsu minzoku shinwa no kigen* (The origin of the myth of the homogeneous nation) (Shinyōsha, 1995) identifies a "double bind" (339) that, on the one hand, insists on the scientific and imperial origin of Japanese ethnicity as hybrid and Asian, and, on the other hand, supports a cultural-national mythology of the divinity and purity of the Japanese emperor, which by extension applied to the Japanese family-state. Oguma argues that this double bind came undone toward the end of World War II and then was completely forgotten afterward. Naoki Sakai provides another way of thinking about this double bind, as "imperial-nationalism"; see his "Ethnicity and Species: On the Philosophy of the Multi-ethnic State in Japanese Imperialism," *Radical Philosophy* (May–June 1999): 33–45. It is important to point out that the vast majority of references to Japanese ethnoracial identity in mass culture discourse in the 1920s and 1930s understood it as hybrid and plural. Representative of this is the main Japanese popular science magazine of the time, *Kagaku Gahō* (Science illustrated), which held the position that modern Japanese ethnicity is the composite mixture (*konkō*) of seven different Asian ethnicities.

41 On the multiethnic, multinational ideology in Manchuria and northern China, see Komagome Takeshi, *Shokuminchiteikoku Nihon no bunkatōgō* (The cultural integration of colonial-imperial Japan) (Iwanami Shoten, 1996), chaps. 4, 5, 6.

42 Dipesh Chakrabarty, *Provincializing Europe: Postcolonial Thought and Historical Difference* (Princeton: Princeton University Press, 2000).

43 Yuasa Katsuei, *Mihei Monogatari* (Banyūsha, 1948); citations in text.

# Kannani (1934)

## CHAPTER ONE

An all-yellow kite, a half-red and half-purple kite, another with a green circle against a white background—numerous kites, like colored paper strewn every which way, were alternately ascending and sinking all through the sky as they were blown by a strong wind. The sky was big and blue with only two or three scattered clouds, like a typical fall day. The kites swam around freely in the clouds while competing for height with one another.

Among all the kites one dyed deep red had broken away and was climbing higher than any of the others. This red kite seemed to be showing off, bragging "I'm all the way up here" as it danced victoriously higher and higher. One kite that lagged behind at a much lower altitude, with a golden circle against the white background shining in the sun, made several jerky motions diagonally upward. When its string just about crossed the string pulling the red kite in the shape of an x, it plummeted down, and now, like a stray, runaway kite fanned by the wind, spun around the red kite's string, causing it to tangle.

A group of Korean boys standing and watching on the bank shouted out "Wow!" The boy who was flying the kite with the golden circle revealed a flush of intense pleasure on his face as he strained to reel in the kite string. Trying to keep the kite strings smooth, every so often he struck the string forcefully against his thighs while reeling the bobbin. His kite proceeded to descend unsteadily and then rise up again. As it did so, the string of the red kite stretched high in the sky and then snapped at the point where it got tangled up with the golden circle kite. After its string snapped the red kite started to float out of human control, dragging its broken string along behind it.

The group of onlookers at the bank shouted, "Wow, it really took off!" and scattered quickly like locusts. Another group of boys who were watching at the river's edge, along with a second group that was on top of the hill, a third group that was playing kick the can near the mud wall, and yet a fourth group that was playing spin the top, yelled out seemingly in unison with the group on the bank, "Whooah, it really took off!" At which point all the groups followed along after the billowing kite, intently fixing their eyes on it.

Although the red kite began to drift over to one side of the mountain, the direction of the wind seemed to have altered its path because it suddenly floated in the opposite direction, toward the river's edge. The boys who'd run off in the direction of the mountain ran down the hill in a flurry, following the kite's shifting course. The boys wearing their customary white clothes[1] streamed down the red clay hill toward the kite, forming the shape of a waterfall with white spray. Just then, the kite with the broken string crashed down into the straw roof of a hut and the string got tangled in a poplar tree. The boys wrestled for position underneath the poplar tree and the hut; finally a scuffle broke out to see who would end up with the kite and the string.

It was New Year's Day. Even boys who weren't involved with the excitement of the kite chase still managed to have fun playing games like kick the can and spin the top alongside the mud wall. The soccer-like game of kick the can is played by kicking copper pennies wrapped up in paper. As they play the boys bend their bodies at the hip and grind their teeth intensely. In convulsions, the tip of their tongue hits the side of their mouth and when they kick the money they yell out in Korean "Did ya see that?" and "That one beat yours!" The other boys watching on the sidelines carefully keep score of the money (that looks like white butterflies) by counting aloud "One, Two, Three." They often place bets on the game. Contestants who win thirty pennies can exchange this amount for two pieces of candy; the winner invariably sprints at full speed immediately to the candy store after the game to claim his prize. Even so, the game played with the top was the more exciting game.

Spin the top is played with a top made out of a sharp piece of oak painted with colors such as red, yellow, and purple. Players spin it by wrapping the top with a five-foot-long string which they then pull with a stick really fast, pulling with their right hand and holding the top with their left hand. When this is done correctly, the top should spin around madly on a frozen road, flaunting its complex seven-color design scheme. As the top juts into a piece of ice, it makes a whirring sound and flies away. The boys chase after the tops, slapping them with the whips they've brought. Sometimes the tops crash into each other, giving off sparks.

Near the mud wall on the road that runs alongside the river, Ryūji and Kannani had been fixated on the tops for some time. Each side had put their team's tops into play and the players were running circles around the tops, grunting with all their strength as the tops let out their whirring sound. The spectators cheered in unison, calling out the names of the boys who were competing.

The Korean boys were having a great time with the tops. To make sure their New Year's poncho-like *dōrumaki* didn't get mussed up, they tucked up the hem and fastened it with a piece of red and purple cloth. These overshirts fluttered lightly like holiday ribbons as the boys ran around the tops. Even the many boys who weren't able to wear the special New Year's black clothing and had to wear summer-like white clothing cut out of coarse cloth put on special rubber shoes just for the holiday occasion. One boy who had on these shoes he was only allowed to wear two or three times a year frolicked about with particular glee. Still another boy was singing a song in Japanese called "It's a New Year" that he learned at the Japanese-style New Year's party at school.

Completely isolated from the frolicking Korean boys, all Ryūji could do was squat down and watch them, disconsolately holding his chin up with his hand. He felt particularly sad because they ignored him completely. Even though he implored the kids "Let me play, will you?" they continued to ignore him. Whenever there were older Korean boys playing, they angrily called him "Jap" in Korean. Even on the rare occasion when they did allow him to play, all the Korean boys would gang up on him and he invariably ended up totally defeated and humiliated. Ryūji thought that this was because of his Japanese clothes and Japanese *geta* clogs. He decided to wear the poncho-style shirts that the Korean kids wore, so that whenever he got a chance to play with them he'd be dressed exactly like them. But it didn't stop there; he also wanted a top of his very own, just like the kind the Korean kids had. Even though up until now his father had bought him whatever he'd asked for, he put his foot down in the case of the top and adamantly refused to buy him one. His father admonished, "Don't pay any attention to those Korean games." So the day before New Year's Ryūji decided to make a top all by himself. He cut off a piece of wood from an apricot tree and tried to whittle it into the shape of a top, but as soon as he tested it out, it spun around only two or three times and fell over. Then he tried to whittle it again to make it spin more effectively, but it turned out as skinny as a pencil. To make matters worse, while he was doing all this he cut his index finger and bled all over the place.

Ryūji tried to stop the bleeding by sucking his finger, but as soon as he did blood started to ooze quickly out of his thin skin. When he tasted the bittersweet blood on the tip of his tongue he felt an inexplicable loneliness. "Doesn't it hurt?" Kannani asked as she brought her face close to him. Her oil-free, braided hair tickled him, and they heard a song off in the distance:

He's clearly the best!
The very best groom in the world
He'll be so happy and proud
When he meets his sweet bride
Covered with ashes from her crown to her feet.

Even though a drunk was singing it, the voicing was melodic and peaceful. Kannani said, "Look, it's the groom's procession," and jumped up abruptly as she ordered Ryūji, "Hurry up! Let's go see!" Ryūji obeyed and took off running after Kannani. The wedding procession appeared to be heading in the direction of the road by the Kakomon River. When Ryūji caught up with Kannani, she was already chatting excitedly with another girl who'd been following along at the tail end of the procession. "Ryūji, I just heard that this is her sister's wedding," Kannani said, pointing at the Korean girl Ŏnyŏnna.

As she was saying this she was already heading down toward the river, dragging Ryūji along by his sleeve. Although the river was frozen over, because the surface of the ice was rough, they hardly slipped at all. They ran across the ice to the other side of the river and then looked back to the procession.

The procession passed slowly along the opposite riverside. At the very front an old man with a ruddy face was carrying a red, purple, and white flag and was keeping time with the rhythm of his singing. A palanquin carried by married Korean men swung wave-like from left to right, filling the entire road. The custom was for these male porters to advance by swinging the carriage back and forth, oscillating from left to right. A big umbrella that stretched all the way from the front to the back covered the palanquin. Young, unmarried men carried this umbrella and they staggered forward under the weight of it, trying to keep in rhythm by swaying their heads back and forth. "They'll circle around Kakomon," Ŏnyŏnna said and dashed ahead to get to the front of the procession. To Ryūji it appeared that Kannani and Ŏnyŏnna were talking about all the wedding outfits, speaking in a super-fast Korean.

After Kannani showed off her pale pink blouse, Ŏnyŏnna proudly displayed her purple *ch'ima* skirt, saying delightedly, "This is the first time I'm allowed to wear this pretty skirt my parents bought for me, cuz it's the day of my sister's wedding. But still, wait 'til you see how beautiful my sister's outfit is! Don't you think it would be great to wear such gorgeous clothes even just one time?" At that point, the procession passed through a small gate with an aphorism written on it in big Chinese characters that predicted: "The first day of spring brings good fortune."

The inside of the reception house was jam-packed. Women servers were carrying dishes cooked in a stove below the floor heater to eight or nine guests sitting together on a wooden floor. A stew made from meat, bean sprouts, and Chinese cabbage, bowls of *udon* noodles, and rice cakes had been laid out beforehand, awaiting the arrival of the guests. Ryūji and Kannani wondered where the bride was. They looked around, but before they could identify her, Ŏnyŏnna showed up with corn cakes she'd brought from the kitchen. After she handed two cakes to each of them she dragged them to the mud wall so they could see the bride. "You can see her from here, can't you?" Ŏnyŏnna asked Ryūji in polite Japanese and smiled. From where they now stood, a little higher than the house floor where they'd been standing before, they were able to see clear into the room behind the stove and the floor heater.

When they peered in they saw the bride sitting on a long rug with her right leg drawn up to her chest and her left leg tucked underneath her. Her hands were gathered up and clasped together inside her wedding dress and her eyes were tightly closed. Her bright golden crown and rainbow-colored collar were especially pretty.

Ŏnyŏnna explained: "Today's the third day. She's waiting with her eyes closed in that position until the groom shows up." Kannani inquired, "And when he finally comes . . . ?" Ŏnyŏnna responded, "She'll have *him* open her eyes." As she sighed and shut her eyes just like the bride, Kannani mused, "That's really sweet. I wish I could be a bride." Ŏnyŏnna, whose eyes were in the same shut condition as Kannani's, burst out, "It costs 50 yen! Fifty yen is what my sister cost." She explained, "The place that owned my sister made him pay 50 yen;[2] the groom had to pay for her." As she grabbed hold of him under the arm, Kannani inquired, "Hey, Ryūji! Would you buy me for 50 yen?" Ryūji responded, "Sure I would, when I grow up." Then Kannani teased him by loudly exclaiming, "I doubt if Ryūji will *have* 50 yen when he grows up." Then she shifted her attention back to the bride. Ŏnyŏnna advised her, "If you become Ryuchan's bride, make sure there's no money involved. Aren't you two sweethearts the most famous couple in this city?"

Kannani brought the loose ends of her sash up to her face, which had turned crimson. Totally embarrassed, she ran as far away from them as she could, ending up next to a mud wall; she shrank down into a crouch and whimpered, "Ŏnyŏnna's so mean."

But Ŏnyŏnna wouldn't stop: "Ryūji's Japanese, so he doesn't need any money to marry somebody. But anyway, it doesn't matter cuz when Ryūji grows up he'll have lots of money because he *is* Japanese. Kannani, you'll be one happy wife married to a rich Japanese. Won't you, Kannani?" As Ŏnyŏnna kept teasing Kannani, she cast a mischievous eye toward Ryūji and laughed. Ryūji cursed her: "You little devil!" Ryūji pretended to sound angry, but his face turned red instantly; one could see he was blushing uncontrollably from the embarrassment.

While Ryūji ran as fast as he could away from the two girls toward the small gate, a strange feeling of delight sprang up excitedly in his body. Suddenly, though, his anger returned even stronger than it was to begin with and he lashed out at a stone with his foot.

He's clearly the best!
The very best groom in the world.

He heard the drunk's wedding song around the corner of the house and figured the procession was coming their way. Rushing out to meet it, Kannani and Ŏnyŏnna were just a little bit behind Ryūji, and farther behind them trailed relatives of the newlyweds who'd joined the crowd after the procession started. The bridegroom appeared from a carriage in the center of the procession, helped along by the guiding hands of the escorts. Family members of the bride strewed sacred ashes from the back of the procession and danced amid them as if the ashes were flakes in a snowstorm. The ashes scattered all over the place and accumulated even on the bridegroom's black crown and on the shoulders of his purple full-length cape. At that point, family members of both the bride and the groom bowed to each other. Just as the bridegroom was stooping down to pass underneath the small gate, Ryūji and Kannani heard another melody being sung, the piercing memory of which they'd be forced to recall over and over.

Ryuchan and Kannani are totally strange
Falling for a Korean slut puts all Japanese to shame.

A group of Japanese grade school kids suddenly appeared rounding the corner from an out-of-the-way path. They seemed shocked and embarrassed to see Ryūji and Kannani so unexpectedly.

"Well, well, look who we bumped into: the famous couple," said a middle school bully with big, round eyes named Katchan. Older than the other kids, he seemed to be the ringleader. So when he picked up a small stone and threw it, about seven or eight grade school kids followed suit and threw stones in the direction of Ryūji and Kannani. The stones missed them, but because Ryūji and Kannani were by this time fairly close to the procession, the stones that suddenly seemed to be coming from all directions struck some of the people in the procession.

"Stupid Japs!"

A group of angry Koreans in the procession responded to the stoning as they jumped out of the crowd toward the Japanese school kids.

"Who do you think you're talkin' to, idiot Yobos?"[3] was the parting phrase the Japanese boys left them with as they took off quickly back down the path. The Koreans in the procession only wanted to scare the Japanese kids and didn't chase after them.

> Ryuchan and Kannani are totally strange
> Falling for a Korean slut puts all Japanese to shame.

That same melody started up again as soon as the kids were in the alley. When Kannani heard it she couldn't control her rage and cursed them in Korean, "Pigs, you're not human!" She realized that this was the first time she'd lost her temper and cursed in Korean in front of Ryūji. Kannani was scooping up stones to throw back as she chased after them. She screamed out, "You're all a bunch of little bastards; I'll kill you!" Finally she gave up, and tears began to stream down her face; she just plopped herself down on the ground and started weeping: "It's a big, rotten shame!" Ŏnyŏnna consoled, "And right now when everyone at our school[4] is so happy for you and Ryūji." Ŏnyŏnna hugged her and stared into her face: "Japanese schoolboys are real pigs."

Ryūji, who'd been standing there impassively while all this was going on, became too ashamed and overwhelmed to deal with anything more and said, "I'm going home," and took off. Kannani followed right after him and when she caught up their small shoulders met. Without saying anything, Kannani used Ryūji's shoulder to wipe the tears from her face.

From the space in between the mud walls you could hear the voices of the happy Korean kids, and young girls were jumping up and down on top of one of the walls with their rose-colored kimonos flapping around joyously. The girls' hair, done up in pigtails, was dressed with special pomade oil; when they jumped down from the wall, their braids stood up toward the clear blue sky. From the opening of the alley, Korean boys were bounding up and down with excitement right into the biting wind, proclaiming, "Wow, it really took off! It really took off!" At this point, even though they were now pretty far away, the voices of those detestable Japanese school kids could still be heard. While maintaining their silence, Ryūji and Kannani walked aimlessly from one alley to the next shoulder to shoulder.

The sky had already gotten somewhat dark, but three or four kites were still floating around in it. The snowfall at Mt. Kwanggyo was pure white and it glittered brilliantly as it caught the reflection of the setting sun.

Ryūji could hear the long whistle of a train somewhere far off in the distance. As he was listening to it, he suddenly remembered the harbor area in his hometown where he played waiting for the freighters to pull in; they blew their horns in pretty much the same way. He daydreamed about all the things that had happened between then and the present time, when he and Kannani had become close, the images passing one by one like the windows of a passing train.

"I wonder whatever happened to Gengobei? He told me I should become the governor-general of Korea." Half-daydreaming, he was muttering all this in Japanese and when Kannani noticed this, she brushed her tear-stained eyes again up against Ryūji's shoulders and inquired, "Are you remembering stuff about Japan? It must be great there, huh?"

## CHAPTER TWO

Ryūji and his family moved into their house last year just around the time the peony flowers bloomed. His father was fired from a tin-manufacturing factory in his hometown on the coastal tip of one of the main Japanese islands, Shikoku, and subsequently came to Korea without his family to look for a job. He ended up finding work as a policeman for the colonial governor-general, a much better job than that of a factory worker. Ryūji heard that his father wrote to his mother from Korea explaining that, the monthly salary aside, he really appreciated the extra 50 percent colonial bonus. This was the time just after World War I ended, and in Korea the system of Japanese military gendarmes was being replaced by a system of civilian police. Because of the troubled period that followed this change, the colonial government significantly increased the number of civilian police, and the government treated them all very well. Ryūji's father told his wife that his new salary was equivalent to a fourth-level junior official in Japan and she proudly relayed this bit of good news to his grandmother. All the family members back home in Japan were delighted with Ryūji's father's success and their house buzzed with pride and excitement. Before long his father sent another letter home to Japan saying that he'd been able to obtain an additional position as one of the private police escorts of the Korean count Yi Kun-t'aek, and he was given a huge Korean-style house in the count's compound. In addition, he received even more perks for this second position and he could afford to send Ryūji—always a very bright student— to a special junior high school. When news of this arrived in Japan from Korea everyone praised father's good fortune. This was because smart children in their small town in Shikoku had to go to a city really far away to get to one of these special schools, making it very difficult for most of them to attend postelementary school. The bratty kids in his neighborhood said to Ryūji, "You get to go to a great middle school!" It was obvious to everyone how jealous they were.

Although their extended family could barely contain their joy, they began to worry when, all of a sudden, Ryūji's mother, Oshun, and Ryūji had to leave Japan to join Ryūji's father in Korea. Naturally, they'd all heard plenty about the anti-Japanese riots that had continued for a long time, beginning way back even before Japan's annexation of Korea in 1910. Ryūji's grandmother was concerned because her daughter-in-law and grandson would soon make the crossing to the so-called hot-tempered foreign country. The grandmother, who was originally from a samurai family, gave her family dagger to Oshun in front of the ancestors' Buddhist tablets, reassuring them, "This is just in case of an emergency." Moreover, just as they were about to leave, they performed a ritual *mizu-*

*sakazuki*[5] and all the family members cried together. Years later in Korea, carrying a string of fish on their way home from shopping on market day, Ryūji's mother would say with a chuckle, "Even though Korea turned out to be this nice, laid-back place where everything is so easy, we had a mizusakazuki before we left!"

Safe and sound in Korea, they were in a good position to laugh in retrospect at all the anguish they'd felt before they left. They remembered how, as the horn of their boat blew signaling the departure, the faces of grandfather, grandmother, and the other relatives waving goodbye to them became hazy. Then, as the big *torii* gates of the Hachiman shrine grew gradually smaller, his mother put her hand more than once in her kimono chest pocket to feel for her dagger. "I can't see the big torii of Hachiman anymore. I wonder when I'll ever return here with Ryūji; we might never see our hometown again if we're killed by resentful, crazy rioters in Korea." She felt so forlorn that she couldn't keep from saying this out loud through her tears to Ryūji, young child that he was.

Ryūji, to the contrary, felt brave and totally alive. "Just you wait; I'll become the governor-general of Korea, so don't worry about anything. A governor-general is like being the king of Korea, so I'll wipe out the rioters right away," he said to reassure his mom. But he was obviously trying way too hard as he soon lapsed into pleasant thoughts about mountains and rivers in Korea he'd never even seen.

Until recently, Ryūji's dream at school was to be a famous general in the Japanese army. But when it was decided he would have to go to Korea, he switched and wanted to be a war hero like Toyotomi Hideyoshi, who'd conquered Korea in 1592. Much of this resulted from being egged on by the village leader's bratty son, Gengobei, a name that made it seem like this kid was a middle-aged man: "In Korea everyone looks up to the governor-general, so you gotta be the governor-general. Go for it! My father said that you could do it, Ryuchan, because you're smart."

So Ryūji immediately became obsessed with becoming the governor-general of Korea. On the day before he left for Korea he and Gengobei had a parting toast to secure their promises at the army fort by the beach, and Gengobei made Ryūji swear that he would be the ruler of Korea, saying, "You have to do it!" Ryūji responded, "I promise you it's gonna happen." Ryūji's wild aspirations swelled even further as he fantasized that when he got to Korea he would care for and love the Korean kids and be respected by all the people, and when he *did* become governor, he would try with all his might to bring glory and prosperity to Korea.

But, never, even in his wildest dreams, could he imagine how quickly his idea of becoming governor-general of Korea would shatter.

When Ryūji met Kannani accidentally on his second day in Korea, his family had already moved into their extraordinary new house. His mother even *complained* about the spaciousness of the house. "To carry food from the preparing area to the family living room with the Korean floor heater in it, you have to walk through another family room eighteen feet long, climb up a stone staircase, and pass through a huge wood-floor room. By the time I get to the family dining area, the hot food'll be cold." Ryūji left his mother behind in the huge, empty kitchen and bolted outside; he was eager to check out all the strange-looking houses in his new neighborhood.

The house of the Korean count Yi Kun-t'aek was so big that its tiled roof ran right straight into and wrestled with the foot of a mountain; Ryūji couldn't even begin to guess how huge it was. He passed under the small entrance gate of the count's house that opened into a wide, graveled garden. The crimson gate, which he'd passed through yesterday, rose up on the left and there was a big yellow gate on the right. There was also a Western-style iron gate directly across from him, flanked on both sides with tall, red brick walls.

Ryūji peeked into the entrance of the big gate on the right; inside there was a garden with peony flowers blooming all over like a red sea. At the top of the stone stairs there was a magnificent mansion like the sea god's dragon palace; a palace that was silent, its doors shut to the outside world. Just as he was about to pass through the gate, five or six Korean workers suddenly stood up from within large beds of peonies. Ryūji quickly lost his nerve and gave up on trying to get inside the mansion.

Instead, he settled for a look inside the iron gate; it appeared that there wasn't anyone around. There were lawn gardens rolling everywhere and a fountain that spit water high in the air, spraying

48

splashes. At the edge of the mountain a chalk white Western-style mansion stretched out seemingly forever.

Ryūji had never before taken in such awesome, luxurious scenery. The Korean houses he saw from the window of the train when he first came to the colonies were really small, like the piles of dirt used for burial mounds. Pigs covered with crap seemed to come and go in and out of these houses no different from the actual humans living inside. Because of that lasting first impression, he never imagined that there would be such splendid mansions in Korea. Not very long after this, he heard from Kannani that Count Yi Kun-t'aek was a member of the Korean royal family and that from a real long time ago the area and the mansions had belonged to him and his family.

"When I become governor-general, you can bet I'll be living in a luxury-type place like this." As he lay down dozing on the soft grass, his dreams magnified limitlessly. However, his dreaming wasn't going to go on much longer. All of a sudden, a girl's piercing scream interrupted his reverie.

"Who's in there?" The girl appeared with a look of terror on her face; she was obviously scared. But as soon as she got a glimpse of Ryūji's face her voice began to calm down. "This is no good at all, grade school kids coming into a place like this." When he heard her say this it became Ryūji's turn to be frightened; he jumped up off the grass and ran up to the girl. "People will get angry when they hear about this and give you a hard time," she said.

When Ryūji approached her she had already regained her composure, although her cheeks were turning red. Despite the blush, she said boldly to him, "Grade school kid, you're the son of the new policeman; your name is Ryūji, isn't it?" Quickly her tone became gentler and she finished her statement with, "Just a little while ago, your mother was calling you in a really loud voice."

"Wow, ya know that I'm a grade school kid and stuff like that," Ryūji said as he stared at this Korean girl who could speak his own language so fluently. He was so shocked at hearing her perfect Japanese he forgot to hide his Shikoku dialect. The girl started to laugh. "Grade school kid, you speak funny Japanese," she teased him and continued, "Japanese kids all get to be grade school students. Korean kids are all just regular students.[6] What grade are you in? What's your last name?"

Ryūji turned rigid and martial as if it were the medieval warring period ruled by samurai and his name had been called out by his commanding officer on the battlefield. Standing at attention, he answered formally:

"I am in fifth grade; name: Mogami Ryūji; age: twelve years."

"What are the characters for Ryūji?"

" 'Ryū' is the *ryū* of dragon; 'ji' is the *two* of one, two."

"Ryū of dragon?"

The Korean girl appeared not to understand. She closed her eyes and tilted her head—was she visualizing the character, trying to write it out in her brain? Ryūji felt compelled to write the character for dragon, *ryū*, on his palm using his finger.

"I get it," she said. To communicate her understanding, she slapped her thigh with the palm of her hand.

" 'Ryū' is the *ryū* of *Ryūzan*, isn't it? For your information, Ryū-zan is the big station at the entrance to the city of Keijo.⁷ My name's Kannani and *I* live in this house. My father is a gatekeeper for Count Yi Kun-t'aek." Actually, Ryūji hadn't been aware until now just how many rooms there were on that side of the big two-story gate; a stone wall divided the rooms from a large garden. At the top of the stone wall melons as big as pumpkins were growing. From inside it, along with the sounds of water one could hear sounds of coughing that seemed like they were coming from Kan-nani's father. Perhaps he was getting water from a well?

Kannani said, "Your father is a retainer in the service of Yi Kun-t'aek, right? My dad is also one of his retainers. We're both kids of retainers." She smiled as she turned her head shyly, showing him her cheek with the dimple on it. "Let's get along well, okay? We will get along well, you know." Then the girl put her hand on Ryūji's shoulder and stared into his eyes. When she did that Ryūji sensed something sweet coming from her skin; her touch was making him feel uncomfortable. Stiffening up, he asked the girl her name for the second time: "What did ya say yer name was?"

The girl burst into laughter once more when she heard Ryūji's dialect. This time, however, she mockingly imitated his soldier-like military pose and stood at attention. She teased him by answering in the style of a rival in a formal gymnastic competition: "Name: Kannani; grade: fifth in the evening session of the regular school; age: fourteen. That's all, sir." Then, demonstrating to Ryūji, who seemed perplexed about the name "Kannani," she squatted down and picked gravel up off the ground; clearly she was about to do something. The garden was completely covered with gravel, and as she picked up the gravel piece by piece, the red soil underneath started to make the first line of a Chinese character. Gradually, Ryūji was able to read the three characters of her name: "ri," "kan," "nan."

"I get it, ri kan ran!" Ryūji proclaimed. Hearing his voice, the girl nodded her head with delight and said, "Mogami Ryūji and 'Kannani,' the Japanese pronunciation of the Korean name 'Yi Kanran.'" Then she promptly threw the gravel that she'd been holding in her hand up in the air, scattering it all over the place.

### CHAPTER THREE

In no time at all Ryūji and Kannani were getting along splendidly.

The morning after they first met, while Ryūji was leaving to see off his father, who happened to be wearing his police uniform, he realized that Kannani was peeping inside his house from in front of their family's small entrance gate. As they approached the gate, Kannani hid in the shadows behind the door of the gate. Saying goodbye to his father, Ryūji left him in front of their second, big two-story gate. When he was sure that his father had waved goodbye for the last time and saw him finally disappear down the alley, Ryūji, half-hoping, wondered to himself, "Maybe that girl is still there in front of my house?" and stooped under the small gate. At that point, Ryūji found Kannani where she was a minute ago, hiding behind the door to his house. She looked embarrassed and her eyes shifted furtively back and forth; then she put the belt-string of her overshirt into her mouth. As she did this, she realized that it was crumpled and tattered, so, out of shame, she bent her stiff arm like a bow trying to stretch the wrinkles out and make the belt-string prettier.

Ryūji's eyes showed his surprise at the fact that although Kannani had been strong and confident yesterday, her attitude was shy and modest today. He called out, "Kannani," and smiled. She smiled back at him, once again showing off the dimple on her right cheek. He yelled out an invitation: "You wanna go play, go play in the backyard with me?" and as he did he started to walk ahead of her toward the backyard where apricots and yusura trees[8] grew lushly.

Kannani followed behind him silently. When Ryūji sat down on the long root of a big ginkgo, she joined him and slid her right foot under her body and drew her left knee out on the opposite side. He didn't have any idea what to say. Suddenly, she broke the ice:

"*Tangshin sunsa adúl ina?* [You're the son of a policeman, right?]" she asked in Korean.

Not understanding her, Ryūji responded, "What did you say?"

"Aren't you the son of a policeman?" she said, this time in Japanese, nodding to herself and giving him a somber look. Ryūji looked at her suspiciously, so she explained to him in Japanese: "My father said that I can't play with the kids of a Japanese policeman."

"Why not?" he asked.

"Because my father hates Japanese; he hates the Japanese military police the most and he hates the Japanese regular police the second most. He says they abuse Korean people and they're mean."

"Policemen don't do mean things. Their job is to *get rid* of bad people who do mean things. Even my father says that. My father also says not to abuse any Koreans. Japanese don't do bad things, because we're subjects of the emperor and also because the great deity of Ise is watching us." With all his might, Ryūji tried to convince her. But she smiled sadly, letting him know she wasn't buying any of it.

Kannani responded, "Even our house, our very own house was ruined by the Japanese. Our family's fields had a brand new Japanese owner before any of us knew anything about it. This couldn't possibly be for real, so we just went ahead and started gathering the harvest, when a policeman came and took my father off to prison. Then they nailed the door shut to the private school my father started, saying that my father was teaching bad things to the kids. Then they forced all the Korean kids who were going to my father's school to go to a regular colonial school, whether they wanted to or not. So, my father had to ask his old friend Yi Kun-t'aek if he could work for him as a gatekeeper. Because of that job, at least we're able to survive."

Suddenly, Kannani jumped up and went to squat down in the balsam blossoms. Even though there wasn't any wind, one petal, then another fell to the ground. Fallen balsamine petals dyed the roots of the stalks red. Kannani picked up some fallen blossoms and crumpled them with her hand; red juice spilled all over her hand like blood. Kannani put some on the tip of her little finger and rubbed it in. From her little finger to her ring finger, then to the middle finger, and finally onto her index finger, all the fingers and tips of her nails were dyed blood red.

"Why are you drenching your hand in blood?" Ryūji asked.

"Oh!" Kannani said, her expression brightening up a bit. She smiled at him and responded, "When they dry the color will be great. All Korean girls do their nails this way."

She wiped the red juice off her fingers with her *ch'ima* skirt, seriously staining its navy blue cloth.

"You know, my dad's right; I don't like any Japanese and I dislike Japanese policemen the most. But still, I really like you." Kannani held Ryūji's face between her two hands and seemed to look directly into his face.

"The Korean word *tangshin* means 'you.' Learn Korean, just like I can speak Japanese. Then we'll be able to talk mixing up both Korean and Japanese. We'll talk about what happened to us at school, what's going on all over the world, and lots of other stuff!"

Then, Ryūji put his little finger inside Kannani's little finger and their fingers hooked and entwined, and he made an oath to her promising to learn Korean and promising to always be friends. Kannani started singing a song and waving her hands around:

> Pinkie-hooking pledge, pinkie-hooking pledge
> Don't break it, don't break it.
> A next-door lady croaked because she broke it.
> If you don't believe it, cut your finger and take it.

Where did Kannani learn such a song?

From that day forward, Ryūji and Kannani played together every day. Even though Ryūji and his mother, Oshun, constantly urged

Kannani to come play at their house, she always refused. So the huge garden on the compound, the street corners, and Mt. Paldal effectively became their playground. Kannani was free to play with Ryūji every day from 2 P.M. to 4 P.M. because there wasn't much cooking work to be done at Yi Kun-t'aek's house during the afternoon. So whenever Ryūji returned home late from his school, Kannani would be waiting impatiently for him in front of the big two-story gate. When Ryūji's figure finally appeared on the street corner, she'd get so excited she seemed to fly after him.

It was hard for Ryūji to deal with Saturdays and Sundays. Even though he knew perfectly well that Kannani couldn't come out to play on those days, from early in the morning he'd invariably wait, longing to see her in the usual place right in front of the gate to his house. The thing they talked about most when they were together was school. So Ryūji came to know all the ins and outs of the school for Korean kids that Kannani went to as intimately as he knew those of his own school.

He learned from her all about the old history teacher, Uemura, who lectured to the Korean girls about how Japan is always good and Korea is always bad; because of his biases Kannani and all the other Korean girls hated him the most. However, even if the teacher wasn't Uemura, no matter who came to Kannani's school to teach history it would be the same story because that's how it appeared in the textbook. Moreover, it was awful for Kannani to hear Uemura lecture about the conquest of the three kingdoms of Korea by the Japanese empress Jingū in the third century A.D.: "If that great era had continued, Korea would have been Japanese territory for sixteen centuries. You students would have been Japanese all that time and you'd be much better off for it."

Kannani displayed her bitterness by mimicking Uemura's speech. But it wasn't only her, about half the girls in the class were dissatisfied with Uemura's history class and on their way home from school they all bad-mouthed him.

The topic of Uemura's next class was "The Japanese conquest of Korea by Toyotomi Hideyoshi." The girls had arranged to interfere with his lecture by whispering and chattering to each other as soon as he began to speak. As the interruption started, Uemura could only stand at the lectern in dumbfounded silence, almost exactly as they'd planned. He was so angry it seemed like steam was coming out the top of his head: "That kind of behavior is why you'll lose your country to us, you demented students!"

A Korean teacher named Mr. Park taught all subjects, and because he was young and hot-tempered he got angry at them a lot; the students didn't like him either. However, in his geography class when they finally learned something about Korea, Park pointed to a map that was hanging in front of the blackboard. Then he said something magnificent: "Today, we are going to study the land that we are living in today, the one that our ancestors handed down to us; in other words, we're going to learn about the fatherland, Korea." The classroom instantly burst into an uproar as if they were at a theater; there was thunderous applause and loud whistling. Then he got flustered and angry and his mood changed dramatically. He tried to calm the students down by shouting, "Be quiet! Be quiet!" Even so, after that Kannani and her classmates made him one of their favorite teachers.

Kannani adored the Korean woman who taught singing, whose name was Kim. With her pretty mouth and great voice she taught the Korean kids happy songs even after school was over, gathering students together around her organ.

Ryūji always looked forward to hearing Kannani's stories about school. She would show him what happened in great detail, performing theatrically with voice, hand, and body gestures.

Kannani liked songs. Although her voice was shrill, it was still quite good. On the big rock at Mt. Paldal, Kannani and Ryūji would line their knees up in a row, raucously singing their favorite songs. As they sang, their songs echoed in the valley and would boomerang right back to them. Kannani and Ryūji laughed because it was so silly, and as they laughed, the laughter doubled back on them just like the echo of the singing.

This was around the time when the chestnuts bloomed. Kannani reported that she'd learned a new song at school and proceeded to sing it merrily. The title of the song was "The Blue-eyed Doll." She sang:

> When they arrived at the seaport of Korea,
> Their eyes were filled with tears.

Ryūji tried to interrupt her, claiming that the real lyrics were "the seaport of *Japan*," but Kannani refused to listen and went on singing. Ryūji tried again:

"That seaport in the song is Yokohama!"

"No way!"

"OK, whereabouts in Korea is it?"

"It's Inchon. In the song they landed at the Korean port of Inchon; Miss Kim said so." She refused to budge even one inch on the matter.

On summer nights Ryūji and Kannani often went to the Kakomon Gate. Seven floodgates were built on the river and whenever they were in the tower above the floodgates they'd feel the cool wind blowing through them. From the tower they watched the foam of the sprays of water falling from the seven floodgates.

While they were up there on the tower, the sound of flutes and bugles could be heard coming from a house in the distance. Every once in a while they could hear the sound of a hand drum played by the watchmen; the famous Korean folk song "Arirang" blended together with "Songs of the South Road" and "Songs of the West Road." The songs—most often it was "Arirang"—wafted and drifted in front of the house and through the alley:

> Arirang, Arirang, Arariyo,
> They cross over Arirang route.
> The farm turns into a road for cars,
> The daughter's sold as a prostitute.

Kannani liked singing this one; the sad melody seemed to stain the fabric of their whole colonial society. Ryūji learned this song, too, and it helped him endure the climb up the hill road with the sad acacias. He would sing it in Japanese:

> Arirang, Arirang, Arariyo,
> They cross over Arirang route.
> The farm turns into a road for cars,
> The daughter's sold as a prostitute.

It rained cats and dogs and the downpour continued nonstop day after day. Five days passed, then a week, but still it wouldn't stop.

Even while the sun was out fat raindrops attacked the tiles of the roof violently, tearing them completely off and scattering them all over the place. The rocky mud walls with stones wedged into them crumbled and toppled over easily. The garden got completely submerged under water. The gingko and cherry trees gasped for air — only their branches were able to breathe above the water's surface. To make matters even worse, water poured right into the kitchen from the garden. And because the kitchen was on a lower plane than the garden, it turned into something resembling a bathtub with jars, pots, and rice paddles floating on top of the water.

The time right before it stopped was the most violent time, as the storms roared wildly; after uprooting everything into the air it sent it all crashing back down to the earth. When an attack of lightning burned the grove of poplar trees and the straw roofs along the mountain's side, the storm let up for the first time. After it stopped, a strange silence took its place; then a blue sky spread adamantly far and wide. Right through the middle of it stretched an amazing rainbow, painting an arch across the entire sky from east to west.

Ryūji had never seen such a beautiful sky in his hometown; nor had he ever glimpsed such an intensely colored rainbow covering the whole sky.

It was right after the annual end-of-July typhoon. Even in this Godforsaken area it came only once a year. Like the rainy season in Japan, it came without fail every July and lasted for two whole weeks.

As soon as the rain stopped, Kannani rushed right over to play with Ryūji. While it was pouring outside, Ryūji and Kannani were forced to spend all their time inside their own homes without being able to see each other at all. Kannani rolled up her long pants to her thighs and her ch'ima skirt up to her chest, fastening the skirt in place with the string of her coat. She approached his house by wading through water so deep it reached all the way up to her thighs. As she waded through it, she balanced a bamboo colander on her head, holding on to it with only one hand; she was using the colander to carry wooden shoes. Looking at her from the wooden-floor room of his house, Ryūji was amazed at how Kannani, who was usually pretty much a coward, could have found the courage to do this. It made him intensely happy.

"Kannani, Kannani, you made it all the way through!"

Because the water was flowing rapidly into the ditch she was wading through, Kannani lost her balance and had trouble advancing any further. As she stumbled she smiled cheerfully and waved with her free hand: "Ryūji, let's go . . . down to the river." She looked toward him as she was saying this and fought with all her might against the strong current of the water. "Ryūji, there's lots of things swimming around in the river: makuwa melons, cucumbers, and watermelons; lots and lots of things floating right on top of the water. Let's go get some."

Finally, Kannani emerged from the water and sat down on a stone at the entrance to the big open room of Ryūji's house. Ryūji and his mother invited her right in, but she paid them no heed. Instead, she showed them her bamboo colander and explained how she placed things inside the sieve and returned home with them completely dry. Ryūji's mother, Oshun, admonished them, "Don't go over to the river just yet; maybe wait until the water has receded a bit."

Kannani protested, "If we wait 'til then all the stuff will already be gone." She clearly wanted to go right away. She hadn't rolled down her long pants and her ch'ima was the only thing covering her legs. "Even entire houses are floating around over there." With that statement, Kannani got their full attention.

"How do you know that?" Ryūji asked.

"Every year lots of stuff is flooded away," she said.

Since the water had receded a bit at that point, Oshun gave in and even decided to go along herself. The road remained entirely flooded out and the water came up to Ryūji's kneecaps. Still with the bamboo colander on her head, Kannani ran out ahead of them, looking back imploringly when they didn't seem to be moving fast enough.

As they came up to the edge of the river they could hear the fierce roar of the water. Kannani momentarily threw caution to the wind and dashed on ahead. There were throngs of people standing by the river's edge; there were even some Japanese people there, although they were just onlookers and not scavengers. The scavengers were almost all Korean and most of them were mothers. The men who were there were holding brooms and rakes and were either wearing only a coat with nothing on underneath, or were completely naked.

"There! There! A ton of stuff is going by!"

The people leaned their bodies forward looking upstream. Houses were crashing down the river, toppling over and into one another. Five burial mounds were crashing into each other and with each collision big clods of mud splattered everywhere.

The very first house appeared to be empty; all the residents must have escaped in time. In the second house there was an old woman clinging for dear life to the front of a floor heater, but as the house tumbled in the waves and capsized, a dying gasp "Ahhh!" was the last thing anyone heard from her; she disappeared inside the floor heater and was gone.

The third house was the most pathetic. A mother and four children were clinging for their lives to their big floor heater. The mother was desperately holding onto an infant, but she must have squeezed it with too much force and accidentally killed it, the child's head and feet were hanging down both sides of the mother's arms. The baby's lifeless face was pale and its eyes were half-closed. But even in such a condition the child's face seemed to look directly at Oshun. Such a rueful eye sent a shiver through Ryūji's mother's body and she couldn't stand to look at it any longer. The mother and four children who were clinging to the sinking house for dear life screamed out a blitz of pleas for help. Their sounds would doubtless cling forever to Oshun's ears; even much later, after she'd returned home safely, she would hesitate in fear before going to bed. For in the darkness she never failed to see those eyes and hear those screams as if it were her very own Ryūji clinging desperately to a floor heater for fear of his life.

Jars, desks, and other furniture were swept along in the current; the water uprooted pigs and cattle as well. A dog clutching onto a small piece of timber howled pitifully. Makuwa gourds, cucumbers, and watermelons whirled by and were swallowed up by the water, only to resurface farther downstream. Although people had rakes and brooms at their disposal to try to snare the various items,

most things were caught up in the swift currents and violent whirlpools at the center of the river and people could only watch helplessly, stupefied. Whenever something valuable swept up close to
the riverbank, the scavengers created a big commotion fighting
over it. Big brawls started out like this and occasionally battlers
ended up being thrown into the dangerous water.

A willow tree on the opposite bank from where Ryūji and Kannani were standing had a trunk that twisted out, hanging over
the water. Because of the ideal vantage point offered by the trunk,
more than ten Korean youngsters had crawled up it and were
hanging down from the branches. The tree appeared unable to
hold up under all their weight. Whenever something flowed by, the
Korean youngsters shouted out with excitement and fished into
the water with their hands.

Makuwa gourds streamed by in bunches, and as they did the
Korean kids' eyes lit up. They hung from the trunk and branches
upside-down by their feet like monkeys and tried to reel the things
in with both their hands. One kid was able to grab something close
to him only to struggle with it, as he was unable to completely
lift the item up out of the water. At that point, something tragi-
cally sad happened. Maybe the kids' weight had become too much
for the tree to bear. In any case, the roots of the willow tree were
washed out by the water and started to uproot. Before you knew
it, the tree—roots and all—came completely out of the ground
and along with the group of Korean kids supported by it fell into
the dangerous water. Immediately, the strong undercurrent swallowed everything up.

"Ugggh . . ."

"Terrible."

Captivated by the screams and wails of the families and friends
of the Korean kids, the crowds on the riverbank could only cry out
in sympathy. There were those who hadn't exhibited much concern before, when they saw things like the little kid dead in his
mother's arms and the people struggling for their lives inside their
own houses as they were swept down the river, and who had eyes
only for gathering the smallest amount of food. But when these
people witnessed with their own eyes the tragic event that just occurred, the ten or so kids falling from the tree to their instant death
in the river, they forgot what they were doing and just let go, crying

hysterically one after another. The crowd of onlookers even forgot about the dozens of rice chests and loads of melons that floated right in front of their eyes. All they could do was chase wildly after the kids drowning under the water, bawling their eyes out.

Suddenly, the drowning Korean youngsters surfaced, sticking their heads out of the torrent trying to catch some air. At that point, just as unexpectedly, their feet were scooped out from under them and they were thrown under the water again. Their parents and relatives yelled out names along the river's edge.

"Kang Suna. Hey!"

At that moment Kang Suna, the child who was being called, popped his head out of the water struggling for his life. He was holding a big melon above his head, desperately trying to pass it on to anyone higher up on shore who could safely grab it. But once again, he was swallowed up by the waves.

No matter how hard he tried, Ryūji couldn't fathom why the Korean children would risk their lives for the sake of a silly melon. He judged this behavior stupid and unnecessarily reckless. Later on, when he asked Kannani why they did this, she seemed unusually sulky and cross. "You'll never understand," she replied, and that was the end of the discussion.

Nevertheless, long after that tragic incident, Ryūji finally understood. Most Koreans didn't get enough food to satisfy their hunger—even with Manchurian chestnuts and some millet, much less rice. When the summer makuwa melons are ripe enough to be picked, they become the everyday food of Koreans, who eat them continuously from breakfast until lunch and right on through until dinner. The makuwa is about the size of a rugby ball, and costs one-half or one cent each. It's about the same price as a foot-long loaf of sponge gourd.

Still, even though the melons are cheap, Korean children aren't allowed to eat the juicy insides. They have to wait around patiently for the rinds left over from whatever the adults eat. When they eventually get their hands on some, the kids put the leftover rinds on their heads and parade around before they start to nibble on them.

Once, Ryūji got to sample a slice at Kannani's house—it was nothing special. The melon was watery, unripe, and had no sweet taste at all. Unlike the other Korean kids, Kannani had opportunities to eat whole slices of melon. The expression on Kannani's mouth at special times like this clearly stated that there is nothing in the world that tastes as good. But it wasn't just Kannani. After buying a melon people would never fail to chat pleasantly with anyone along the roadside as they made a show of eating it. Whenever someone with money came by to invite their friends, "Let's go eat melon," they'd hold a garden party, forming a circle around the rich person's crate of makuwas. It finally dawned on Ryūji that only on these occasions do poor Koreans feel happy, like they have something valuable in their life.

## CHAPTER FIVE

On the way home from school one day, a swarm of grade school kids formed a tight gauntlet on a tree-lined road of Akashya. Amid the raucously laughing schoolboys the shrill screams of schoolgirls reverberated. The husky schoolboys, probably in sixth grade or higher, circled around the schoolgirls, who appeared to be trapped in the middle of it.

Ryūji ran up and wedged his way inside. Bullies were known to tease and harass girls on this out-of-the-way street. Maybe a tomboy or two had become somewhat interested and started to half-play along with the teasing. Ryūji was wondering if that's what happened as he pushed his head between some tall boys.

"*Omoni, Tasukete!* [Mommy, Help!]" A cry sprang out from inside the boys' circle in mixed Korean and Japanese, at the same time as a girl's head stuck out of the crowd.

Four big Japanese schoolboys were forcing two Korean schoolgirls to the ground. The boys were grabbing one of the girls by her hair while a second was being shoved around; after a struggle the second girl finally fell into a pile of white dust and sand. As the four schoolboys pinned her down, they started throwing handfuls of dirt into the girl's face. Using his wooden clogs, one schoolboy kicked the schoolgirl being held down by her hair in her side. "Oww!" The girl struggled to get up. The girl who'd been knocked off her feet was also kicked really hard: "Ahhhh!"

Amid these shrieks the girl who was being grabbed by the hair focused all of her energy into getting up. When she finally managed to, she rammed into the circle of attackers head-on. As she came face to face with one of the schoolboys, she kicked him really hard in the shins with her wooden shoes. Tossing away her shoes that were already falling off, the girl dove nimbly like a squirrel into the center of the ring of schoolboys. The fierce-looking gang suddenly couldn't hold their line. Thanks to her bravery the second girl escaped. But the brave heroine left behind was now in a much worse situation. Two boys who'd been surprised by the attack and a little humiliated by the girl's escape angrily joined their two friends in the assault on the remaining girl. Apparently as a result of her struggling with all her might to get up, the string of her underpants broke. As she pulled on the leg of the schoolboy holding her ankles, her skirt slipped further and further from her body. Her blue shirt peeled off and was trampled on. Now the boys could see her bare legs and buttocks shining like white cucumbers.

As soon as he saw her exposed body parts, one schoolboy whose hands were unoccupied roared, "Yeah!" This was Katchan with the big round eyes. Visibly excited, with his knees shaking, it appeared that he was looking along the ground for a tree branch. Finding one, he held up the branch and said, "Hey, I'm gonna do ya with this!" He squatted down and forcefully spread her thighs apart. Then he stabbed into her vagina with the tree branch.

The girl let out a heart-rending scream: "Ahhhhhhh!" Startled, the boys pinning her legs and arms to the ground released her and jumped up. Then, with the main perpetrators in the forefront, the whole gang of boys cheered loudly in unison, "Banzai, Banzai," and retreated from the girl like a receding tide. For just a second, Ryūji wondered if the girl might be Kannani. Since she was concealing her eyes and nose with her hands, he couldn't see her face.

The girl turned around, rose up unsteadily like a *daruma* rocking toy, and pulled out the tree branch. As she did that, the blood-covered tree branch sprayed blood around her crotch and thighs. She picked up the branch again and hurled it away into a barbed-wire-enclosed mulberry field and ran off quickly toward the mountains in the opposite direction from the branch. She crossed a small valley, came to a little hill, and suddenly screamed in Korean, "Ahh, Mommy!" As she cried out, she collapsed. Ryūji thought for sure that it was Kannani. He called out to the girl: "Kannani . . ."

Weeping loudly, he crossed the small valley and came to the small hill. From the girl's crotch two lines of blood trailed over her white thighs—a pitiful sight. Ryūji wiped the blood off the girl with a handkerchief. He looked at the girl who'd been running and falling down hysterically, all the while covering her face with her hands. Her eyes and nose were still covered by her arm as she lay on the ground, seemingly unconscious. He moved her arm gently, attempting to wipe the blood off her face. Suddenly, completely awake, she bit into Ryūji's hand. "IEEE." Letting out a terrified sound from her windpipes, she scurried away up the mountain.

It wasn't Kannani. With a sigh of relief, Ryūji watched the girl flee. Her underpants were puffy and baggy and hung down around her ankles, making any movement difficult. She climbed up the mountain hill at weird angles like a madwoman.

Ryūji found it impossible to tell even his own mother anything about what had happened, let alone Kannani. Talking about this horrible act carried out by his Japanese schoolmates made *him* feel ashamed. By that same evening, the place where the girl had bit him turned purple and swelled—it stung. So his mother wouldn't notice the wound, he rushed through his supper and left the table in a real hurry.

However, the next day at school during his free composition class, Ryūji made up his mind to write down in his journal everything he remembered about the events of the day before. He concluded his testimonial with the following: "I've heard that we Japanese govern Korea justly and fairly, but actually this isn't true; I'm very depressed about this. Kannani, the Korean girl who lives in the house next to mine, says she despises Japanese people. The closer I get to Kannani, the more I understand her feelings. I like Kannani; I like her very much. There's no better friend than her. I despise the Japanese boys who bullied the poor Korean girls yesterday and who humiliate Korean friends like Kannani. It would be better if the Japanese who do things like that are thrown out of Korea. Our school principal told us that we must be good friends to Koreans and that Japanese who marry Koreans are great heroes. I truly believe this."

After the free-writing period, the teacher normally designated three or four students who are good at writing to read theirs out loud in front of the entire class, and then gave evaluations. On that particular day the teacher chose Ryūji to go first. So he read out loud his freshly inked words with the heightened emotions he'd felt yesterday welling up inside him once again. The students fell dead silent as they listened to the whole story. Ryūji was quite good. "The truth always wins out," he thought to himself as he finished, then looked to his teacher for the standard evaluation. However, the teacher had turned pale as a ghost; his hands had been shaking with fear. With blank eyes, the teacher looked at Ryūji's eyes and then lowered his gaze down to his desk. Finally, he said sullenly, "Fine, that's enough for today," and exited the classroom, leaving the stupefied students just sitting there without any supervision.

Ryūji got really scared by this unexpected response. He was sure he'd get into trouble with his teacher, and maybe even suspended from school. But in the end, neither Ryūji nor his parents heard a single word from the schoolmasters pertaining to Ryūji's composition. Moreover, from the very next day on his homeroom teacher conducted class as if he knew nothing at all about it. However, his classmates drew the conclusion among themselves that "the six-graders and middle school kids who attacked that little Korean slut are in for big-time trouble." Since there had always been tattle-tales in situations like this, there was no doubting that the schoolmasters knew who the troublemakers were. However, the perpetrators received no punishment of any kind. At the same time, the situation led to more and more unexpected developments.

First, beginning with the ringleader, Katchan, and then followed by the other three troublemakers who'd taken part in the incident the other day, they began to taunt Ryūji and Kannani regularly with their chant going to and from school.

Ryuchan and Kannani are totally strange
Falling for a Korean slut puts all Japanese to shame.

After a while, under the direction of the troublemakers, the number of participants in these demonstrations increased to ten and then twenty students. Eventually, there were some thirty kids who took part in the daily event. These school kids yelled out the same lines over and over:

Ryuchan and Kannani are totally strange
Falling for a Korean slut puts all Japanese to shame.

They would even chant this in unison right in front of the big gate to Yi Kun-t'aek's compound, then scream out, "Geeet," and disperse with a wild glee.

Ryūji's mother, Oshun, didn't hear about this until much later, finally learning about it from the wife of the police chief Noguchi, who'd transferred to their neighborhood three months earlier from the station at Kangwon-do. "It's just kids' pranks, that's all. There's no ill will behind it," she said, chuckling. Then her tone turned serious and she advised Oshun, "Nevertheless, you have to be careful about your son's involvement with the Korean. Everybody says that Korean girls' temperament turns bad; and she's older than him, too." This was the topic of conversation during teatime, but for Oshun, the topic was bitterer than the tea. That night she discussed the situation with her husband, Matabe, asking him, "What shall we do?"

"Do nothing," was his response. "Just leave them alone." He clearly wanted to hear nothing more about it. But because Oshun was a woman she couldn't just forget about it. The following day, she waited impatiently for Ryūji to return home from school. As soon as he arrived she started to lecture him: "Right now everyone's really rude. Things seem really nasty at school, too. But the school principal said that fifth-grade kids like you who do well on their grades would go directly to middle school next year without having to go through sixth grade. So why not just forget about playing with Kannani? You should study instead. If you do, I bet you'll forget about her in a hurry."

Ryūji listened to his mother in silence, mumbling "Uh, huh" every so often. But Ryūji disappeared that night just after her speech. By dinnertime and then by bedtime, he still hadn't returned home. What happened? He and Kannani obviously had disappeared somewhere together, but their whereabouts were unknown. Oshun felt attacked by evil premonitions and couldn't stand the waiting. It was doubly unlucky that her husband, Matabe, had left her alone to go to Seoul. Why of all times did he have to go now? Desperate, Oshun flung herself out of the house to ask the police to get a search party together. Although it was the middle of the night, she knocked wildly on the official residence of Police Chief Noguchi.

"It's Ryūji; Ryūji might be dead. Ryūji, he might be dead." Repeating the same words over and over like a crazy person, she burst out crying in front of Noguchi.

However, by the time morning rolled around and the sun's red face appeared over the mountain, Ryūji and Kannani returned from wherever they'd escaped to. With looks on their faces that communicated they were clueless about the police search party, they appeared in front of a downhearted Oshun, who was squatting down on the root of a gingko tree in front of the hospital. The two of them had been walking around in circles all night and when they saw Oshun's face they cried out in unison. Ryūji's mother was absolutely speechless with relief, but when she tried to stand up to hug them her legs gave out beneath her and she collapsed in a heap on the ground.

The previous night, Ryūji and Kannani had met by the pond in front of the North Gate. They sat on a small hill covered with pine trees, casting fishing lines into the pond. They didn't catch much: two skinny spider crabs and a carp no bigger than a little finger pranced about inside their fishing creel. Ryūji finally spat it out: "Starting tomorrow, I have to study; next year I'm going to enter middle school. I'll get back at that stupid grammar school of mine."

Kannani asked, "You mean you won't play with me any more?"

He answered immediately, "I can't; I have to study. My mom yelled at me."

"That's mean," Kannani said as she threw a small stone that plopped into the shallow marsh; the ripples from the stone radiated.

"But it will suck if you go to middle school and it will suck if you become governor-general or some other big shot. Because when you go to Japanese middle school they'll teach you to bully Koreans . . ."

The sky darkened little by little. A gray, thick fog enveloped the North Gate. There was something in the distance, maybe a funeral procession. Cries called "mourning wails" drifted toward them, alternately loud and soft. This moaning seemed to convey the sad, miserable existence of this town that had been stained by such darkness.

The two of them turned their heads away from it.

"Look at that sky; look at how crimson it is, so pretty." The setting sun hung out over the hill on the cape. It resembled a big lump of fire falling toward the mountain. As it shone on the cirrocumulus clouds, they reflected various colors like the shell of a giant abalone inlaid right into the sky.

From the far side of the cape came the sound of a gong; the commotion of happy and boisterous people was carried along with it. It was the Harvest Season Festival. Every autumn, whether the harvest was good or bad, farmers traditionally carry faded banners boasting "Bumper Crops." They form a long procession and dance wildly with their heads twirling back and forth, left and right, and round and round. They dance along with the procession waving their wrists and contorting their ankles. The sound of the gong brought to mind vividly the image of people dancing.

"Want to go take a look?" asked Kannani. Ryūji stood up like her and faced the cape: "Toward the cape; it looks fun and lively."

Ryūji weighed in on the matter: "Oh, that place. But if you want my opinion, I hate that Suwon town." Kannani responded, "OK, let's go someplace where there's no bullying; Ryuchan and me, just the two of us. Let's go somewhere we'll always be able to play together." So they went out on the opposite side of the cape. All the commotion of the Harvest Festival could now be heard coming from a totally different direction. The side of the cape that Ryūji and Kannani were now walking around on was much more beautiful than the opposite side.

Night fell. Lost among bushes in unknown paths, the woods stretched all around them with no exit in sight. Ryūji and Kannani felt helpless and a little scared. But before they even realized what was happening, the moon came out. The moon seemed to be rising from the direction of Suwon; it shone serenely. In the mirror of the moon's reflection, Ryūji thought he saw his mother.

Suddenly he determined, "Hey, we could be devoured by wild beasts." With lightning speed, anxiety took hold of his heart and shook him. "Let's go home." So Ryūji took Kannani's hand and they ran down the hill so fast it was like they were tumbling head over heels. They cut through the meadow and dashed across the frozen river, wandering around all through the night.

## CHAPTER SIX

Four days straight of warm sunshine began. Roads that had been frozen over crackling with ice just the day before were now thawing little by little from the sunshine. It was right around the time of day when Ryūji normally returned home from school. The surface of the road had white bubble-like things on it and a faint vapor was rising up from them.

In their wooden geta clogs, Japanese walk with a lively bounce. In spite of the sound of the dry, crackly ice road, the tips of the geta get caked with wet mud. One, then two days pass like this. On the last day of the four warm days, the road is so soft that the tracks of the horse carriages sink right into the slushy mud. Then, as always, comes the three days of cold weather in the cycle. The subsequent freeze encases in ice the carriage tracks and even entire footprints left by the bottoms of geta clogs during the thaw, sketching in ice the direction of the people who'd passed that way previously. Until it snows or rains again, people can check for their own footprints made during the fourth day, when everything melted.

Although it still snows occasionally, it sometimes rains as well. At the end of warm spells like the present four days of sunshine, a somewhat strange phenomenon often occurs: it feels as if a sudden summer shower is falling, but the rain quickly passes. Around the same time, water will flow down into the ditches like a waterfall from the high point of the center of the road. As the water runs into the ditches, it freezes solid, just like someone was conducting a scientific experiment.

This represents the biggest pain in the neck for Japanese wearing the geta clogs because the bottom grips of the geta tend to slide sideways. If you're careless you'll fall into a ditch. And when you do your best not to fall into the ditch—oops, you fall right on your butt. Middle-aged women wearing coats often fall face-up this way, and when they do, the turned-up red hems of their kimonos scattered all over them attracts unwanted attention.

Since Koreans wear shoes made of straw they don't slip a lot. But even they fall sometimes, heaving a sigh, "Ahhhh," and looking around to see if anyone saw them. "Just my usual bad luck," they joke, and pick themselves up off their behinds. Even when there's nothing stuck to their clothes, they wipe off the area around their behinds carefully, just in case.

The rule promising that three cold days have to be followed by a fourth warm day turned out to be correct again this time. During the three days of awful cold, the north wind blows across the frozen water and the telephone poles clang like distant thunder. After a while, as these cold days end, the first of the heartwarming days of sun brings with it the feeling of something finally having melted and loosened up inside one's body.

When Ryūji got as far as the corner of the American church, he suddenly recalled that today was market day. In the area at the end of Four Roads, waves of people were gathering like whirlpools. As Ryūji looked around, even people just passing through had bunches of dried fish tied up with rope and bundles of cloth for sale hanging down from them. There were also people carrying flat, large Korean pans on their backs making them look like the turtle that Urashima Tarō rode in the famous Japanese fairy tale.

"Kannani is waiting for me," Ryūji thinks to himself as he bends forward trying to negotiate his way through the crowd. On market day, Kannani always stands at the same crowded corner of Four Roads waiting for Ryūji. As she sees Ryūji, she makes the usual signal to him with her eyes twinkling and, taking the lead position in front of him, proceeds to walk ahead. So he won't lose sight of her, Ryūji follows close behind trying not to look too conspicuous. Until they come to the entrance of the marketplace, he continues to follow behind her. In the area just in front of the household goods shop on the corner, they'll raise a cry of "Hurray!"—once they've entered the marketplace they know they'll be safe; there definitely won't be any Japanese bullies there. So, at Four Corners Kannani is actually more cautious than she has to be; she looks around obsessively to check if there are any bratty schoolboys who might have seen them. If things aren't completely safe, they can't proceed with their plan.

At Four Roads the people are packed in together and move quickly like whirlpools. It's so crowded that Kannani can't be seen standing in front of the glass door of the general store.

Today, for some unknown reason, strange-looking people are all over the place. A person wearing a thick, swollen-looking rice planting straw hat walks by. Three people wearing only short, half-length coats over coarse hemp kimonos in the cold weather go by. Later on, Ryūji would ask Kannani why they were dressed this way, and she said they were in mourning for a dead parent and they had to wear these mourning clothes whenever they went out in public for three whole years.

But when he arrives this particular time, Kannani is nowhere in sight. She's not in her usual waiting spot in front of the glass door of the general store; not on top of the rock next to the meat market; not even at the corner of the Rising Sun Petroleum Company.

Slouching down underneath and slipping through the arms of the adults, he walked all over the place looking for her. Up to that point, Ryūji hadn't paid any attention to what was going on inside the whirlpools of human beings. However, once he realized that Kannani wasn't anywhere to be found he figured he'd sneak through the gantlet of adults and check out what was going on in the middle of it all. There he saw a fight happening between a man in a black coat and a man in either a brown or what was once a white coat, now turned filthy. The two stood there as if they were actors in some kind of theatrical farce, exchanging words. While they were having words their eyes didn't show any anger; they were merely making grand, impetuous gestures. It was totally different from a Japanese fight, which can start only when someone physically strikes his opponent.

In a Korean fight, the combatants just stand there without wrestling each other and exchange words stubbornly, persistently, for what seems like a long time. This is followed by a period when their voices gradually get louder as they begin shouting at each other. But even here, when the pitch reached this level, neither of the fighters seemed at all bloodthirsty. Every so often, they would turn toward the spectators and ask for their take on the situation, with the fighters taking turns telling their own side of the story. The audience nodded for more, laughing among each other. To a few audience members this intermission seemed to be going on too long, and one finally stepped out of the crowd toward the fighters to spur them on to real battle. This seemed to work, as at last the fighting spirit returned for both of them and one of them grabbed his opponent by the collar and pulled him close.

However, right away the peacemaker stepped in and, once again, the two were separated. One headed off toward the market and the other stormed off with his friends in the opposite direction toward South Gate. After heading off in separate directions for a while, it seemed that being separated from one another only meant lonely frustration, so both sides looked back and glared wide-eyed at each other.

Next, the black-coated man from near the market raised his voice.

"Hey, I wish I'd fucking killed you. Your mother is no better than a pig in shit, a real loser." When the man who was walking toward South Gate heard that, he asked, "What the . . . ?" and turned to go back. This time the fighting ring moved from Four Roads to the marketplace, so the waves of people quickly pulled away from Four Roads and spread out into the marketplace itself.

Fights normally start at Four Roads and after some whirlwind negotiations move to the marketplace. The final climax invariably takes place at the market entrance, at the end of which one or both of them will be on the ground half-dead. After letting them sleep it off a little, people return to help them, throwing water on them and then taking them to get something to eat and drink.

Typically, Korean fights are for enjoyment and seem to be controlled more by the spectators that the actual combatants. Nevertheless, every once in a while Ryūji would see a small, pitiful man being dragged around from morning to night with blood flowing all over his face, the sight of which made him sick to his stomach. Ryūji thought that the Korean way was terrible; he compared this to Japanese fights, where blows are exchanged—Pow! Pow!—and people leave immediately afterward; the Japanese way is clearly much better.

As the fight gets underway, the theater ticket taker, a man with a long face like a Korean pumpkin, comes over to mediate. There are pockmarks around the edges of his big, round eyes. Whenever that man enters the fighting ring, even if it had been a clean, honest fight up until then, he transforms it into a theater for a struggle over life and death.

Today, the pockmarked, pumpkin-faced man isn't around, which is fortunate because the fighters will no doubt be quickly brought over to the food joints for some cheap booze and munchies. Ryūji leans against the Raijin-Gusan Oil warehouse facing the general store waiting for Kannani, but she doesn't arrive. On a street corner a candy hawker interrupts Ryūji's waiting with a loud call for customers:

> Get your first-class, first-class white candy,
> Buckando date candy
> Japanese Osaka millet candy.

He gestures ostentatiously while belting out his sales pitch. Ryūji had heard of but never actually seen Osaka millet candy.

Three or four Korean kids gather around the candy hawker, brushing right up against the front of his wide box of sweets. They each bought one stick of white candy, broke it, and brought it up to their eyes, concentrating on the number of holes in the candy. The rays of the sun shine brightly through the narrow holes of the stick of candy; this is actually the best part of it for the kids. There were some kids who actually got three small sticks. But children aren't the only ones enjoying the spectacle of the candyman; adults, too, pressed forward to one side and were absorbed in all the fun.

Ryūji had never eaten this kind of top-shelf sweet. Once before he was given round, black sugar candy from the Japanese candy shop. And every once in a while he got thick candy striped with red and white lines from visitors coming from Seoul, the capital. Still, Ryūji wanted to try this stick candy just once, and it would be great if it was smothered all over with sesame. He'd begged his mother to buy him some, but she frowned disapprovingly and told him that because Koreans use spit in their hands when they make candy, Korean-made candy is dirty and unhealthy. He replied that if that's the case, if it's in fact sesame, than it must be good since you can't see the candy under the sesame. But with a stern face she'd replied that *all* Korean-made candy, including sesame, is made with spit and anyone who eats it will soon after become infected and die. Ryūji thought, "How sad, all Korean kids will get sick and die just from eating candy." But when he thought more carefully about it, he realized this didn't make much sense because these same Korean kids always looked healthy and lively. Moreover, he'd never heard anything from Kannani about Korean kids dying after eating candy.

## CHAPTER SEVEN

A loud, mellow-sounding echo of "Khah, Khah" could be heard coming from the direction of the general store. Upon closer inspection, there was a person squatting down in the front of the store who was tapping fingertips on the edge of one particular Korean kettle among a whole stack of them. For some reason, Koreans feel that it's necessary to tap on kettles before they buy one; after they hear the kind of sound the kettle gives off, they decide whether to buy it or not. The person squatting down testing the kettles apparently had slid her hand from one kettle to the next, and in so doing, accidentally collapsed the neatly stacked display of kettles, causing the loud sound. Just as that accident was happening, Kannani finally appeared in the front of the store. Ryūji yelled out, "Kannani!" but, maybe because she was so far across the road, she didn't seem to hear him; as usual she was facing toward the school. Because lots of people were passing by, Kannani was standing on her tiptoes with her mouth open slightly, struggling desperately to locate him. Her beautiful white teeth were all shining in a row. From directly behind her, the glass window contributed to the brilliant effect she gave off as it received the sun directly.

After waiting for a while she slouched her shoulders in disappointment with an expression that said "He's not coming," and, tentatively, she decided it was time to leave. Sliding her left arm underneath her armpit, she caught it with her right shoulder and walked away with a self-consciously broken-hearted, theatrical performance.

She crossed the street and went to the front of the candy store, selecting one piece at a time: first some sesame and then some stick candy. Finally she grabbed some date candy and put a two-cent coin down on the counter. The candy store owner picked up his scissors and, with first-class precision, he concentrated his energy into cutting off a piece of date candy for her: "That's right, Buckando date candy, with a fantastic taste that comes right from the island." Saying that, he sliced off a piece on a big board and handed it to her, but it was only as big as a marble. She took it, and once again crouching down in the direction of school, she held it up to the light. Finally releasing from the crouch, she stood up and this time reversed her direction and went off toward the storehouse where Ryūji was waiting. Ryūji was planning on surprising Kannani when she arrived, so he was deliberately silent. He was having trouble breathing with his lip zipped up like this, so when he almost bumped right into Kannani when she finally got close, he felt like his voice was so hoarse, he couldn't shout even if he wanted to.

At last Kannani noticed Ryūji and she greeted him with a squeal. At that point, her body was trembling intensely, and after some time in this state Kannani finally breathed a sigh of relief. Kannani queried, "What's up, Ryūji? What are you doing in this kind of place? You surprised me; why didn't you say anything?" He responded, "I did call out to you once, but you didn't hear me. The next time I tried to nothing came out; it was like something in a dream." Kannani broke the date candy and the sesame candy exactly in two and handed half of each to Ryūji. "Please eat some; you said before you wanted to try it."

Although Ryūji took it, his mother's warning about the dirtiness of Korean candy was sounding in his ear and he was unsure of what to do. Kannani placed the marble-like candy in Ryūji's hand and said, "Please eat it, Ryūji; it's *not* dirty, you know." Then, after a few seconds had passed, she looked at the hesitant Ryūji and then put the red, dried sesame into her mouth and Snap! bit it in half with her teeth. Taking the bitten-into piece, she put it right into Ryūji's mouth. The soft scent and feel of the sesame on his tongue was delightful. Although he wasn't sure that Kannani's saliva was on the candy, he thought that he detected some and he felt that it was even more delicious than the candy itself. "It's sweet, isn't it, Ryūji?" Kannani asked with her head tilted inquiringly to one side. She was looking right at Ryūji and noticed that he had a smile on his face; she turned and immediately started walking ahead of him.

Ryūji realized that he had never tasted anything as good as that gum, sesame, and stick candy. The knotted, angry brow on his mother's face seemed kind of silly to him right now. The ice seemed to disappear just as they stepped onto the road, and mud soon began to cake thickly on their wooden clogs. The sun was burning bright and strong and they thought that spring was already approaching.

Countless oxcarts moved slowly past them. In the gaps between them slowly trudged oxen, loaded down with pine needles. It was probably owing to the fact that it was so close to spring, but the road seemed unusually crowded.

Perhaps she was enjoying sucking on the candy too much, because Kannani wasn't walking as briskly as usual, and as Ryūji was scraping off the mud that had stuck to his geta clogs and socks, they found themselves surrounded by a crowd of people. The people involved in the fight stretched all the way from the electrical company up to the edge of the bridge to the market. Trying hard not to look at the fighting, Ryūji turned the corner and found Kannani waiting by the front of the grocery store, three buildings down from the corner. People were pulling their loads down from the oxcarts and human traffic was clogging up the area in front of the store. They were unloading something strange, something red.

Shifting her attention, Kannani said, "Ryūji, do you know what it is?" and pointed right at the thing. Ryūji twisted his head around to where she was pointing and said, "I have no idea what it is, what do you think, huh?" Kannani exclaimed, "It's an octopus. Look, there are lots of legs. I'm telling you, it's an octopus." Ryūji doubted her. "What? This thing?" He opened his eyes wide and stared. There were circular wart-like things attached to it, warts one after another as big as two-cent copper coins. Kannani opined, "People can catch these in Ryūji's country, in a faraway place." Ryūji answered, "You think so, huh? This is completely different from the kind of octopus that swims around in the beach of Hachibanhama in Japan. I wonder where these things live around here, these monsters." She suggested, "I learned about it in geography class. It comes from that Japanese island north of Honshu, Hokkaido." Ryūji reminisced, "Ah, Hokkaido." "Yeah; I bet they caught it in Hokkaido and then brought the octopus here after a long journey."

With regard to things in the market area, Kannani seemed to know all the ins and outs. Most likely, it was because she'd often come here with Yi Kun-t'aek's cook and maid. There were stores that had pollack fish in stock and stores that had displays of sesame candy. What looked like white sugar coming out of a straw bag at one store turned out to be something called baking soda. And surrounding this congested area was a jumble of smaller roadside stands.

Kannani was playing with the hand mirrors that had blossoms attached to them. Then she started counting the seashell buttons and was checking to see if the needle points were sharp or not. "Ryūji! Ryūji! I'm going to make you a coin purse, OK?" Ryūji answered, "No, you don't have to do that," and Kannani shrugged her shoulders figuring he wasn't that enthusiastic about it. But she persisted and told him that in Korea you make a coin purse for the person you like and then give it to them. "Even if you give it to your brother or sister It's OK. Ryūji, you're my brother, you know, Kannani's younger brother. So, I'll make you one, OK?"

Although Ryūji nodded his head "Yes," he wondered if Kannani could organize all the things necessary to make such a complicated present. On New Year's Day Korean kids carried around embroidered coin purses. Among the young Korean men there are always several who'd been given beautiful purses embroidered with a pair of mandarin ducks swimming side by side. Still, Ryūji wasn't sure if Kannani was capable of making such a thing, or if she had enough money for it. Kannani whispered "Ryūji" directly into his ear, and smiled. A sugary smell transmitted into Ryūji's ear and a sweet emotion melted through his whole body.

Kannani burst out with: "Kannani is a wise *yanban*[9] today, a three-penny yanban!" Ryūji responded, "What's a three-penny yanban?" Kannani explained, "Yi Kun-t'aek's old uncle is a yanban, but he's a real one. Me, Kannani, I'm a three-penny yanban."

Ryūji understood at last. Finding the whole thing amusing, he laughed. Kannani laughed as well, with the sound ringing out from her whole throat. Ryūji realized that he'd never seen Kannani in such a good mood. Kannani was exuberant. "Yeah, because I'm rich today, this three-penny yanban will treat you to whatever you want." Ryūji replied, "No, it's OK; you don't have to. You should hang on to your money."

Usually, he tried to avoid streets that were filled with the smell of food. Still, it was always on his mind and he couldn't help stealing peeks at the food that was there even though he usually didn't have the money to buy any of it.

Although there were soy sweets, sesame sweets, and fluffy bread available to anyone with money, and Ryūji, who'd been offered a treat by Kannani, was pretty hungry, he turned his head away stoically pretending not to be interested in food. Instead, he gulped down his spit in preparation to say something: "Let's turn at the dry goods store and go down to the river just like we always do." Kannani nodded. But before departing, she finally bought a yard each of red, blue, and yellow thread after lots of haggling over the price. She obviously bought them with the intention of making one of the coin purses for Ryūji.

Off to one side of the general store was a vendor standing with some chickens, their legs and wings tied together with rope. The chickens were picking at tidbits of food spilled on the ground from the grain merchant across the street. There was also a rabbit and two small pigs. While they waited for someone to buy them they ate their feed. A little farther down was a vendor who was selling eggs, with ten eggs wrapped up in a package of straw and tied at the top. The vendor would hang these down from a line in singles and pairs of ten. These people stand in the street like this all day until they've sold all their wares, the lined-up shacks looking like mushrooms with their straw roofs sitting atop exposed support beams.

When people turned the corner and entered this area—the *real* market—they could already taste the delicious smell of cooked oil fat in the air. And the smells sure did travel. The vendors' shacks stretched out one after another; these didn't have any walls, just poles stuck in the ground; they were porous and wide open to the world. Today, long kitchen tables and kitchenware were lined up on big display stands, and they stuck out beyond the borders of the store. Off to one side, large Korean kettles seethed unsteadily over a blazing bonfire; pig flanks were simmering and the sides of oxen were jutting out over the fire.

The smell of the meat cooking and the smell of the sliced onions rose up leisurely from the steam inside the cooking pot. Pulled in by these smells and the dizzying allure of the food market, crowds of adults would gather around to sit cross-legged on the ground, bringing food steadily into their mouths with chopsticks and spoons. It's hard to comprehend how great the enjoyment is that the market day (which comes only once every four days) brings to these neighborhood people. Even when people are broke there's always plenty of them hanging out on seemingly every street corner of this area; they just show up carefree and penniless and somehow manage to amuse themselves until nightfall.

There were ruddy-faced drunks around, some of them slapping their thighs while singing raucously and others contorting their shoulders and bodies wildly while dancing. Among them Ryūji saw the man with the black coat who'd been fighting just a little while ago and let out a startled cry. There was a big wound on this man's face and covering it was some kind of brown stuff that looked like dried grass. Just below the scar were streaks of caked, black blood. Ryūji told Kannani that this was the guy from the fight, but she didn't seem to think it was such a big deal. When he asked Kannani what was up with the dried grass all over the guy's face, she replied that it was tobacco. Ryūji asked Kannani, "I wonder why they fight like that?" Kannani responded, "Because they're bored." Ryūji quizzed her, "What? You're telling me they only fight because they're bored?" Kannani elaborated, "The young men who fight still have energy left to do other things. My father said he wishes he still had that kind of spunk." But Ryūji couldn't really get his head around much of the meaning of any of it.

For some time Kannani had been staring over in the direction of some eggs cooking. They were being dropped into a small pig-iron pan that had yellow-colored oil spread on it. Little by little, while the yokes of the egg opened up, onions were dropped into the pan.

One Korean kid rolled the food up, paid, and left. An old lady who seemed like she didn't have anything to do with any of this was relaxing on top of a rock, sitting with her legs crossed. Kannani went up close to her and put up two fingers, then she called Ryūji to come over. Ryūji asked, "Those things are omelets, right?" She answered, "No way! They're not, Ryūji." Kannani's eyes shone with the pleasure of having complete control in this situation. "It's called *butchigi*: soybean flower, green soybean flower—it's delicious. It's fit for a king. Hold it together like this." So Ryūji copied exactly what the Korean kid had done a little while ago, and then checked the taste. Somehow he didn't think it was all that delicious.

Just then, they heard the sound of horses' hoofs shuffling to a stop. From the direction of the river they saw two Japanese military police on horseback gallop up to one of the eating places and dismount. Because the waves of people who were milling around in that spot moved quickly out of their way, Ryūji and Kannani were nearly crushed right into the military police. The old woman of the butchigi store was holding a pan and a ladle; she stood up quickly. Then she began her preparations to get out of there in a hurry.

The two Japanese military police dismounted slowly and then went into the middle of the pub. By now there were tons of people around and it was impossible for little Ryūji and Kannani to see what was happening inside. Then suddenly they heard something that sounded like a whip, or maybe a rope. "Oww!" came what might have been the heart-rending sound of a grown man in pain, but because the sounds were all jumbled together it was hard to be sure.

The wave of people moved unpredictably and chaotically in several directions; they had grown into an awesome tightening whirlpool of humanity, even bigger than the crowd attracted by the fight earlier. "Anyone who starts any trouble will end up pushin' up daisies—this person here is a common criminal!" barked the Japanese police, barely audible above the collective crescendo of the crowd. Although the police said "criminal," it was unclear who the criminals were. In no time at all, a sound resembling the Bang! Bang! of a pistol burst out. With that sound the huge wave of people began to shake hesitantly, finally moving toward Ryūji like an avalanche. When they realized it was coming right at them, Ryūji and Kannani took off together.

They had been holding hands, but when the Bang! went off, before either of them fully realized it, they let go and were separated in their flight. When they finally stopped running, they rested underneath a willow tree on the riverbank. Then Ryūji impetuously grabbed Kannani's proffered hand and she wrapped her arms around him. Kannani trembled nervously; Ryūji wasn't sure if it was her trembling or his own that he was feeling. In this position, they both somehow felt safe.

Suddenly two or three Korean youths came running so hard toward the riverbank they almost fell into the river, whereupon they changed direction and joined a crowd of people going in the opposite direction of the bridge. Just after that, somewhat like a topknot that was hacked off at the base and was shaking all over, an old man who had just left the area arrived at the riverbank where Ryūji and Kannani were positioned. He plopped himself down on the ground, relaxed his head, and breathed a sigh of relief, "Ahhh." Because it was sort of strange to see the man there so close to them, Kannani and Ryūji moved further away from him in a real hurry, putting some distance between themselves and the guy. Ryūji's face was a little red from blushing and Kannani was blushing as well. Then, something happened that was typical of embarrassing situations like this: their voices became noticeably louder than normal

Way back in the middle of the human wave the so-called criminals had been handcuffed, manacled, and put on the backs of horses one after another. Then the Japanese military police galloped away with them. Although the whole thing happened in a flash, it was clear that the Korean man who'd had his face bloodied in the fight was not among the people handcuffed and led away. The military policemen's pistols were put safely back into their leather holsters.

The old man near Ryūji and Kannani said "Oh, no" as he saw them off, then he stretched his legs and said to them, "I asked back there if anyone was killed. They told me that nobody was killed; the cops just fired their guns into the air." Ryūji's lips were still trembling a little as he asked, "I wonder who they're looking for?" The man replied, "I'm willing to bet it's not just a 'common criminal' or robber, like the Japanese cop said." Kannani's words and facial expression said that she understood exactly what had happened.

Kannani and Ryūji walked away indignantly on a road lined with willow trees, heading in the direction of Kakomon Gate. Kannani analyzed the situation: "I wonder what they did, huh? What did they do? Did they do something good or something bad? Sometimes they arrest Koreans for doing good things, too, you know."

Although the surface of the river had begun to melt, the middle was still frozen. Nevertheless, the portent that signaled that water would soon break free and flow was somehow audible. You could hear its message in the metallic sound of the ice, coming from the depths, far away.

## CHAPTER EIGHT

The next day Ryūji went to school and learned about something that had taken place unexpectedly. After the third class session, the entire school was called to the courtyard for a talk with the school principal. That day, March 1, was the funeral ceremony for the Korean king Yi Sun-jong. Lots of people from all over Korea attended it, including Ryūji's father, Matabe, who left for Seoul on the first train that morning, so early the sun hadn't even come up yet.

The funeral procession for King Yi in Seoul was supposed to proceed to the imperial burial ground in Gold Valley from the old royal palace and the Tongdae-mun, passing through Chong-ro. It was rumored that there'd be tens of thousands of people from all over Korea in attendance, watching from alongside the funeral route. Ryūji fretted and whined, saying that he wanted to go, too, but Matabe refused to listen. Besides, he had school and, moreover, nobody knew how many hours the people in attendance would have to wait before actually seeing any of the funeral procession. While they waited the attendees would have to stand up straight on their feet or sit perilously on rooftops to get into positions where they could see anything at all of the procession. And then there was the problem of where Ryūji would go to the bathroom during all this time; apparently he would have to pee into a beer bottle. Ryūji wasn't sure if his dad was serious when he held up a beer bottle and showed how he'd have to pee if he went to Seoul, but anyway, in the end Ryūji resigned himself to not going.

According to the principal's address in the schoolyard, while the procession was going on in Seoul, a maelstrom of protest had broken out from the middle of it, when someone yelled out: "Three Cheers for Korean Independence!" Apparently the cheers spread infectiously from one to another, and in a matter of minutes the cheering had spread throughout the whole crowd. The principal warned them that more and more Korean people were joining in the uprising against the Japanese and that the demonstration seemed to be spreading to the outer areas far away from the capital city. Seoul itself was in riotous turmoil. He said because of this they would have to cancel school for a while. Then he instructed the students on how to return to their homes safely. First, students were divided up according to where they lived: those who lived in front of the station and those who lived in the new, model town area; those who lived inside and outside the old castle wall; those who were from Tsubomura and those from Engawa hamlet. The older students were supposed to guide the younger students. The principal insisted that on the chance that the Japanese students see some Korean kids on their way home, they were not to get into any fights, but behave themselves properly and proceed directly to their homes quietly. All the students went back to the classroom and got their schoolbags and shoebags and lined up in the schoolground. Ryūji's group included all the kids who lived inside the castle wall area and it followed the group of kids from outside the wall area. The student leader of this group was named Watanabe. He was in the second year of middle school and was quiet and shy. Katchan, the kid with the big chestnut eyes, was another of the leaders. The general idea was that the older students, middle school and above, would form a protective line in front and in back of the younger students, sandwiching them loosely.

Because of the principal's warning, everyone kept quiet until they exited the school gate, just like *they* were in a funeral ceremony. While they walked down the slope in front of the gate the group of kids who lived in front of the station, the one with kids from the strategic area, and the kids from Tsubomura hamlet all split off from Ryūji's group. So the bigger group decreased by half, and as a result, they felt unprotected and a little scared.

It wasn't long until a group of three or four Korean school kids appeared. The leader, Katchan with the big acorn eyes, started singing "Ryōyō Castle," a song from the Russo-Japanese War that was the famous Japanese war hero Lieutenant-Colonel Tachibana's song. Even though they were young they knew it very well because it was sung before they played competitive games like push over the stick and attack the territory, to energize them as they faced off against their opponents. Katchan was the song leader and all the other kids accompanied him. The group of kids from outside the castle wall and from Engawa hamlet all sang it really loud together, so loud that three or four Korean kids got scared and avoided them by scurrying to the side of the road like mice. When the Japanese kids saw this they got pretty confident and one bragged, "Those Korean kids are nothing; it's easy to conquer them cuz we have the spirit of Yamato." Another kid seconded him, saying, "That's right, we have the Japanese spirit so we can do anything we want." Not all of the students acted up, though; some followed the principal's orders and didn't pay any attention to the Korean kids.

They passed by an American church, a French church, and an Anglican public orphanage; these had continued to operate in Japanese-controlled Korea. There they came across an equal number of Korean students. But instead of saying anything to them, they passed through this area in silence. Next, they moved through the street where all the official residences were located and, because the group from outside the castle wall and the group from Engawa hamlet had separated and taken the main road, the only group that went via the back road was the group from inside the castle—Ryūji's group. Because everyone was going in different directions, the main group had shrunk to only fifty-three students. They were disheartened and a little scared. On all sides of them in the neighborhood they were in mulberry fields that fed into tree-lined roads. Korean-style houses with straw roofs were scattered here and there; except for these there was nothing else in the area save a storehouse for a sake production company.

By the time they arrived at the area where the Japanese school-boys raped the Korean girl, they were all hoarse from signing the war song. "Sing it one more time! Sing it like you're going to fight your last fight." While Katchan was egging them on further, they heard some shouts coming from the middle of the mulberry field; stones had just been thrown at them from bushes in the same area. Katchan said, "It's no fair, it's no fair! Our enemies are using flying weapons!" as he took off toward the mulberry bushes. Some middle school students and sixth-graders followed him into the field. But Watanabe made a stern, determined face and said, "The rest of you guys all just follow me," and he started running. First-graders, second-graders, and a few girls followed him silently; they were all biting their lips, trying hard not to cry. When they got to Holegate, it appeared that people had started a fight back where they'd just retreated from. Somebody said, "Katchan's been knocked down!" Indeed, two Korean kids were beating up Katchan and his hat flew off. The fifth-graders were wondering if they should go rescue him, but Watanabe said firmly to them, "No way." He yelled, "Hey, don't even think about! We're all going home," and led them back in their direction home. When they passed under Holegate they came across another group of Korean kids that was a little bigger than their group. This group of Korean kids was clearly itching for a fight, but just as they were about to pounce on them one of the Korean kids said, "Don't do it, one of them is the Japanese cop's kid!" He added, "That kid is Ryūji, you know, Kannani's boyfriend." Thus, one Japanese group was able to escape danger.

Three policemen riding bikes approached them rattling their swords and brandishing pistols. One of the police was Onoda's uncle and another was Sumikawa's uncle; yet another one was a Korean gendarme named Kim. Watanabe asked them for help, explaining to them that the older students were being beaten up. The policemen nodded their heads and took off in that direction.

After everyone split up, Ryūji finally arrived home to the familiar two-story gate of Yi Kun-t'aek's compound. Evidently, no one had heard anything about the uprisings that were going on all around them. From the morning right up until when Ryūji got home, people were mourning the death of the Korean king; they'd been crying and wailing all day long. Regardless of whether they were actually sad or not they continued on like this. The wailing and crying was almost like the singing of a chorus, with high notes and low notes somewhat in the manner of a religious hymn.

They were mourning the death of the king who had reigned until very recently. This was the same king who'd lost his country; the same king who people were angry at for selling out Korea to the Japanese. He was a sad, pitiful king. Maybe it was because he was such a tragic, sad king that these people kept crying and mourning in the same way they would over the death of one of their own relatives.

Ryūji became inexplicably sad and he almost started to cry himself when he pushed open the red door of the cherry gate. "Why do Japanese people and Koreans have to fight each other so often? Why do even Japanese and Korean *kids* hate each other so much?" He looked everywhere for Kannani, but she wasn't around.

He crossed the courtyard and returned to the gate of his house. He felt unable to take the side of the older Japanese students who were being beaten up, but at the same time he didn't feel comfortable watching approvingly as Korean kids—even though they'd clearly been bullied by Japanese kids—got their revenge. Somehow, this inability to take sides made him feel so depressed that he hardly had enough energy to push open the door to his own house.

CHAPTER NINE

From that evening on, the sounds of mourning transformed decisively into the "Three Cheers for Korean Independence!" Maybe everything in the world had changed dramatically.

At the cherry gate entrance of Yi Kun-t'aek's compound, the terrible sounds of tossed stones falling on the steel locks and scraping the metal fixtures of the gate were audible. At the small gate entrance of Ryūji's house, too, the stones flew right past all the way up into their inner courtyard. Ryūji's mother, Oshun, was muttering "This is horrible! This is terrifying!" as she hastily fastened and locked tight the front door to their house. She added spitefully, "This is why I didn't want to come to Korea in the first place."

Strangely, Ryūji's father hadn't returned home yet; apparently he was still in Seoul. Finally, though, when the moon began to get full, he returned home, whereupon the adults got immediately absorbed in discussions about the nature of the demonstrations in Seoul. He was so late because he had gone to report to the official residences before actually coming home.

Ryūji was getting sleepy and in his semiconscious state he couldn't understand what his parents were talking about. But it was clear that while the huge and beautiful funeral procession was proceeding, from somewhere off in the distance the sounds of "Three Cheers for Korean Independence" were reaching a boiling point. His dad was disturbed by the fact that even people who had pulled themselves up onto roofs near his location just to watch the funeral procession were quickly energized by the cries for Korean independence and pumped their fists up into the air as they started to cheer in unison with the other Koreans.

The next morning Ryūji woke up to discover that his father wasn't at home. Only when night fell and it got really late did his father return. On this particular day he was wearing his official Japanese uniform, but the next day he changed into regular clothes. On the third and fourth days his father changed once again, this time into some Korean clothes that he had somehow gotten his hands on. Naturally he put away his military sword and kept only a pistol, which he kept hidden inside his Korean clothes. When his father came home at night, he reported, "I saved several people today," a figure that multiplied quickly to "I saved twenty or thirty people today."

Ryūji's family was sad and angry when they heard some of the stories going around, like the one about the Japanese man Matsugawa, who was stammering on and on how about he'd built his orchard himself and no Koreans were going to steal it from him; and the one about the old man who owned the Nagasakiya hardware store who was swinging his military sword around dangerously, practicing so he could use it on Koreans. On the other hand, though, positive stories like the one about Ryūji's father appearing in front of bloodthirsty people like that sword-wielding hardware store owner and the angry Matsugawa and calmly rescuing Korean people from certain danger made Ryūji's family very happy.

Ryūji's father detested the police fencing instructor. This guy was always waving a wooden sword around in the fencing area. Even though Ryūji had actually seen the instructor browbeat and force an alleged criminal to confess to a crime he hadn't committed, the true character of this man was even more horrible than that—the fencing instructor's face made him look like the devil incarnate while he was terrorizing that man. The instructor arrogantly showed off his fencing talent, and he reportedly was using a sacred, ritual sword to murder live prisoners.[10] It was said that this butcher was increasing the number of victims of his atrocity by one a day: yesterday he did it to two people, today three people, and so on. Maybe it was revenge on somebody like the Korean ringleader of a group that assassinated Japanese people in this way. Whatever the case, Ryūji's father spoke out strongly against perverting the ancient art of Japanese fencing for these ends, especially the practice of butchering people with new swords who hadn't even committed a crime. But Ryūji's father was also skillful at fencing and he was sure he could defeat the man if they dueled, his father said, slapping his arm muscles for effect. When the present disturbance died down, he would quit his police job for good. Sitting around sipping hot tea to soothe his tired and aching body, Ryūji's father confessed that he wanted to get out of police work altogether and go into some kind of business instead. The sooner, the better.

Ryūji's mother had a splitting headache and had been in bed sleeping all day long. However, when Ryūji tried to take one step away from the Korean floor heater, she called out, "Ryūji, get back here," which was proof that she hadn't actually been sleeping. Even when he had to go to the bathroom he was forced to ask permission each time, to ensure that his mother could keep constant tabs on his whereabouts.

While the human sounds of the demonstration for Korean independence were alternately moving closer and receding like the roar of the ocean, snow had started to fall. The snow was dry and fine. Probably they were in for a three-day cold spell. Even the rowdy voices on the street got perfectly quiet while the snow was falling.

Thanks to the snowfall, Ryūji's mother was able to relax, and after the days of insomnia she needed to make up for lost sleep and totally collapsed. When she woke up, she applied both her headache compresses as well as an *umeboshi*[11] to her head (it looked like she thought the umeboshi would help with the headache); Ryūji thought she looked pitiful.

As he stepped out of his house to get some snow to eat, he thought he heard a voice like Kannani's saying "Ryūji, Ryūji." When he looked to see who was there, he noticed that a hole had opened up in the thick Korean paper door at the side of the back courtyard. He moved toward it and although he could only make

out one of Kannani's pupils, it rotated around and seemed to follow him. Finally she said, "Ryūji, let's go play outside; it's stopped
snowing."

Ryūji nodded his head in agreement and tiptoed back across his
main room so as not to alert his mother. He quietly put on his
geta sandals and then went outside to the backyard. There were yusura plum trees everywhere and their small flowers were covered
with snow. When Kannani saw Ryūji she put her finger to her lips
to shush him and then she ran into the middle of the yard. Ryūji
understood that this meant that he shouldn't speak; he nodded
and followed her.

Kannani went to the mud wall and grabbed a sumomo plum
tree branch; she was standing up straight on the mud wall with no
problems at all. The snow on the branches dropped on her face and
chest and she brushed it off her. Then she grabbed the branch and
shook it and the white powder sprayed around as if it had actually
snowed once again. As the snow powder gradually disappeared
like the lifting of a fog, Kannani was smiling and beckoned him
to come closer.

Ryūji shivered, trembling with excitement. For him to go beyond the boundary of the mud wall meant that he'd be outside
the area of his mother's supervision; he didn't know what kind of
things would be in store for him. But it didn't take him long to
make up his mind—Ryūji took off toward Kannani like he'd just
left the starting blocks for a track race. Then, just like Kannani had
done, he grabbed the plum tree, did a pull-up on it, and climbed
up to the top of the mud wall. But he wasn't able to accomplish all
this as easily as Kannani.

To help Ryūji all the way up the wall, Kannani grabbed Ryūji's
body and finally pulled him up by his hands; then she turned in
the opposite direction. All they had to do was jump over the ditch
to get to the hill beyond the mud wall and they'd be free from all
parental surveillance. Kannani counted "One, two, three" in a soft
voice and jumped off the wall as Ryūji jumped off with her. They
managed to avoid falling into the ditch and took off to climb the
hill together, holding hands tightly. Ryūji was breathing heavily as
he climbed up the hill. When they reached the big rock, Kannani
suddenly let go of his hand and hugged him. Embracing him she
blurted out, "Hey Ryūji, what were you doing day in and day out

all that time?" Ryūji heard something like sobbing in her voice; he felt tears welling up in his eyes, too.

They weren't embarrassed any more. Kannani was blushing intensely but she didn't pucker up her lips for a kiss. But she didn't cover her mouth with her belt or turn her body away either. Then she exhaled and hugged him again. Ryūji put his arms around her and held her soft back. Their chests were touching; it was sweet and painful at the same time. Kannani said, "Hey Ryūji, I kept watching you while I was squatting down behind the door; I don't even know how many hours I was waiting for you in that position!" She released his arms and looked at him petulantly. Ryūji noticed for the first time how big and beautiful her eyes were; they seemed to be growing bigger and rounder. She explained, "That paper in the sliding door sure is thick, cuz even after I put some spit on it and tried to soften it up, I couldn't make a peep hole. The paper was frozen solid. But I put my ear on it once and heard you singing that song about the battle of Ichinotani.[12] But the problem was that if I called out to you in a loud voice your mother would have been able to hear it, but if I spoke too soft *you* wouldn't have been able to hear it. But finally you showed up, so Kannani leaped out at you! Anyway, what were you doing day in and day out all that time, huh, Ryūji?"

CHAPTER TEN

When Kannani and Ryūji climbed up the mountain hill the town below was white all over from the snow. Because of the snow cover the houses looked like hair let down out of a bun, or like small mushroom stools, or even like balled-up pieces of confetti. All of the gates—east, west, north, and south—the tower of the church, the bridge, and the storage facility all looked like they were covered with white sugar. They thought it looked like a picture in a magazine from some country in northern Europe.

While they were looking down at the scenery, both on the small hill facing the gate and on the small pinewood field beyond the river, they saw some Koreans gathering together making fires. One after another, they heard the shouts of "Three Cheers for Korean

Independence" cross the valley of the town below and echo in the mountains.

Kannani's eyes were sparkling as she said "Look, they're all out." Then she asked suddenly, "Hey Ryūji, do you know what the Monroe Doctrine is?" Ryūji answered, "No, I don't." He was a little disappointed that he didn't know anything about something so important-sounding that she appeared to know lots about. Kannani explained: "It's what President Wilson of America said. The Monroe Doctrine says that each race of people should determine its own affairs." Ryūji didn't understand what she was talking about at all. "Silly, it means that Korea will be independent. If we continue yelling out the 'Three Cheers for Korean Independence' President Wilson will come to Korea in an airplane and save us." Ryūji asked, dumbfounded, "In an airplane?" She said, "Yeah, Ryūji, in an airplane; isn't that awesome? He'll come save us in his airplane."

On the small hills scattered around below them, people were rising up and chanting "Three Cheers for Korean Independence!" Those voices came all the way up to the mountain, bounced off them, and rebounded back down again. Kannani raised up both her arms and cheered "Hooray!" in Korean and Ryūji also put his arms up and in Japanese repeated, "Hooray!"[13]

Kannani was bubbling over with optimism: "Because Kannani said it in Korean she said 'Manse!' and because Ryūji used Japanese he shouted 'Banzai!' Isn't it great that we did it together? If we keep doing it like that, Korea can be independent, you know."

Kaboom! Off in the distance they heard an explosion. Maybe it was the American President Wilson? They looked up into the sky. But the airplane that he'd promised to fly in to liberate Korea was nowhere to be seen. In truth, neither of them really understood exactly what an airplane was. Whenever there was a picture of one in a magazine, it looked like either a huge dragonfly or maybe a black kite that had spread out its wings.

It was now apparent that the explosion had come from the middle of the road on the facing small hill. Two automobiles prowled the area like ants. When they stopped, soldiers in khaki uniforms got out. The soldiers lined up on the snowy hill, their guns pointed up to the sky. It seemed some Koreans on the hill had been throwing stones and cheering for Korean independence somewhere around that area. Suddenly gunshots rang out: Pow! Pow!

While Ryūji yelled out "Soldiers!" a feeling of incomprehension came over him. Just then, a wave of Koreans fled from that area, cutting through the field of snow. The soldiers followed after them, opening up a gap between them and the Koreans. The Koreans scattered over the small hill started to merge gradually into one large group and when their numbers reached a critical mass, several of them became emboldened enough to turn around and throw rocks at the Japanese soldiers in hot pursuit. In no time at all, the number of the soldiers increased as well.

This time the soldiers were definitely not just shooting into the air, but were starting to shoot at people. Kannani turned white with fear and clenched her lips together. "Ryūji, what should we do? Should we go back home, or maybe go inside the church? The church is American, so they'll protect us." When they looked back they realized how far away from home they were, but the church was in sight. When they descended down the hill toward the church, the groups of Koreans that were chanting "Three Cheers" had moved in succession from the road to the direction of the church, seeking refuge inside. Although it was not yet time for the church bell it began to ring; suddenly, voices singing hymns could be heard emanating from inside the church. The high-pitched tone was probably the result of there being so many women singing.

When they arrived at the base of the hill they could see the roof of the French church right in front of them. Finally, the Koreans stampeded into the church like a snow avalanche had descended on it. Chasing after them were the military police in hot pursuit.

Kannani urged, "Ryūji, I don't think it's very safe around here either; let's go home." The two of them changed direction again and crossed the valley from the direction of the hill. They crossed two valleys and climbed up a small hill; from there they could see flames rising from the church. They weren't sure from which one, but the women's beautiful singing voices continued to echo from inside a church.

Kannani asked, "Ryūji, I wonder if the people who escaped into the church are being burned alive?" Her angry face got small and seemed to transform into the shape of a fist. As she spoke she saw fire and black smoke billowing from the church. Abruptly, on the white snow there appeared black smoke and red flame; it was quite vivid and strange. When they got to the same rock corner where they'd been shouting out their "Hoorays" just a little while ago, Kannani grabbed both of Ryūji's hands, gave him a sad look and said, "Hey, Ryūji; Wilson isn't coming, is he? It's not looking so good for Korean independence either, huh?"

In Ryūji's ears both the cheers and the sad cries over the Korean king's death stuck, but he couldn't distinguish one from the other. The church burned completely down to the ground. They thought that all the people must have been burned to death, too, so Ryūji took hold of Kannani's small hand with both his hands and held it tightly. He didn't know any other way to respond to her depressing question about President Wilson and the tragic murders except by holding her hand. Kannani sat down disconsolately at the rock corner and looked up into the sky for a while. Then she said in a surprisingly cheerful voice, "Oh, Ryūji, I have something to show you," and started to look for something in her sleeve. She continued, "I'm making something nice for you," and she took out something that looked like a small bag and showed it to him. It was a piece of white coarse material and on it were two doves lined up next to one another. Their bills were red; the outline of their bodies was blue; and their feet were yellow. She stitched it all together with some string she'd bought when they were at the market. "They're Ryūji and Kannani," she said as she pointed at the two pigeons, smiling wistfully. She promised, "It'll be all finished after I sew their mouths and put the cord on it; then I'll give it to you." Ryūji felt really happy and caressed the rough Korean cotton.

## CHAPTER ELEVEN

"Knock, knock, knock" went the sounds on the door; there was someone outside knocking in some kind of rhythm. It was a humble way of calling someone and therefore easy to tell how constrained the person was—it was an extremely timid knock for sure. Ryūji sat up in his bed and listened as the knocking sound continued in the same rhythm. After the knocks went on for a while, Ryūji heard someone's hoarse, frightened voice in between the beats of the knocking. Someone was calling his father in Korean: "*Yongam. Sunsa, Yongam* [Mister. Policeman, Mister]." At that instant Ryūji thought that it might be Kannani's father. Ryūji called out, "Daddy, Dad," and woke up his father, who was sleeping beside him. "What?" Ryūji's father asked. Ryūji responded, "Someone's calling you; I think it's Kannani's *aboji*."[14] Ryūji's father said, "Could someone be here this late at night?" Ryūji's father, Matabe, turned on the light and tried to see what time it was. He said, "You must've been dreaming, Ryūji, go back to sleep and keep quiet." As he said that, Matabe picked up the clock and he put it to his ear, saying, "God, is it already close to five?" Ryūji's father put a cape on over his pajamas and went outside, and Ryūji followed after him. Snow was falling in the darkness, falling silently like a bird's feather.

When Ryūji and his father opened their small entrance gate, Kannani's aboji floated into their house like a piece of paper. He said to Ryūji's father, "Mister, Kannani hasn't come home yet! We waited all night, but she still isn't back." Kannani's father was staggering and he kneeled down in the snow and begged, "Please look for her, Mister policeman! She might have been killed!" Kannani's father raised his arms high in the air in supplication and, continuing to kneel in the snow, rubbed his hands together begging for something to be done.

Ryūji felt like an electric shock was running up and down his spine; he was unable to utter a sound. Ryūji's father said, "She's not back yet? That's terrible."

Matabe looked up at the sky filled with snowfall and said, "OK, I'll look for her, don't worry. Is there anywhere she would've spent the night?" Kannani's father responded, "No; there's no place she would do something like that. From yesterday until the middle of the night I was visiting acquaintances asking everywhere for her, but she wasn't anywhere to be found."

Ryūji's father tried to calm Kannani's aboji. However, turning to go home he let out one last heart-wrenching sob before he finally departed. Ryūji's legs were trembling with fright. Ryūji's mother came into the room where they were and probably had been listening to the conversation because her lips had been bitten purple.

She said, "It's been one bad thing after another since yesterday," and she covered her face with her sleeve. Matabe said to her, "Make some rice balls," and he started to get ready to go out. He said out loud, "Maybe the civilian clothes with the stand-up collar would be good, huh? I'm all done with the cop business for now."

Ryūji's mother took out a rice tub wrapped up in a futon and started making rice balls. Ryūji said, "Mom, make some for me, too." As Ryūji said that her facial expression got stern. "What in the world are you talking about, child?" Ryūji said firmly, "OK then, I'm going even if I don't have any lunch."

When Matabe noticed Ryūji's determination he agreed to let him come: "OK, I'll take you along with me." Matabe said to reassure his wife, "It's not dangerous out there anymore. All the disturbances have pretty much quieted down." Nevertheless, Matabe put his pistol in his pocket before he took Ryūji's hand.

It was getting light outside and the snow was hardly falling at all anymore. Ryūji and his father went looking for clues to Kannani's whereabouts all the way from behind the mountain to the rock corner; from the rock corner to the back of the church; concluding by going through the castle wall before finally arriving at the West Gate. At the West Gate, they saw some men following a policeman with their hands tied behind their backs. Ryūji's father was talking to the policeman, one of his coworkers. After the conversation he seemed miserably sad and he pulled Ryūji away again and headed for the North Gate by way of the castle walls. Ryūji asked his father, "Were those some of the guys yelling 'Three Cheers for Korean Independence?'" Ryūji's father responded, "Yeah, the cop said they were the ringleaders." Ryūji's father didn't seem to want to say any more about it.

Ryūji called out "Kannani," and when he did that his father joined him, calling out her name with his loud, deep voice: "Kan-ran-eeee!" There was no reply. At the root of a big pine tree there was a sudden rising incline almost like somebody was buried there. Sure enough, when Ryūji's father brushed away some of the snow there was a man's dead body with his decapitated head next to him. Matabe said, "This is terrible. But if the old police chief Noguchi hadn't been shooting off his gun yesterday, his head wouldn't now be separated from his body like this." Noguchi went out to the countryside to suppress a Korean uprising single-handedly, and before any Koreans did anything, he got scared and starting firing his gun. That's probably why the Koreans responded by throwing rocks at him; he was hit with so many rocks he ended up being mashed into a flat piece of pulp.

Ryūji's mother later went to Noguchi's wake, but when she saw his body she was completely horrified. His eyes, nose, and face had been smashed in beyond recognition, and when Oshun tried to console Noguchi's wife, nothing would come out of her mouth.

Ryūji and his father passed through the forest from Kakomon Gate, and they headed in the direction of the Japanese military training grounds, going through Rainbow Flower Gate. Ryūji's father kicked at some flurries near the root of a pine tree; a chestnut-brown mushroom appeared from out of the snow. "Wow, a winter mushroom, huh." Around the same area, five or six more had sprouted in cracks between the ice and frost. "Look, this is really beautiful." When they checked out the next tree root, Ryūji noticed something: "What the heck is it? Wow, it's covered with blood; it's filthy . . ." Ryūji's heart started pounding a mile a minute when he picked up the discarded fragment and examined it.

On a coarse, white Korean cotton bag were two figures lined up next to each other; the doves were completely drenched in blood and had turned bright red. "Kannani." With a sob, Ryūji embraced the bag and collapsed into a squat on the ground. Ryūji's father was taken aback by his son's strange reaction and asked, "What's going on? What happened?" Ryūji exclaimed, "It's Kannani's. She'd put this by her tummy, underneath her skirt." Ryūji's father tried to take the thing out of his hand, but Ryūji refused to let the doves out of his grasp and only showed it to his father. Ryūji wanted to be the only one to touch and embrace it. Matabe took a deep breath of air, but even so, he was barely able to get these words out of his mouth: "If it's really something that belonged to Kannani, I'm afraid it could be a pretty strong piece of material evidence."

Resigning himself to the reality that Kannani had undoubtedly been killed, Ryūji felt a sinking sensation, like he was being dragged down and thrown into a deep valley. What compounded his pain was that he figured it must have been one of his own countrymen that killed her, somebody like that old man Noguchi. "If she was killed, her body should be around here somewhere."

Although Ryūji's father said this while he was looking around the area, all that was visible was a cover of white snow blanketing everything. The forest seemed to continue on with no end in sight, without any further breaks or irregular drops.

Ryūji's father said, "The jerk who killed that poor little girl isn't around either, huh. It was probably a young Korean kid having himself a little fun." When Ryūji heard this, he was overwhelmed by attacks of pain and remorse. "Kannani! Kannani!" He screamed out her name like a madman and began looking around for her furiously. Ryūji thought to himself, "The guys who killed Kannani were definitely those crazy Japanese swinging their swords around like lunatics."

The snow had continued to fall, as if to bury Kannani's beautiful corpse for eternity. Matabe, feeling terrible for his son, searched around for her like *he* was a madman: "Kan-ran-eeeee!"

The thick snow was now mixed with some moisture and it continued to fall on the two of them. As spring was already approaching, the snow seemed to be melting.

### Notes

1   The "customary white clothes" signify that all these children are colonized Koreans.

2   About U.S.$200 today, but it would have been two or three times the annual income for colonized sex workers in Korea. The common situation of women sex workers in Korea at the time was that they were sold at a young age by their impecunious farmer families to a house owned by usually Korean, but sometimes Japanese, men and they had to work many years before they would be free of the contract. As in China and Japan, in Korea rich men would sometimes buy out the contract of women they wanted. Working-class women who were in the relatively privileged position to have their labor waged at all, through more in-dependent sex work and streetwalking, despite the fact that this labor was sold at super-exploitative levels compared to its wage, were at least free of the nonwage, slave-like conditions involved in being under con-tract to a house. This situation of women under contract to independent houses was one of the ways the Japanese military could claim until the mid-1990s that they played no direct role in the recruitment of Korean women sexually enslaved as so-called comfort women.

3   *Yobo* was the racist Japanese colonial word for a Korean person.

4   The young Korean woman Ŏnyŏnna uses the phrase "futsū gakkō" to refer to the school for colonized Korean children. Japanese colonialism established a system of public education for Koreans, Taiwanese, Okinawans, and Chinese that was fairly fluid in the beginning but that solidified in Korea and Taiwan as four to five years—the futsū gakkō or regular school. For the most part, Koreans could not advance into the next level or middle school, especially in the first decade and a half of colonial rule. All Japanese children growing up in the colonies and inside Japan, like Ryūji, were required to attend six years of school. Most middle-class Japanese children then went on to the next level of education, hence the designation of the ringleader bully Katchan as a middle school kid.

5   A centuries' old ritual where families drink from a sake cup together at what might be a final parting with someone going off to war or on a dangerous trip.

6   Again, she's referring to the two-track Japanese colonial education system in Korea, Taiwan, northeast China, and the South Pacific, whereby Japanese children usually went to elementary and then middle school, and Korean and Taiwanese students normally had access to only the five years of futsū gakkō.

7   Keijo was the Japanese colonial name for the present capital of South Korea, Seoul.

8   Yusura trees are a species indigenous to Korea similar to small palm trees.

9   *Yanban* were the intellectual, aristocratic class in Korean Confucian society.

10   *Tameshigiri* is the Japanese compound that I've translated as "using a sword to murder live prisoners." However, the barbarity of testing the strength and cutting power of a newly minted or sharpened sword on a living prisoner of war isn't really captured in my translation. Its widespread practice in China from 1937 on incited international outcries against the atrocity.

11   *Umeboshi* are pickled plums sometimes used for medicinal purposes.

12   Ryūji was singing "Aoba no fue," a 1906 children's song about the defeat of the Heike military clan in 1184. Special thanks to an anonymous reviewer for catching this.

13   Here Ryūji and Kannani are basing their voicings on the same Sino-Japanese character compound, read as "Banzai" in Japanese and "Manse" in Korean.

14   The Korean word for "father" is written in the Japanese *katakana* script and given no Sino-Japanese character translation.

# Document of Flames  (1935)

### CHAPTER ONE

The train slides into the station of Shimonoseki and Nuiko is pushed onto the platform by the waves of people to a place where she can see the ocean; from here the strong smell of the sea tickles her nose and the roar of the ocean is audible in the distance. As the travelers hear it, too, they look through the dark surface of the salt water with anxious eyes. Checking how heavy the rainfall is on the platform with the palm of their hands, they murmur to each other, "This is going to be a rough one." One passenger chips in, "Yeah, after all it's the Sea of Genkai and the waves are bound to be crazy." As people talk back and forth among each other Nuiko's heart starts to pound. "We better hurry up or we won't get a seat; we'll be bouncing all over the place the whole trip if that happens," someone says, trying to get his companions to move faster. The travelers all rush to the platform for the good seats on the connecting ferry.

As the other people continue to run ahead for good places, before she can even advance three meters or so, Nuiko starts to feel heavy chest pains and leans up against a column on the platform. She gets dizzy, so with downcast eyes she crouches down on the ground. As she sees the people around her carrying baskets and heavy trunks on their shoulders she thinks to herself, "My body has gotten weaker." Following along behind her are couples pulling along kids and old folks who have given up any hope of getting a good space upstairs. *accents, spoken language no better visual cues*

*· Stereotypical, racialised, this is how police are operating*

Threading her way through the crowded platform for the Tokyo Express is a girl dressed in sailor clothes selling flowers. She pushes her overflowing cart and yells out in a clear voice: "Carnations! Roses! Sweet Peas!" As Nuiko walks to where she can see the connecting ferry, which seems like a kind of ark bound for Kyūshū, people are waving goodbye. An old woman yells out some last advice: "The boat trip to Korea is pretty rough so take good care. After about fifteen minutes you'll get used to the tosses and turns."

The long platform extends right up to the ramp of the connecting ferry to Korea. At each column at the platform there are men in Western clothing who don't seem to be travelers. They're just standing there observing everyone; their eyes keenly inspect the crowds of people by the loading docks whenever a boatload arrives, paying attention to the newcomers arriving by train as well. Nuiko feels herself shudder each time she senses the men's gaze on her. But without any luggage or possessions she walks as if she were just going out for a casual stroll, telling herself, "I'm no longer under police surveillance and I don't have any dangerous contraband." Nevertheless, every time she notices the surveillance looks of the undercover police her throat gets dry. She already feels as though she's been made to walk for thirty minutes and hasn't yet made her way through the long gantlet of gazes. Finally, she finds herself at the bottom of the ramp and identifies the gigantic body of the yellow connecting ferry; relieved, she feels the blood rush back into her body. Even though the icy rain claws into her back, she doesn't mind at all; she's almost made it out of Japan to finally return to Korea.

However, descending the ship's stairs to the third-class cabin Nuiko is stopped. "Your name?" a man with bushy eyebrows asks her. She looks up to find four or five men in Western clothing standing assertively in front of the cabin. They pester her with questions like "Where are you going? What's your business? Where are you coming from?" and state, "This is the passenger inspection." Directly in front of her Nuiko overhears an interrogation happening: "Kinoshita Saburō is a false name; your real name is Yi Mi-yŏng. If you don't quit with the bullshit now, we won't give you any breaks later." It appears that a Korean-looking student is being hassled by the inspectors. There's also a man in Japanese clothing being hassled and checked out. "Say fifteen dollars, fifty cents!" the police inspectors demand. When the man responds meekly with a slight Korean accent "Fiteen dollars and fitty cents," he's hauled off somewhere.

Nuiko cleared the procedures quickly and slipped past the men down into the main cabin. Once inside, she finds the cabin is so completely packed that even in the women's area there isn't room enough to put one foot down. A steward yells, "For all those who don't have seats, please go down to the lower cabin." So she has to go further down into the bowels of the ship. When Nuiko puts a foot onto the staircase leading down to the lower cabin, she almost *garlic,* faints from the intense nose rush of garlic. Inside, almost every- *pepper,* one is Korean, with the exception of a few Japanese sprinkled here *kimchi \** and there without seats and trying to squeeze in somewhere. They complain in Japanese, "The wooden deck would definitely be a lot nicer than this." A few of them are admonishing the crew: "Clear out some room so we can sleep on the floor of the passageway by the Japanese cabins."

Nuiko goes to the corner of the women's section and squeezes in next to an uncomfortable-looking Korean mother sitting quietly with a worried look on her face. A Japanese woman with a friendly face peeks her head out from in between three or four Koreans and greets Nuiko, "Well, what do you think about these first-class digs, huh? There's no way we're going to get any sleep here." The woman seems eager to move closer to her, possibly because there are only Korean strangers surrounding them. Nuiko smiles weakly and, trying unsuccessfully to be sociable, answers, "I know what you mean," but lies down shamelessly anyway, excusing herself with, "Sorry, but I'm really exhausted and weak." Nuiko has just gone two days and two nights without rest; her head is aching and her feet, hands, and hips are numb as she thinks to herself, "I want to rest my body, I want to sleep."

As the ferry disembarks a big bell rings and a rusty whistle blows; one can also hear the sound of the splashes of the rising tide hitting the bottom of the boat. As Nuiko begins to doze off she thinks, "I'm getting sleeeeepy. How many months has it been since I've slept all stretched out like this?" In fact, for seventy days over a period of about three months from July to September Nuiko has been passed around from one detention center to another for

. Koreans on lower decks (mostly)
- also what/how much stuff you have

interrogations. If the telegram hadn't arrived when it did, her release from prison would probably have been delayed for another ten or twenty days.

Telegram: *Mother dead. Come back to Korea immediately.*

When they showed Nuiko the telegram in the interrogation room of the prison she was surprisingly unaffected. Her reaction went something like, "Oh well, Mother has died." Even thinking back on it now, it all somehow seems like a lie and she doesn't feel particularly sad or alone. Her head feels completely empty and no matter how much she reflects on it, it doesn't seem like such a big deal. She remembers thinking at the time: "Anyway, I've been released, that's what counts."

The person in charge of her interrogation said to her, "You've politically converted into a patriot for Japan and, furthermore, out of respect for your mother's death, we've decided to let you go free."[1] He added spitefully, "If you had given up your left-wing activities and returned to Korea earlier you would have seen your mother before she died."

For some reason, just at that moment the churning sounds of water outside seemed to rise even higher — perhaps it was because the interrogation room was so silent. Or maybe it was because her head was so empty. Whatever the reason, nothing mattered at all; not the kindness of the person in charge who was allowing her to go back to Korea, nor her mother's death. The last interrogation room she'd been sent to was just above sea level and while she was detained there Nuiko remembered how pleasant the scent and sound of the tide seemed to be. After about ten days, she learned from someone who had been interrogated there several times how to differentiate the size of the waves from their sounds.

Nuiko wonders if her present condition of actually being on the connecting ferry on her way back to Korea isn't just a dream. She thinks to herself, "I can hear the breaking waves roaring. And doesn't that thumping sound mean there's someone beating up on somebody above me in the criminal holding area? And isn't that the stink of that woman who'd been arrested three times previously, that they tortured for ten days straight?"

*"Oh no! An earthquake! It's like an awful earthquake. Tōru, hurry up and get out through the garden. No, that's no good, no good just holding onto the desk. I've packed up all my papers; now please get your stuff together quickly and let's get out of here! We can't take everything. Hurry! Hurry! Oh wow, I'm getting thrown into the closet. This is the first time I've ever been in an earthquake like this; we'll be crushed any minute, crushed any minute." Nuiko dashed down the stairs— and then the next dream: "Tōru, you have to get out right now! They're coming into the house from the back door. All those cop uniforms. I wonder how the police knew? Burn them! Burn those papers so the cops don't get them. (A sound of an explosion comes from the fire.) I don't want to die right now. Tōru, I don't want to die right now!"*

Bumping her head on the floorboards of the cabin, Nuiko wakes up. She thinks that maybe the ship has capsized and is sinking, as it tilts rapidly at a dangerously sharp angle. All the ship's passengers are pulled onto the same incline and the body of the ship screeches and grates as waves crash against the side of the upper decks with a huge roar.

When the ship tilts back in the direction of the window Nuiko feels OK again because she slides down feet first. But when the ship tilts in the opposite direction, away from the window, she feels a rush of vertigo to her head and can't help but bump her head on the floorboards again. She feels nausea but fights it down; her stomach starts to spasm with cramps. People roll on top of her and wooden headrests and baskets fly up in the air; the sounds of people screaming and vomiting gradually get louder.

Nuiko clings to the floorboards for dear life and stiffens her body to fight the steepening incline. Without intending to, she calls out "Mother!" Suddenly she has a flashback to when she was living with Tōru: It was about four days after I'd left Korea. I don't know why but my stomach was so upset. With a weird unease I said a kind of prayer, and with the sense that I had to cling to something for safety, somehow the night passed. The next morning as Tōru brushed his teeth, he chuckled and told me, "You kept saying 'Mother,' you know."

Much later, during a police questioning, the cops themselves started laughing when, as they started to use force in their interrogation, she also cried out "Mother [*Kakashama*]" in terror. She wondered in which part of Japan people used "Kakashama" for "Mother"; Nuiko wasn't sure. Didn't it come from Kyūshū, somewhere around her mother's birthplace of Fukuoka? Ever since she was a kid Nuiko understood that just by saying the word "Kakashama," she could feel her mother's presence.

Abruptly, a child starting crying from somewhere on the ship: "This is scary; this is scary, Mommy."

The first time Nuiko's mother brought her by ship to Korea, the weather was just as bad as it was today. In those days people carried all their household possessions when they boarded. That must have been the time their wooden chest tumbled open and grains of rice escaped and scattered all over the cabin. Because she was a lively kid at age five or six Nuiko didn't get sick the first time she crossed to Korea. She remembers, though, that as she clung to her mother she yelled out, "I'm scared, I'm scared, Kakashama!" She threw a temper tantrum and insisted she had to go to the bathroom, so her mother, who was getting sick and looked like death, finally brought her to the men's bathroom. Unfortunately, because the ship was rocking back and forth, when she finally squatted down to go she got completely soaked in piss. Her mother wasn't mad at all, though, and cleaned her up. But then her mother vomited violently, and she had to squat down, holding onto a pole because she was unable to stand upright. Her mother's hair was all messed up and her eyes were welled up with tears. Even after all these years, Nuiko can still vividly recall her mother's appearance at that time. Without a doubt it was one of the most depressing times in her mother's life. Even now, when people say that this woman isn't her real biological mother, Nuiko thinks they're lying.

Nauseous bile shoots into her mouth and Nuiko barely manages to swallow down that sour and bitter liquid. "I must not throw up," she thinks, but now it seems impossible to hold it back any longer. Isn't there some thought she can escape into? "Kakashama's dead. Kakashama's dead," she says to herself. Kakashama's life was a tempestuous one, and the road that she followed was as stormy and violent as the terrible storm Nuiko is presently enduring on that ship.

*[handwritten: Father Critique of patriarchy]*

Nuiko couldn't remember her father's face. The fact that he hadn't made any lasting impression on her probably meant that he had a plain face. Years later Nuiko heard her mother say, "Father was too popular with the ladies," so maybe he was actually handsome. In all the stretch of time that Nuiko and her mother spent together they hardly ever talked about him, but it was obvious that her mother hadn't forgotten him. When Mother would start to utter, "Your father . . . ," she'd stop herself abruptly from saying anything further. It would have been impossible for Mother to have completely forgotten about him, if for no other reason than that it was Father alone who drove her into her present circumstances in colonial Korea. Still, Mother wouldn't allow Nuiko to say anything bad about him. When Nuiko *did* say something critical about her father, Mother would simply say, "Men are just like that," and add more sternly, "Don't bad-mouth your father that way." From these incidents Nuiko discerned that as time passed, rather than hatred Mother couldn't help feeling more love for him. Through all the ups and downs of Mother's life, right from the first time she fell in love with Father, she continued to be obsessed with him as if he were a Greek god or something. Despite the fact that Mother had once sworn she would get revenge for what he did to her she was still crazy about him, even after he'd walked all over her, beaten her to the ground, and pushed her to the brink of death.

Nuiko wasn't sure whether it was six months or one year after the concubine started living at their house that she and her mother left for good. The concubine had been coming to their house every once in a while to see Father when, before they realized it, she just became part of the family. After the woman moved in permanently, Mother and Nuiko slept in a separate room all by themselves. This room was probably the small tearoom, because the space wasn't long enough for them to spread out their whole futon. Occasionally, in the middle of the night Nuiko would wake up to find Mother's place beside her empty. Then she'd usually hear Mother screeching from the next room. Father was either silent, not responding at all to Mother, or talking to her gently, trying to calm her down. During these incidents, he rarely raised his voice and never hit her. As a child Nuiko remembered think-

*[handwritten right margin: economics: success]*

*[handwritten: Mother can be replaced with concubine]*

*[handwritten: importance d' male inheritance - can't give children]*

*[handwritten: - once divorced, she has no prospects]*

*[handwritten: Okay for man to have mult. partners - sexual expectations]*

*[handwritten: woman's place is within the home]*

*[handwritten: this is all Legal, so the mom is technically breaking the law, stealing daughter, and moving to Korea (more opp.) = new life HOPE]*

ing to herself, "This is not something a kid like me should have to deal with," and proceeded to bawl her eyes out, pulling a futon over her head. Invariably, Mother realized that there was no use trying to pressure Father into getting rid of the concubine and she would return to their room shaking with rage, rip the sliding room divider (the one separating theirs from the room where Father and the concubine slept) out of its frame, and furiously . . .[2] Then, silently, she'd crawled back into her side of the bed. Father would then calmly put the sliding room divider back in place and a suffocating silence would ensue. At times like this Mother would suddenly yell, "Daddy has turned into a beastly monster," and hug Nuiko so hard that she'd almost crush her. At that point she'd sob uncontrollably.

One particular night, that room divider was ripped out and put back in over and over, until finally the situation escalated to where Mother and Father were just opening it and shutting it one after another. Father and the concubine together tried to keep it closed with their combined strength, so Mother couldn't open it even when she gripped it tightly with all her might. In the end, she couldn't open it so she broke into a tantrum, screaming, "Take a look at this, jerk!" and in a rage started to tear into the room divider with her bare hands. At that point the concubine shouted to Mother in her high voice, "You've lost it, woman!" Mother then grabbed the wooden frame of the thick paper room divider and replied indignantly, "You better believe I've lost it! How could I not when my man is sleeping with another woman in the room right next to me?" Then with a burst of energy, Mother tore right through the room divider into the other room. Nuiko was so traumatized she couldn't even let out a peep, she just stood dumbfounded in front of the hole that Mother made in the door.

At that point Mother physically attacked the concubine, who was much taller. Mother dragged her around by the topknot of her hair, and the concubine bit right into the flesh of Mother's hip. They battled wildly like this, shrieking at each other. Father, completely fed up, tied Mother down with her own undergarments, scolding her in a low voice. Mother cried out with a weakened voice, "I'm the wife! I'm the wife!" By this time the sun had already started to come up, and the morning factory whistle blew in the distance.

During the day Mother had a completely different attitude, working hard and appearing to put up with any insults from Father. For his part Father would go on the offensive during the day, opposite to his usual relaxed demeanor at night. Although he wouldn't shout at Mother, he'd taunt and scold her. After really bad nights, he'd follow Mother around and criticize her every chance he could, for whatever reason. In these encounters, Father's eyes would light up like a wild man, with dark threatening veins popping out of his skull. These veins looked like worms and Nuiko got scared when she saw them. No matter how many times he told Nuiko to get out of the way and go play, she refused to leave her mother's side, saying, "I'm scared; I'm scared." Only when Nuiko declared her terror verbally like that would Father stop abusing Mother. It was clear to Nuiko what kind of danger her mother would be in if she weren't around. So Nuiko would hang on to her mother even more closely than usual and peek her head out from underneath her mother's arm to stare at Father, as if to inform him that she was protecting Mother.

Whether it was one of those days or not she couldn't be sure, but it definitely was one night during dinner. Mother and Nuiko normally sat across from Father at the dining table in the servants' seats close to the kitchen, while Father and the concubine would sit next to each other on the opposite side in the standard places for husband and wife. At that dinner Mother (whether it was intentional or not was unclear at the time) dropped a rice bowl while handing it to the concubine. Mother got startled and turned pale; Father looked at her overbearingly, as if to say, "Look what you did, you failure of a woman!" But in later years Nuiko came to believe that the concubine pulled her hands away prematurely on purpose, causing the bowl to fall. Father divorced Mother shortly after that incident. Maybe the whole thing was just a ploy by the concubine and Father to give him a reason to separate from Mother. Nuiko was certain that it wasn't Mother's fault: even after being victimized by such demeaning treatment, Mother had been careful not to make a mistake so as to give Father and the concubine an excuse to banish her—so strong was her desire not to be thrown out of her house completely. So at least during the daytime, far from bad-mouthing or treating the concubine disrespectfully, Mother focused her attention on each and every activity so as not to incite Father and her further. That's why Mother had even decided to put up with the added humiliation of washing the concubine's underwear.

One sizzling hot day, Mother was happily doing laundry and Nuiko was blowing bubbles from the overflowing tub. The larger bubbles burst into many smaller bubbles and shone in the sun. "You're so pretty, so pretty," Nuiko said as she chased around after the bubbles. While Nuiko frolicked, Mother hummed a famous, upbeat song from Shikoku about a boat traveling to the Kumbira Shrine: *The Kumbira boat boat, hurling its sails in the wind. Scrub-a-dub, Scrub-a-dub.* Mother scrubbed harder and harder as she sang and talked in a childlike manner. Nuiko begged Mother to allow her to scrub along as well, and when she joined in the bubbles grew even larger. For both mother and child laundry and cleaning time was the most fun part of the day.

The well for cleaning was down a ways from the house and going there provided a welcome opportunity for Mother and Nuiko to escape the thick, oppressive atmosphere of the house. However, their pleasant routine was soon destroyed. The next time they did laundry, Mother grimaced abruptly when she pulled out another pair of the concubine's underwear. It was the concubine's white flannel underwear; for some reason the concubine wore flannel even in the hot weather they were experiencing then. Mother seemed to have come across something awful because she cried "Disgusting!" and with all her might threw the underwear into the muddy gutter and spit on it. Then something unexpected happened. As if she was taken aback by what she'd done, Mother ran to the shed to peek into the house, made certain that nobody was watching, and fished out the muddy underwear with a long bamboo pole and tried to clean it up. Even though she was just a kid, Nuiko realized what was happening and why her mother had lost her head and was overcome with such disgust toward the stained underwear. Nuiko felt an unbearable hatred and rage toward things that caused Mother so much distress. Nuiko suddenly threw the underwear back into the muddy gutter and was so taken aback by what she did, she started to cry loudly. Mother ran to the edge of the muddy gutter and watched the underwear get washed away with a stunned look on her face. Then she squatted down beside Nuiko and spoke to her as her tears fell into the oily

water of the ditch: "Nuiko, when you become a bride, you'll realize there's a big difference between a woman who can give birth
and one who can't. If you can't have his baby your husband will
treat you horribly, and you'll be tormented by him and treated like
a fool by his pig of a whore."

At that age, of course, Nuiko couldn't be expected to grasp much
of the meaning of those words. But once she was older she realized
that her father used her mother's failure to conceive a child as a
pretext for his abusive treatment and his debauchery. Nuiko even
remembered her father shouting at her, "You barren woman! You
barren bitch!" Mother was taught that if a barren woman adopted
a child, even though she wasn't able to conceive until that point,
she'd suddenly be able to have her own child. Nevertheless, when
she adopted Nuiko she still couldn't conceive. Having a concubine
around and watching her husband treat her as if she were his real
wife all stemmed from the fact that Mother couldn't give birth to
a child of her own. Father would routinely chastise her by saying,
"If you can't keep my family line going, then get the hell out of
my house!"

That evening when the bowl fell on the low dining table, spill-
ing food on the concubine, he again screamed at her "You barren
bitch!" and picked up the bowl and threw it at her. He missed,
and the bowl flew right by her ear into the kitchen and shattered.
Then, with a smirky grin on his face, he flung the *entire* dining
table at her. Bowls and dishes flew right toward Mother's face and
she ended up covered with hot stew from head to toe; there was
even a steaming piece of kelp stuck on her that stretched from
her left ear all the way to her neck. Mother jumped into the air
screaming, "It's boiling!" In a panic she wiped the fish stew off her
kimono with her apron. Her neck ended up badly scalded. Right
up until her death, that burn left an ugly mark on her neck that
never went away.

Shortly after this last incident Mother disappeared completely.
Even after evening came and went she still hadn't returned home.
The concubine saw Nuiko crying and after tea brought her from
the tearoom to lie down between her and her father, saying, "Start-
ing today I'm your Mommy; it's OK." Nuiko responded with, "NO!
I won't! I don't even know you. I don't know about any of this.
Please call Kakashama for me." Nuiko cried and cried all night

long and Father finally lost patience, putting a lollipop in her hand and sticking her in the closet. Nuiko refused to give in and pounded on the closet door, crying even louder than before.

One early evening (it was probably autumn) Nuiko was watching the older children play a version of London Bridge is falling down in the big field overgrown with silver pampas grass. As the kids let down the bridge, suddenly an adult appeared and, without any hesitation, walked right toward Nuiko, a stranger in nice dressy clothes. She stood next to Nuiko and holding her by the shoulder asked, "Were you lonely?" as she stared into Nuiko's face. Nuiko grabbed onto her and blurted out "Oh, Kakashama!" and she jumped up and down with excitement. But her mother hushed her up by placing her hand over Nuiko's mouth; then she took Nuiko's hand and they ran off together.

It seemed that they dashed through fields and ran down evening roads; Nuiko felt adventurous and excited. However, at the same time, Mother's worried and anxious face and the feeling of floating in space made her feel a little uneasy.

Suddenly, she found herself on a train. When the train began to annoy her Nuiko decided she wanted to go home: "Let's go home. Let's go home now!" she whined. Mother gave her orangeade and licorice candy to try to quiet her. As those things weren't sold on the train Mother must have bought the candy before she kidnapped Nuiko; she must have planned the whole thing beforehand. That's how conscientious and careful Mother was. But the sweet treats couldn't make Nuiko forget about home, and she dragged her feet along the ground, insisting she wanted to go back. At her wit's end, Mother started to cry, too, and finally blurted out, "Kakashama was divorced; I can't go back to the house! I don't care if I die. I'll never go back!"

## CHAPTER THREE

The connecting ferry *Ikimaru* was still tilting and reeling from the severe storm on the Sea of Genkai when it finally docked into Pusan, Korea. Nuiko's condition at the end of that journey, feeling like a lost child, probably mirrored Mother's own condition when she first arrived here. After they left the boat and Mother had taken in a little of the different customs of the streets of Pusan, she stopped and hugged Nuiko tightly. Mother made a pledge to Nuiko that went something like: "We're going to plant our flag here and make a success out of ourselves and someday look back at that horrible concubine and that monstrous father with a feeling of superiority."

Right after mother was divorced, while they were still back in Japan, she went back to her parents' house. But she wasn't welcome there because her family was just a poor bunch of farmers and they were scared to death of food shortages. Of course, there wasn't a divorcée anywhere in Japan who could return to her family without being ridiculed by pushy, annoying relatives. This was especially difficult in a small rural town like hers, and with an uncle who was especially bothersome. Strangely, people didn't think it was disrespectful for a man to have his own concubine. In fact, it was just the opposite. In her hometown, to be rich enough to have a concubine was something for a man to be proud of. But for a woman like Mother the only choice was to either get back together with Father or get married to a different guy. So a fairly well-off but elderly man was proposed as the best candidate for her remarriage. Once it was absolutely clear that she would never get back together with Father, her family tried to force her to marry this run-down old man. Mother would say out loud, "I'd rather die than go back to Father." Nevertheless, she refused to even consider marrying the old rich man. Desolate and desperate, one day Mother went out to the cliff with the intention of throwing herself off into the water. However, that day there was a clear blue fall sky with a beautiful view of the nearby islands, where the leaves were changing color. This dream-like vision of the distant islands on the fog-shrouded horizon kept Mother from suicide.

They said that Korea was located somewhere just beyond that water. Mother wondered to herself, "That beautiful, dreamy island behind the fog—is that really the up-and-coming Korea?" In reality, there's no possible way anyone can see Korea from the shores of Fukuoka; it was probably just some island in Mother's field of vision. Nevertheless, that island unleashed Mother's hopes. She mused, "If I'm going to throw my life away anyway, then I may as well do it trying my hardest to make a living in that undeveloped land. Maybe some great job'll just drop into my lap. No matter what, I'll try my hardest until I shatter into a million pieces." A flame that had been just about to burn out forever started to smolder again in Mother's heart.

But even that undeveloped peninsula wouldn't be very welcoming to the itinerant mother and daughter. The only work that Mother could find after a long search was as a brown rice bread peddler on the street. She would put the freshly steamed bread into a red soapbox and pound on the steaming box hanging in front of her like a drum, shouting: "Freshly made brown rice bread from Santokudo!"

It was probably around this time that Mother started to wear a red bandana and a red vest with advertisements for the brown rice bread. She'd put a megaphone to her mouth and sing a jingle as she danced, with her shoulders moving back and forth in rhythm: "Boys and girls, today we have freshly steamed brown rice bread! It's easy to digest, high in nutritional value, and cheap!" In the streets of Pusan at that time there were only redheaded Russian brown rice bread sellers, Chinese noodle sellers, and Korean candy sellers. As there were no other Japanese, the itinerant mother-and-daughter team became instantly popular. Wives from the upscale part of town would be there early to wait for them, with mobs of children following behind them, and young Korean men would come to flirt with the young woman with beautiful eyebrows. The new brown rice bread was a surprise hit. Mother was invigorated again and as she quickly counted her money, figured out that if she worked incredibly hard for another year or two she'd be able to open up her own candy store. Mother constantly concocted new sales pitches and often trudged all the way out of town to factories and distant construction sites to try to expand her market.

Winter came rushing in and Nuiko and Mother didn't have the luxury to even breathe a sigh. After trudging home in the early dusk and the bitter cold from selling bread at the faraway factories, using distant streetlights and houselights as guideposts, they tried their best to bear the cold and fatigue stoically. But no matter how much she tried to be strong, cries and whimpers invariably escaped from Nuiko's mouth. At times like this, Mother would hug Nuiko and ask, "Tell me what you want to be doing

Pros/cons_
success
due to
exoticism
(the only
Japanese
sales-
woman)
Japan = exotic?

telltale
signs of
development

this time next year?" Nuiko replied in a shivering, meek voice, "Candy. I'll be working hard in our candy store." Mother encouraged her, saying, "That's great! That's fantastic!" This formulaic exercise would temporarily energize them, and they'd take off down the dark mountain road chanting together: "Candy, candy, work hard!"

Notwithstanding their dreams, the days got colder and colder; telephone poles screamed in the wind and icicles hung from roofs and houses. The number of people in the streets of the city began to decrease and sales went down drastically. The brown rice bread that they brought out to sell was no longer piping hot; instead, it quickly froze solid. As New Year's approached people completely lost their interest in brown rice bread because they made their own rice cakes at home. Nevertheless, Mother would leave Nuiko at home and go outside to brave the elements anyway, only to return home with purple lips and ears. They moved out of their first rental house in Pusan by a mountainside and moved into a dirtier, mixed Korean and Japanese neighborhood closer to the bay. By springtime they'd moved again and settled into an all-Korean neighborhood that smelled of flowers, sewage, and rotten kelp. There they rented a small longshoreman's room with heated floorboards. The wax paper lining the heated floorboards was worn away in places, and the newspapers used to patch it were covered in soot. Smoke leaked out through the gaps and cracks to fill the room. For sustenance they ate *kimchi* (pickled vegetables) given to them by the Korean grandmothers of the longshoremen for days and days on end. Once they ran out of rice they boiled brown rice bread into water and poured the porridge into their mouths—there was no taste or flavor whatsoever. In no time at all, steam from the porridge upset their stomachs. Even the mere *sight* of brown rice bread made them nauseated. Nuiko even had nightmares about being completely smothered by brown rice bread piling on top of her.

One day Nuiko went out to fly a kite with the Korean son of one of the dockworkers, named Ton-su. This was a kite that he found abandoned in a poplar tree. For the first time in weeks Ton-su was able to fly a kite of his own. The kites around them were all red and purple but Ton-su's was gold. Ton-su and Nuiko were so excited that they jumped up and down as they let the kite loose. The kite danced along with them as it flew high in the sky—"Look at mine go! Look at mine!" Ton-su yelled as he proudly flipped the kite over in midair. But suddenly his fortunes changed as Ton-su said in Korean, "Oh no, this is going to crash!" and started to reel the string in, but the kite slammed into their faces. He stopped reeling in the string and blindly reached out for Nuiko's hand and said, "Let's go home." Nuiko tripped over some small pebbles as she was walking and unexpectedly went blind. "I don't want to go blind! I don't want to go blind!" she screamed as she latched onto Ton-su tightly for support. Ton-su tried to cheer her up and said, "I know! I'll help. It will be like a three-legged race!" So, they tied Ton-su's left leg and Nuiko's right leg together and started walking toward home, but suddenly the darkness became complete for Nuiko. It was dusk when they left but she knew that there was no way the darkness could fall that quickly. "Usually, I can see houses and poplar trees even at night," Nuiko thought to herself; "I must be going blind." As soon as she had convinced herself that she was blind, Nuiko became terrified and started to sob. Ton-su asked, "What, you've lost your eyesight? Don't worry, you'll be able to see again once tomorrow comes. Recently I've been going blind around dusk, too. Lots of my school pals go blind then, too." Nuiko wouldn't let herself be comforted by him. She thought that Ton-su was just saying this to make her feel better. As though her life were over, she felt a dark despair and collapsed on the side of the street. Ton-su picked out the way back home by following the mud walls. She still didn't have enough energy to stand up and continued crying. Nuiko's mother found them eventually and took them home, telling Nuiko with a concerned look that she probably just had night blindness.

Beginning the next day, they fed her fish intestines that the dockworkers brought. She also ate raw pig gizzards that Ton-su's mother got from somewhere. Very soon her eyes did get better, but she came down with typhoid fever and suffered in agony for thirty days, wavering on the brink between life and death. Ton-su's little sister, who was sick at the same time as Nuiko, had already died by the time Nuiko recovered. Ton-su's mother had bathed his sister in the sea, thinking she might recover if she could bring the fever down by cooling her.

At some point Mother became a dockworker herself. Years later, when Mother was asked why she stopped selling brown rice bread, she answered, "Because the brown rice bread boss told me to become a prostitute." She refused to go into any further details about it. Reflecting back on this after a long span of time, Nuiko realized that the boss used to come over late at night around the time Mother stopped selling brown rice bread. He was a man with a square head whose lower lip hung down in a totally disgusting way. One evening Nuiko came home after playing all day and ran into him, but he was in such a hurry to leave that he didn't even notice her. When she entered the house, seeing that there were broken dishes everywhere and the serving tray tipped over, she realized the boss had done something awful. Out in the back yard Mother was vomiting and spitting something out of her mouth out on the ground: "Peh, peh, yuck!" She pinched salt from a jar and rubbed it inside her mouth. However, Nuiko realized that this wasn't the day that Mother quit selling bread. This much she was sure of: Mother's last day was definitely when she completely exploded in response to the construction crew's lewd catcalls. Some people said that the workers were also sick of the brown rice bread and harassed Mother when they had absolutely no intention of buying any. "You know, I sure would like a . . . brown rice bread, heh, heh," they joked, leering lecherously at her. The brown rice bread that Mother sold was shaped like an egg with a crack right down the middle. This must have made the young men think of . . . The only worker who bought any bread (probably because of what the bread reminded him of) smirked and held the steaming bread to his genitals and turned to show the other workers. . . . The other men clapped appreciatively and burst into laugher. One of them said to Nuiko, "This is your mother's . . . !" When Mother heard that she yelled back, "You stupid idiots," and threw the whole box of brown rice bread at them, screaming, "Stop treating women like that!" The mushy brown rice bread stuck to the men's faces. Flustered and in some pain they protested, "This is hot; this is burning!" Mother and Nuiko quickly left with the men cursing and grumbling.

narchy cont'd thru 3 + 4
1lar to Karauki (how women stereotypically
me involved in sex trade, Jap. persp. at the
time) ← first
line in
chp 5

CHAPTER FOUR

spite all that, why did Mother become a dockworker? Was it the promise she made to herself ("We're going to plant our flag here and be successful") when she and Nuiko landed in Korea? Why was someone like Mother—who, when she even thought about men, got really angry—doing a man's job to survive? No matter how much energy she expended, she could never keep up with men. She looked pitiful, like a kid trying to compete in a world of adults.

By this time Nuiko was already in grade school, so on her way home from school she would watch her mother at work stooping and squatting as she unloaded cargo in front of the storage shed. Nuiko noticed that one of Mother's male coworkers had a big scar on his forehead and another had a big snake tattooed on his arm; Mother stumbled around them, bent over like an aronia rose, carrying loads that were much too heavy for her on her shoulders. It made Nuiko sad to watch her mother work like that and she was sure that the heavy loads would eventually split her body into pieces. For that matter, Mother didn't want Nuiko watching her. She told her to go home every time she noticed Nuiko spying on her; she hated it when Nuiko saw her performing this kind of drudgery. Even when Nuiko was off studying quietly at school, she would have visions of her mother being crushed by large loads of crates, so, holding her breath out of fear, she'd dash off to her hiding place behind the storage shed and spy on Mother to make sure she was OK. One day she discovered something: one of the longshoremen was picking out smaller, lighter-looking loads for Mother than the ones the men carried. This particular man who was trying to make life a little easier for her was called Scarface. Although initially Nuiko was afraid of Scarface, after she made her discovery he started to grow on her. When the dockworkers all sat around chatting during work breaks, Nuiko would sit in Scarface's big lap and fall asleep as she listened to them. Something about Scarface's body odor reminded her of her father. Before long, more than anything else in her life Nuiko looked forward to the time when she could go to sleep in Scarface's lap.

Every day around dusk Mother would come home exhausted to the point of crawling from a long day on the job, but their life never seemed to get any easier as a result of all her efforts. On days when it was raining or storming outside, Mother just didn't seem like herself as she slept all day on the heated floor with a grim look on her face. These kinds of days seemed to go on and on, and like the times when they had to eat brown rice bread every day, they had to eat rice with Manchurian chestnuts flavored with pickled kimchi from Ton-su's house. Sometimes, though, there were big chunks of pickle and leftover fish in the kimchi. Mother always made sure that Nuiko got all the big chunks.

One day after a stretch of many rainy and stormy days, as she left for work in the morning, Mother promised Nuiko that they would have white rice for dinner. So Nuiko waited excitedly till dusk for Mother to come home with money, and when she did, they dashed out to the rice store by the shore to get some. Upon receiving the precious rice in a wrapping cloth, Nuiko insisted on carrying it home all by herself. She thought of the beautiful, white tooth-like grains of rice inside the cloth as she carried it over her shoulder, skipping happily on her way. She called to Mother, who was lagging behind in the sand, "Come on! Hurry!" After the storm, the beach sand was washed clean and the moon smiled down from above the grove-wood forest. Nuiko tried to leap all the way over a creek and somehow dropped the wrapping cloth. There's a rule that states that during bad times, terrible things happen one after another, so when the knot of the wrapper came undone and before Nuiko realized it, all the grains of rice had poured into the sand of the creek bed, where they were swept away. Even Nuiko herself couldn't fully recall later how it happened; she thought that Mother had surely tied the wrapping cloth up tightly at the rice store.

Nuiko was so shocked at this tragedy that the moment it happened she didn't even cry; all she could do was watch the rice sink into the creekbed. Then she just sat down in the creek and kept thinking how cold the water was and how beautiful the moon looked reflecting on the shore. Suddenly the shadow of the moon's reflection on the creek's surface trembled. Mother was on her belly desperately scooping out the rice from the oily water. The grains of rice were camouflaged in the silver shimmering rocks and shell fragments in the reflection of the moon in the water—there was no telling which was a grain of rice and which wasn't. As Mother weakly threw a handful of sand back into the puddle in resignation, she and Nuiko held their breath and stared into the water. The shadow of the poplar trees in the water swayed comically. Suddenly Mother raised her head and asked, "Nui, are we going to die?" Nuiko felt a shiver up her spine as she watched her mother's intense look. "No! No! I don't want to die!" Nuiko responded.

As Nuiko turned to flee from this scene of desperation toward the bay, her breath stopped as she felt her mother's hand on her back. When she ran a little further she stopped and looked back to find her mother crouched down by the puddle with her face down. Nuiko had been so terrified at the thought of death that she'd only imagined being chased. There was a large dark shadow wavering uncannily behind Mother's back. This contrasted sharply with her mother's petite shadow screened by the shimmering shore and reflected in the moonlight.

Nuiko couldn't remember whether it was that winter or the next, but it was winter for sure because the longshoremen's stove was flaunting its scorching red belly, and the raw heat from it produced a burning sensation on her back. It was around that time that she got into the habit of having pleasant dreams whenever she dozed off in Scarface's lap. Icicles cracked and crinkled outside; inside, stoves blazed crazily and people sat around telling stories. The same exaggerated, unbelievable war stories would be told over and over, yet produce new laughs each time: like the one about almost killing a man in a Kyūshū coal mine, or the one about capturing two German hostages at Qingdao in the German-Japanese conflict during World War I. These types of hero stories eventually led into obscene ones that Nuiko didn't understand. One day during a pause between stories, Scarface complained about his glaucoma not getting any better; it was even starting to get infected. People responded with advice and opinions like "Wash it out with salt water or University brand eyewash—it's made by famous doctors at the university. Not that I'm being paid to promote it or anything!" and "You have bad karma from whoring around so much." Then a heavily tattooed man interrupted: "You know I've heard that the medicine that works best is women's vaginal . . . Yeah, you get a gob of it in your hands and rub your eyeballs in it six or seven times for a heavenly experience. It's an old custom from my hometown." Then Scarface swallowed his spit and said, "Then

I would have to use Tokichan's . . ." The men broke into collective laughter and started gossiping about Mother's body: "Yeah, yeah, Toki's thing must work best for this because it's washed in the ocean breeze." Even though she was still a child, when Nuiko realized that they were teasing Mother in such a demeaning way, she felt disgust and fear run through her whole body. She became so angry at the men that she started to punch Scarface's chest with all her might. She remembered clearly that she noticed that his naked chest was bigger than the bottom of a boat and as hairy as a horse's mane.

Looking back on it now, Mother was probably already selling her body to those men then. She remembers that Mother had the luxury of skipping work altogether and just sleeping during the day; there were even days in a row when they were able to eat white rice with beef and vegetables. Nuiko recalls all of this now with humiliation.

*[handwritten note: Nuiko can go to school due to mothers work, above starvation line, has aspirations, gossip → wants mother to stop it (clients even at house)]*

## CHAPTER FIVE

It was right around this time that Mother started selling her body in the red-light district. Isn't this always the place where women go when they have nowhere else to turn? Nevertheless, the flame was still burning in Mother's heart, and later on, she told Nuiko that she was preparing financially for their future. She didn't have any outstanding loans and she figured that with only two years of sex work she could save $1,000. Mother thought to herself, "I don't have anyone to save my body for anyway. I'll save all my money for two years and then buy us our own candy store." At night when she and Nuiko lay in bed together, their dream of owning a candy store would expand into the goal of having their own drugstore full of makeup and beauty products. They also fantasized that they'd carry a few things for students, since the place they had their eye on was a vacant house right in front of a school. Mother's head must have been overflowing with all kinds of glorious ideas at that time.

When Nuiko first saw her mother in the red-light district she mistook her for a much younger woman, as her shiny lapels and

*[handwritten note: • physical transformation of mother (even how she smells), weird transition of Tokiko]*

*[handwritten note: Nuiko vs Ohashi = example of class struggle]*

nice clothes hid her sun-tanned skin she got from working outside with the longshoremen. Because of her drive to be successful, Mother was immediately popular with the other sex workers
and they called her "Big Sister." Even though she was young,
Nuiko understood that her mother was also very popular with the
male clients. The room where the women slept with clients was
called "The Store" and when Mother came home from there, her
footsteps were no longer heavy and depressed, they were light
dance-like steps filled with excitement. Mother would walk into
Nuiko's room mimicking some dance and making melodic shamisen sounds with her mouth. Then, as she opened the shōji
screens, she'd bad-mouth her annoying clients just like her coworkers did: "That guy's such a jerk!" Nuiko didn't like her mother
acting so casual and flighty, and at times like this would roll her
eyes at her mother—in the exact same way that her mother used
to roll her eyes at Father. When Mother noticed Nuiko looking
at her so condescendingly she'd get hurt, but she kept right on
bad-mouthing people anyway and telling work stories. Speaking
of being hurt, the burn mark on Mother's neck would get uglier
and more noticeable as she tried to hide it with makeup. Then one
time Mother came home from a long stay in the hospital. Nuiko
remembers seeing the big, open, red wound on Mother's upper
thigh when she changed her bandages from the operation. After
it healed, it left a scar on her thigh as ugly as the one on her neck;
it made Nuiko that much sadder to see the second scar.

The women Mother worked with had even worse scars than
Mother. When they had breakouts of detestable red sores or pim-
ples on their chest, arms, or thighs, anywhere on their bodies,
the common treatment was to squeeze the pus out of them (they
groaned while doing so) and have leeches suck it up. Every time
Nuiko saw the leeches, creatures that seemed a weird cross between an insect and a fish, it gave her the chills. Watching the
women have blood sucked out of their thighs or seeing a bowl full
of leeches knocked over and spill squirming out onto the straw
tatami mat of their sleeping room never failed to make Nuiko
shriek and run away. She was sure that for a long time she'd be
completely unable to put even one foot into the room occupied
by the leeches. But the worst part was that when she did return

in the evening after fleeing from the leeches, she had no choice but to retreat into that same room and sleep. On nights like that she'd be haunted by a repeating dream in which pencil-size leech monsters attacked her. If Mother weren't right next to her when she woke up, without fail she'd scream loud enough so that she would hear her from the next room. When that happened, Mother always dashed right to Nuiko with a bowl of leftovers to comfort her, even if she was right in the middle of seeing a client. Mother never failed to bring her a bowl of *nanzewanze* Chinese vegetables that had been left over from a client and, because Nuiko loved these vegetables so much, she always felt better after eating. Nuiko would then fall asleep in Mother's arms listening to a lullaby like she did when they lived by the shore. But the smell that Mother's body gave off was not the same odor that Nuiko was used to from the shore. It had been replaced by a man's greasy body odor mixed with a strong antiseptic, the smell of which went straight to her nostrils. These new smells had the effect of making Nuiko feel even lonelier.

Eventually Nuiko entered fifth grade. At that age her classmates began to have some idea of what kind of a place the red-light district was. The time was somewhere around the ceremonial day after the Chinese New Year so it was probably the seasonal equinox. After the ceremony the kids rushed back into their classroom, scrambling and fighting over sweetnuts, which caused a huge ruckus. Nuiko was the class president and she'd just had a meeting with her teacher, so she entered the classroom a little later than the other students did. As she walked into the classroom it seemed that her classmates had been waiting in preparation for her entrance; when they saw her the ruckus and banter increased all the more. They were making too big a deal for it all to be related to the sweetnuts; they were going to joke with her about something. But when someone directed her attention to the blackboard she just stood there in amazement. Someone had put on the board a kid's drawing of a man with a derby hat hailing a rickshaw and next to it was a quote that said "Cab driver, how much is it to Midorichō?" and the cabbie says, "Hey?" and scratches his head. Midorichō was the name of the red-light district where Mother was working at that time. Nuiko swallowed her breath and looked at the next picture, which was the picture of a two-story house with paper lanterns hanging from the second floor. It probably meant the house where Mother worked as a prostitute. From the balcony of the second floor there was a grandmother and a young girl dressed provocatively and waving. "Machida Nuiko" and "her Mother" was written on the board next to the two figures, and just above their names was scribbled "Prostitution." The drawing didn't actually resemble Nuiko's mother at all; it looked more like an old lady. Her classmates giggled cruelly and stared straight at Nuiko. From then on there was one kid who would come right up in Nuiko's face, hold his nose, and say, "Filthy! Filthy!" then run away. Students began to gossip wildly about her, and these rumors spread through the school like wildfire. Male students from the high school approached Nuiko and asked, "I heard that one of the fifth-grade students is a prostitute?" And once during a break between classes, one of the older students brought Nuiko to the back of the school and said to her "I want some of Nuiko's . . . too."

Humiliated, Nuiko cried in a corner of the school's courtyard, screaming out, "Who and why would anybody draw something like that?" Then some of Nuiko's classmates came outside, gathered together around her, and confessed that it was Ōhashi who had written that cruel stuff on the blackboard. Nuiko knew that Ōhashi Michiko, the daughter of the general manager of a rice-importing business, had moved to Korea from Tokyo just last year. As soon as Michiko transferred into their school she generously handed out notebooks and pencils to all the students with pretty ribbons on them saying "from Tokyo," and quickly became the queen of the class. Her grades were relatively good and her father had a respectable position, so she was elected class president for the first semester of fifth grade. But their teacher was suddenly relocated, and once the new teacher was assigned to the class Nuiko became the class president again. At first the general manager's daughter went around saying "Teacher's Pet! Teacher's Pet!" and all the other classmates followed her lead and taunted Nuiko in the same way. Then Michiko started writing graffiti about her on the board. Nuiko thought to herself one day on her way home from school, "I'm never going back to that school." Then she plotted, "When Mother comes home I'm going to tell her how sad I am and let her know what kind of humiliation I have to put up with in school; then I'll beg her to stop doing that kind of work. Then I'll throw a tantrum."

While she was planning this on her way home she overheard some ladies in their neighborhood gossiping about her mother, using Mother's maiden name: "That poor thing, Ageha, huh? She's so young, but she has to take care of that little kid, and I hear that she's not even her real kid?" This information made Nuiko's heart drop: "A . . . A . . . Adopted? Muh . . . Muh . . . Mee? Me, Nuiko, adopted? That's crazy! I've never heard anything so dumb! It can't be true!" But at that point the whispers of the women started getting faster and faster until they climaxed in a crescendo of loud cackles. "Maybe they are laughing about me?" Nuiko thought. When she remembered that they were accusing her of being adopted she suddenly flew into a rage. Then she ran up to the door, pulled it open, and screamed at the gossiping women: "Kakashama is my real Mommy! Nuiko is Kakashama's own kid!" First they all looked at each other, then at Nuiko, as if to say, "You poor thing." When Nuiko saw their eyes she felt like her safety net had been cut right out from underneath her, sending her into free fall. "Maybe I was adopted after all," she realized, and then she recalled how people at both the red light district and at the longshoremen's job had always said they saw no similarity between her face and Mother's. Gradually this all began to make some sense. Nuiko considered that Mother had an attractive long nose while she had a flat nose, and furthermore, the structure of their faces had nothing in common. Realizing this made her sad and she wondered, "Where could my real mother be?" After thinking for a while her thoughts returned to her mother: "Things are actually fine the way they are; I have no need of another mother." She never let out one peep about the details of the women's gossip; it was way too scary for her to think about. Nuiko reassured herself with the thought that she couldn't have asked for a better mother.

Mother finally gave in to Nuiko's whining and mother and daughter abandoned the streets of Pusan for good. Mother no longer entertained the dream of having her own drugstore. She resigned herself to the fact that there was probably no place where poor people could settle down and live a normal life. Mother wanted to wander.

When they left Pusan a violent rainstorm hit them, the same storm that hit the Sea of Genkai the night before. They were on a Mukden express train named *Hikari* headed north to China and the windows screamed out as if they were in pain from the heavy rain that struck them. But as soon as they entered the territory between the small mountains that followed the course of the Nakdong River the weather cleared and there were empty chestnuts burrs hanging on branches right next to the window. Off in the distance the top of a mountain threw back its shoulders proudly, leaving only one bluish rock protruding dangerously.

Nuiko was starting to doze off listening to the sound of the storm but woke up when she heard the station master bark out "Milyang!" There were hawkers walking around the train holding up baskets of pears and apples to the windows, trying to make a quick sale. Even though this was the main junction with the Umayama train line it was still a cold, sleepy little rural town with wide plains surrounding the Nakdong. It didn't have much to offer except for the hawkers with the fruit baskets at the station selling gifts to bring back to Japan. But since Mother had made the decision to abandon the kind of life she'd led in Pusan to become a wandering small-town geisha, this was the first stop on the journey. So, they settled down here for a while and using this as her home base she went off to parties in the nearby towns. From then until Nuiko was viewing it now in the present, the town had hardly changed at all. Even now, from the window of the train she's riding on, Nuiko can see the restaurant that she woke up in every morning many years ago. Nuiko reminisced that even the way the restaurant sign tilts somewhat to the left hasn't changed. Behind the poplar trees a wide ribbon of white smoke emanates from the pier where the Nakdong River runs, where Nuiko and Mother used to go fishing. At the pier you could see clear through the fog to the opposite shore. Sometimes a whale would lose its way and swim up the river, which would excite the people on the shore.

Mother and Nuiko drifted around from one place to another along the main train line that runs from Pusan to Seoul, wandering from Samyangjin to Milyang and then from Milyang to Kŭmsun, Mother with her three-stringed shamisen in hand. During all the moving around, somehow Mother had managed to find time to teach herself traditional Japanese folk songs and customers would compliment her on how professional she sounded. She was able to play almost all the songs they requested, including old songs in the Hakata style from Kyūshū. No matter what town she was in she was popular, sometimes too popular—invariably there was a customer who got too involved with her and wanted something more than she was selling. When this happened she would immediately pack up her things and tell the manager of the establishment that was sponsoring her, "See you later." Nuiko didn't go back to school; her mother bought her magazines and she lay around all day in bed reading them on the second floor of the restaurants where Mother was employed. Sometimes she would go fishing by herself, like a boy playing hooky, and catch all sorts of fish. She used to catch a big, round fish called a *donguchi*, which can be found only in that region. She figured she'd had enough school in Pusan and didn't want to go back.

Suddenly, the sound of kids yelling interrupted Nuiko's reminiscing and she moved up close to the window to see what it was all about. There were five or six Korean kids swinging water buckets above their heads and shouting at the train. Behind them water was everywhere, stretching all the way toward the other side of the red- and ocher-colored mountain. Here and there were footpaths and heads of rice were popping out of the flooded rice paddies. Were those children actually trying to scoop water out of the flooded paddies with those tiny little buckets? Then right in front of Nuiko's eyes a group of adults appeared scooping out water as well. Four men would fill a boat the size of an oil tank with water, fasten a rope to it, and then tip the boat over to drain the water out, repeating this over and over. The four men worked while chanting a slow folk song, steadily repeating each part of the operation. Sometimes when trains went by they'd rest for a minute and watch them with their mouths hanging open.

One particular time, a train was running alongside a branch of the Nakdong River. With a vicious roar the crimson water created a vortex-like current in the center of the river as it sprayed out a mist. Just when Nuiko caught a glimpse of a castle off in the distance, she also noticed something floating down the river from the same direction. What was swirling around and bobbing up and down

in the wild current was an entire roof that had become detached
from a Korean-style house. There was a man holding on to the roof
for dear life and screaming for help; his mouth was open as wide
as his whole face and he was screeching at the train. As soon as
the man's sunburned face flashed into view it dropped back out
of sight and into the recesses of Nuiko's thoughts. There was a
big flood like this the summer Nuiko was at Milyang. It seemed
that the flood was especially bad that year; there were twenty or
thirty houses from the village side of the mountain washed off
its slope and forced into the river. Whole families would be hanging on to one rope attached to their roof as they were helplessly
washed along with the torrential current. These people yelled out
as loud as they could to onlookers, "Where the hell are we now?"
Even kids and women holding small babies cried out to people
standing on the shores, "Where are we?" The people on shore
yelled in reply, "There's still a long ways to go until you hit the
Nakdong River." The people had probably been desperately plead-
ing for information about their present location for many kilometers already. When the bystanders in other villages answered
them they must have cried out the name of their own village. However, Milyang was the only village that answered "a long way to go
until you hit the Nakdong River." Actually, the main streams of
the Nakdong weren't that far away; it flowed along the outskirts
of the city. Once these people reached the point where the two
main branches of the Nakdong meet, they'd have to deal with sav-
age cross-currents crashing into each other; their roofs would undoubtedly be crushed by angry waves and they themselves would
be swallowed up by the surf. Even as young as she was, Nuiko
understood why these people were asking where they were instead
of begging for help. She ran to the edge of the water and, with the
other Koreans who were looking on, cried out with pity for these
people as they floated away.

Whether it was the divorce, abandonment, selling brown rice
bread, working on the docks, prostitution, or working indepen-
dently as a traveling geisha entertainer, each time they seemed to
be on the brink of sharing the fate of those people and be drowned
by a huge flood. Nuiko and Mother took what seemed like their
last breath and waited for the end. With her aggressiveness and determination Mother fought back against this malevolent torrent

of life, only to find herself thrown back each time into the river rapids with more war wounds and bruises than she had before. By the time she realized this, the river had widened into something that was absolutely unbridgeable. If she were to continue to be washed downstream in these wild currents, the only thing awaiting her would be the gaping mouth of the great river's raging billows. Mother, who had by this time been working solely as a geisha, barely got through each day, and each day seemed more hopeless than the one before it. She couldn't predict when the end was waiting for her somewhere around the corner. Just like the Koreans thrown into the swollen river, Mother must have been screaming "Where the hell am I now?" through her worried eyes as each day passed. But what exactly was it that pushed her so far out into the deep end, day in and day out? This question grew stronger in Nuiko's heart as she grew older, and she searched diligently for an answer. It was her search for an answer to this that gave shape to Nuiko's way of seeing things at their most basic level.

Was it the force of her father's abuse alone that sealed her entire life's fate together with the one that had crashed in on her mother? The destiny of the people screaming "Where the hell am I now?" as they were washed away wasn't merely coincidence—they were the targets of a more violent storm than one with mere natural causes. The storm caused such destructive flooding due to a host of reasons dating way back to their ancestors and the oppression of ancient governments that had forced them to strip the mountain bare. They also weren't fortunate enough then to have the right equipment to deal with the flood, as the colonial government didn't provide ditches or dams to protect the people living in the area. But more than any of those other explanations, the main reason for their suffering was that they were just too poor. Every year they were beaten to the ground by Mother Nature, yet they didn't have the luxury of taking any precautions whatsoever. They had only just enough to get through each day. But the causes weren't just poverty. There was something more fundamental flooding and overflowing the foundation of their existence. In Mother's case, for example, this was the basic fact that she had no legal or civil rights. After escaping from her male-dominated, so-called home in Japan, Mother faced a feudalistic system that didn't offer her any sort of social support. She was forced to live with her husband's concubine in her own home merely because she was unable to conceive a child and couldn't continue her husband's paternal line. A single notice of divorce forced her out of her own home. Things like this happened as a matter of course amid the feudalistic floods of those days. A divorced woman in Japan is labeled undesirable and treated as absolutely dishonorable. Even if she were to drum up enough confidence to look for a place to work, there would be no occupation that would pay her enough to live an independent life. If she worked as an equal to a man in the same job, her wage would still be less than half of his. As a final insult, more often than not she ends up in places where women are sold like pieces of merchandise. It's a fitting irony that Mother finally found some respite from being on the brink of starvation all the time—by becoming a commodity to be bought and sold.

If Mother were to continue on her journey as a traveling geisha her fate was sure to force her onto an even worse path than the one she was presently on. Mother could easily end up squeezing pus and blood out of breakouts of boils and sores all over her body, a body that would have nothing left on it but skin and bones. She'd probably end up buried, fertilizing this foreign soil, like the other prostitutes traveling this kind of dead-end road. However, she was carried safely to the other side of life's torrential river by a mysterious stroke of good luck: Mother became an upstart colonial landlord.

After drifting from town to town, Nuiko and Mother settled in a small city called Suwon. On their first night there, the man who would eventually turn her life around requested Mother. He had an impressive farm hidden in the woods about forty kilometers outside of the city; his wife had passed away about six months ago. They found out later that the local Koreans believed that his wife had died from possession by a vindictive ghost. Even when the dead wife was in good health, she'd be attacked by fits and end up rolling around on the ground and foaming at the mouth, reaching out to grab at nonexistent things in the air. According to their servant, before she died her body convulsed like a harpooned fish as she screamed out gibberish hysterically. The local Koreans were certain that her death was a punishment for the way her Japanese husband committed acts of evil against them, and they guessed that he didn't have much longer to live either. What the Koreans called his "black magic" was directly related to his business practices. This Japanese guy appeared nonchalantly in this Korean town one day about twenty years before. After inquiring with the Japanese colonial government authorities about the land title for the huge mountain forests (which in the past had collectively belonged to the village), he found out that they'd never been officially registered as anyone's property. So, he boldly purchased the forests as his own private possession. Of course, he didn't do this without consulting the Korean villagers. As soon as he arrived in the village, he started to research the property situation of the villagers and he wrote down the figures and calculations in his ledger book and asked around. Even though taxes had been going up annually he thought that buying the communal forest outright might make a good business investment. Of course, the villagers let him present his offers but didn't take him seriously. There had never been a time when a Japanese proposed a reasonably fair offer to them except for the time when . . . But still, there was no way the villagers wanted to be paying more and more taxes each year for that barren, pitiful mountain that produced only a few skinny pine trees. Moreover, these poor Koreans were already finding it oppressive to pay taxes on the fields that were right in front of them. The villagers figured that if they unloaded the mountain on the Japanese guy they would still be able to get much-needed firewood and pine needles from the other mountains nearby that they considered their collective property. But they were completely taken in. That Japanese man had claimed every mountain in their village. He put wire fences around the mountains and built small shacks as police stations. Just to get firewood for their stoves in the winter, they now had to go to faraway mountains. But even these more remote mountains were gradually taken over and occupied by compatriots of the Japanese man. So the villagers were forced to purchase the fuel they needed at an exorbitant price from this swindler, because he now owned every single one of the mountains and was even beginning to plant new pine trees. When these grew tall enough to be telephone poles he harvested them and sent the load down the Han River to Seoul. Weaker trees were pruned each year to allow the strong trees to grow even taller, and it was rumored that he made $3,000 or so a year on these pruned trees alone. He also planted a large orchard and, in the end, took over the very fields that the Korean villagers were struggling to pay taxes on. In no time at all, he became a big landowner and all the local people could do was look on in amazement.

After his wife died, he went to Suwon every night to drown his sorrows. That's when Mother suddenly appeared in front of him. A little later on, when he'd get drunk, he had the habit of drumming on his belly, saying, "Ya know, Mr. Saigō[3] was different from me. Saigō tried to conquer Korea but couldn't do it. I'm a small man, but . . ." He shyly rubbed his long, shaved head and continued, "I'm small but I more or less conquered this whole area." Once after this performance he put Nuiko on his lap and said, "Ain't I an excellent man?" Nuiko rolled her eyes at him, and as he brought his face closer to her, misreading her reaction, he said, "You have such a cute face, kid; don't you like me?" and smiled at her.

About this time it was decided they would leave Suwon and Nuiko was taken to the man's house with Mother and settled in there. It wasn't a very impressive house for a big landlord. Moreover, there was no wedding or wedding reception of any kind. Starting right the next evening, the man drank sake in his living room as Mother played the stringed shamisen. There wasn't anything dramatically different from the situation in the restaurant except the actual place itself. However, one evening, before even one month of this arrangement had passed, the man suddenly died. He was on the verge of passing out while Mother played his favorite song. He tried to stand up to go to the bathroom but somehow lost his balance and fell on his back. He never got up again. A vase fell over when this happened and Mother went to wipe up the water that had spilled on the tatami carpet. She thought he'd just passed out from drinking too much—his usual routine. But when she tried to put a blanket over him she realized that he was cold. Even though his previous wife had died from tuberculosis, the doctor said that his cause of death was an aneurysm resulting from high blood pressure. His will was another strange matter. He had only one nephew living in Japan, in Kagoshima, so the fortune was split into real estate and household goods, and the will stipulated that Mother could pick whichever she wanted. Although the goods were more valuable, Mother surprised the man's relatives by taking the real estate. People wondered what a woman could possibly do with all that property, and the relatives felt sorry for Mother.

## CHAPTER SEVEN

Their new farm was located at a point where the boundaries of the three provinces of Kyŏngsang-do, Ch'ungch'ŏn-do, and Kyŏnggi-do meet, alongside the Han River that runs west rubbing up against the folds of some small, white mountains at the point where it runs down from its source in the distant Odae Mountains. At the location of Mother's farm the Han was wide but narrow enough for people to yell across it. It stretched about 120 kilometers down toward Seoul, by which point it manifested the guise of a great river, but it extended even farther out toward the west, forming a gulf in the Yellow Sea.

The forest property that just fell into Mother's hands spread out some forty-five kilometers on both sides of the Han River. As it was almost completely covered in pine trees, the idea was that they'd clear-cut one section of the forest each year and fourteen or fifteen years later would return to that section when the saplings had grown into trees large enough to be harvested. The lumber they cut down was piled up and sent down the river to Seoul to become telegraph poles. If you looked to the south with the forest behind your back there were three thousand square kilometers or so of orchard-covered hills, and beyond the orchards, where the land was more flat, there were rice paddies and fields.

In the beginning Mother just went around the farm in a daze. It was autumn and there were apples and pears hanging from every tree in the orchard, and there were radishes popping out of the ground in the fields and top-heavy ears of rice in the paddies, too. It must have been strange for her. She strolled through all this newly acquired wealth accompanied by caretakers, supervisors, and other employees. When she returned Mother lay right down in bed and took some medicine for a headache. She made pathetic faces as she complained of dizziness and kept telling Nuiko stories of the hardships she had to deal with during the time she worked on the docks. Maybe she had hallucinations of avalanches of rice falling onto her as she watched the rice sway in the wind of her ripening paddies. Or maybe she couldn't stop recalling that painful time in her life when they almost killed themselves on the beach over that small bag of rice Nuiko spilled. For two or three months running she remained in this dazed condition, just playing her shamisen in the corner of the living room. But eventually Mother came to and rediscovered the will she had when she chose to be a big landowner; that old flame in her heart rekindled once again.

First she took charge of the orchard. Mother wore a thick work jacket and participated in all the major tasks: from wrapping the blossoming fruits with pest control bags, to applying pesticide, to finally packing the fruit together with her Korean workers for shipping to other areas. The packaged fruit was stacked onto an oxcart that left around dusk, arriving in the city of Suwon the following day at noon. Here they dropped off part of the shipment and the rest was sent to Seoul on the railway. However, after traveling for two or three days, Mother's "20th-Century Pears" wilted and decreased in value, becoming hard to sell. So the next year, she sold off part of the forest and bought a motorized boat at Hapyok River. This cargo boat had an airplane-like propeller attached to the bottom. With the new boat they were able to deliver their shipment to Seoul in four or five hours. They realized how profitable the orchards could be thanks to the new propeller boat and the next year they increased the stock of 20th-Century Pears in addition to expanding their peach orchard. Mother's assertive character raised its head over and over again, and eventually she was personally directing everything that went on in the farm. She took the lumber, fruits, and rice to the market herself and learned how to bargain with the sly merchants in the process. Soon she developed a reputation for herself as "the lady who's a wizard with the abacus." She always carried around an accounting ledger with all her calculations recorded in it, and if she were even one cent short in her total, she'd whip the abacus out and figure out the deficiency. People gossiped that she could still be living comfortably without doing any of the work herself, and they predicted she'd double her worth in no time at all.

With Mother reversing their fate so quickly and unexpectedly, Nuiko got the chance to enter a private school for girls, where she was no longer the pathetic little poor girl that she'd been during grade school. She was now more like that confident and privileged daughter of the wholesaler who'd been the most popular kid in her grade school. Mother prepped Nuiko so that she wouldn't feel inferior to the daughters of the businessmen and government officials she was now mingling with at school. There was nothing at all remaining of that old dark shadow hovering around Nuiko. As she hit tennis balls across the school court in her pure white uniform, she'd been fully transformed into an attractive young woman with big, bright eyes. She amused herself and her friends with silly tricks like buying candy from the second floor of the dormitory by tying a coin to a string and lowering it down to the candy store below. During summer and spring breaks Mother would pick her up in the propeller boat after making her deals. The boat was painted white at Nuiko's request, which made it look like a swan floating down the Han River. That's how it got the nickname *The Swan*. On the deck of *The Swan* Nuiko wrapped her arms around Mother's neck and sang things like her school fight song and "I trained my body in the North China wind" at the top of her lungs.

And so a few years passed like this. Then one day a slip of the tongue by Minister of Finance Kataoka during a National Assembly session triggered a chain reaction where big corporations like Suzuki Merchandise fell one after another. There was a run on the banks that began in Taiwan and spread throughout Japan until a moratorium was declared on withdrawals. Throughout the whole of Japan's empire a kind of chaos erupted, like when someone pokes a beehive. Leaders of the left-wing unions yelled from their soapboxes, "Finally, the end of capitalism has come!" At any rate, a kind of terrible storm swept over Japan. At first, the rough Sea of Genkai seemed to prevent these problems from spreading to Korea. Mother said confidently, "The homeland may be suffering a depression but it hasn't come to Korea yet." She was certain that even if Korea were hit by the storm, her business would be the only one strong enough to weather it. In fact, even to Nuiko it seemed that Mother's business was expanding at an enormous rate, as she added a large-scale pig farm and a pasture for cows behind the farm. She also got involved in a coal mining enterprise somewhere far away. But maybe spreading themselves so thin left the core of the enterprise weak. One fall evening a few years later, a violent rainstorm stripped the forest of its pine trees and the orchards of all their ripening fruit. As if this were an omen of what was to come, Mother's business began to lose its stability. Although the storm winds had hesitated right before crossing the dark Sea of Genkai, they finally attacked Korea. When the depression hit and as their businesses began to go under, they had to deal with their crops being stolen as well. Even in the farming villages, the number of starving Koreans increased alarmingly and those people set their hungry sights on Mother's crops.

It was sometime after Nuiko graduated from school and returned home that she suddenly woke up in the middle of the night to find Mother's bed empty. It was around two o'clock in the morning and the air was still; the only sound was the howling of wolves off in the distance. Although the wolves were shy about coming into their village, tigers' footprints were still sometimes found in the village, so people closed their heavy gates before going to bed. Midnight in the country house was quite eerie for Nuiko. After four or five years in Seoul she was used to living with bright lights and bustle. She lay motionless in her bed and held her breath, but Mother didn't return. Suddenly, she heard a rifle shot coming from the orchards. Then two, three, and four more shots rang out. It dawned on Nuiko that it might be Mother firing those shots. Nuiko ran to the back and the door squeaked as she opened it. She wondered if something had happened to Mother, so she woke up the maids and workmen and ran outside. Sounds of people running around were audible in the distance; then they heard a man's voice and Mother's angry voice yelling in Korean.

One of Mother's menservants ran straight toward the voices. Nuiko couldn't stop trembling. She squatted down and started to urinate, but even though she had to go really bad hardly anything came out. Finally Mother returned with a man who was yelling out something, and her pistol was pointed right at his stomach. Some of the other men from their house who'd been searching through the fields returned as well. Patrol officers from the police station arrived and took away the man Mother was pointing her pistol at. The bullets that Mother had in fact fired were shot harmlessly into the air. But a rock or something had hit her and there was blood running down her forehead and into her eyes. Nuiko cried helplessly as she tended to Mother, who could only say, "Business sure is lousy." For the first time, Nuiko realized that Mother had been guarding the orchards every evening wielding a pistol.

Nuiko watched uneasily as Mother ran around in circles desperately trying to rally her failing businesses. Since there was plenty of money for them to eat and get by on, Nuiko didn't exactly understand why Mother dedicated her body and soul to the businesses. She sometimes tried to take Mother's mind off the troubles, but Mother would hear nothing of it. It was also around this time that farm rents fell in arrears for several years due to a severe drought. That fall Mother put up "Keep Off" signs in front of the rice paddies and it was then that the incidents started. Ignoring the warnings, her tenant farmers would enter the paddies and harvest them illicitly anyway. Eventually Mother apprehended their leader, but this only infuriated the farmers more. They responded by stoning her big farmhouse and selected a representative to go inside to negotiate with her. The representative and Mother faced off in her front yard while just outside close to two hundred farmers screamed out in protest and boldly confronted the police. Every so often a rock would come flying in Mother's direction and the crowd cheered. But in the midst of all the Koreans' rage Mother remained firm; she refused to withdraw the prohibition on entering the rice paddies, even if she had to ask for help from the colonial police. Mother said that she and the farmers could work out an agreement on some of the issues and she would take 10 percent off their rents. But she was determined not to budge one inch beyond this offer.

Nuiko came face to face with all the typical characteristics of a stubborn landlord in Mother's behavior and she wasn't happy with it. She tried to convince Mother to be fair with the Koreans, but she refused to listen to anything. She responded by lecturing Nuiko: "A woman can rely only on money and the law." Only recently had Mother begun to protect herself by taking advantage of the feudalistic laws, the same ones that had, in fact, been oppressing her most of her life. Nuiko saw all too clearly the way Mother was using the law to her advantage, especially when she relied on a colonizer's privilege to become a powerful landowner.

In the five or six years after becoming a landlord, Mother's face and personality transformed in frightening ways. Even though her skin's complexion was refined and polished when she was a traveling geisha and while working in the red-light district, it had recently turned rough and coarse without any trace of how pretty it used to be. Moreover, there were red fatty deposits broken out all over her wrinkled skin, the kind of things only men were supposed to get. The shape of her eyes had narrowed and sharpened from constant anger and her body got plump from alcohol, which caused her belly to stick out from the long years of drinking that began during her geisha years. Her voice, the way she talked, even the way she walked became more and more masculine. When Nuiko sat down and thought about their relationship now, it occurred to her that Mother had started to think of her more as some kind of . . . than as her child.

Nuiko wanted to attend an upper-class prep school in Tokyo, but Mother furiously opposed the idea. When Nuiko imagined her lonely mother abandoned in the countryside, she gave up on the idea herself. Instead, Mother took Nuiko to Seoul in the motorboat for lessons in traditional Japanese flower arrangement, tea ceremony, and *koto*—to try to train her to become more ladylike. This didn't last for very long, though, and Mother made Nuiko quit even these lessons. She refused to let Nuiko out of her sight for even one second, and forced Nuiko to console and comfort her every time she took a break from work. Now, not only Mother's three meals a day, but also teatime snack had to be prepared exclusively by Nuiko—not by any of the maids. Moreover, whenever Nuiko left the house to go to a friend's place, Mother refused to eat from that morning until she eventually returned in the evening. And if there was ever an unavoidable errand that would take up most of the day, Nuiko was forced to make dinner and occasionally even breakfast in advance before she left the house. Although Mother wore work clothes and dressed like a man, she made Nuiko wear first-class silk gowns and other ladylike outfits, even as casual attire around the house and yard. Mother also insisted that Nuiko always have on makeup. In the evenings, Mother drank with her sake cup in hand while she made Nuiko play the string koto for her, gazing intently at her daughter's hand and nape while she did this. Since Nuiko was a grown-up young woman now, she didn't want to sleep on the same futon with Mother at night, but Mother insisted that she do just that. Although she agreed to sleep with Mother she did so only reluctantly; Nuiko no longer enjoyed being held in her arms like when she was a little girl. Similar to the time when Nuiko despaired for Mother when she became a prostitute, there was now a strange masculine body odor coming off her that was really different from her old smell.

Once when Mother came home in the middle of the night from an evening gathering, even though she was worn out and drunk she insisted on embracing Nuiko. When Mother hugged her tightly, Nuiko felt something suspicious about Mother . . .

Mother screamed and yelled hysterically from Nuiko's reaction and . . .

For Nuiko, this was . . .

"No way, no; I hate people like Kakashama," Nuiko exclaimed . . . and burst into tears as she ran into the room furthest from where Mother was. As she was crying, she noticed how bizarre her weeping was. While Nuiko was weeping . . . her mother's . . . faded . . . she realized she felt a kind of strong comfort. Also something inexplicably sharp made Nuiko's whole body numb and she let the sobs pour out of her mouth; lukewarm tears rolled down her cheeks. In an odd way Nuiko found herself enjoying this sensation.

The feeling of . . . that Nuiko experienced that evening with Mother was very close to how she felt when she met the young man Tōru. Tōru entered Nuiko's world just a few days after the incident with Mother. The agricultural high school of Suwon sent Tōru to her area along with ten other students for training. They met for the first time while Nuiko was brushing a calf under an apple tree on her mother's estate. Ears of corn were rustling below as a young man wearing a school uniform emerged from between the hills. He swerved to avoid a hillock and almost crashed right into Nuiko, who seemed to have appeared suddenly right in front of him. He gasped, blushed strongly, bowed his head down, and said, "Hello." Then he took a few steps to start running away from her with his head still pointed at the ground, embarrassed. Suddenly, he turned around to face her, still appearing to blush, and asked, "Excuse me, where is the farm office?" For some reason, Nuiko felt her throat choke up and she couldn't get her voice out. "Um, that way," she finally managed to say as she pointed toward the office. The student made an incredulous face and as he looked in the direction her finger was pointing, he inquired again for clarification, "That house with the red roof, right?" All Nuiko could do in reply was give him a big, slow nod. The student responded back with a nod and ran off toward the office. Tōru recalled this incident later with her and they laughed about it: "Where is the office?" he'd ask, and mimicking Nuiko's reply, answer "Um, that way."

Even though their encounter was brief it entranced Nuiko. She deliberately stopped herself from staring at Tōru as he ran away. Flustered, she gripped the brush again and continued combing the calf's soft coat, but the image of the student's thick nose kept appearing in between the strands of the animal's hair. "What's wrong with me? I'm not acting like myself at all," she mused as she tried to snap out of her stupor. At that moment, a frightening premonition ran through her blood and struck her heart.

The students stayed at the building next to Mother's business office for a week and helped out on the farm; there was a going-away party for them on their last night. The students got red around the eyes after drinking a little and began to argue. When their discussion topic turned to "Women are _____ (fill in the blank)," a student from Kyūshū started to tell a story. "In Kyūshū women are only considered baby-making machines. For instance, let's say there's a whole fish bein' served for dinner. The father takes the best meat from the head, then the oldest son, then the next oldest, and so on—with all the boys taking the best meat from the back, toward the tail. Then the girl in the highest position, which is the youngest, gets the fat and whatever meat's left. So the oldest daughter and the mother are left with only the scrap meat on the bone or they pour hot water on the plate and slurp the water. And the father, who ate the best meat, is not even remotely concerned with the fact that his wife can only slurp soup off a plate." Another student jumped in: "Yeah, yeah; that's the way it is. My father owns a mine and there's a bath for the mineworkers. There's a log dividing the men's and women's sections of the bath, you know. The mineworkers are so filthy that a little scrubbing with warm water just won't do the job. So they lather themselves up and jump in the water, then scrub some more. Even the deep pockets inside their nostrils are black so they stick their soapy wash clothes in their noses and then blow. Their private parts are in the same condition so they take off their loincloths and scrub totally naked. Well, obviously the water gets black like ink with all that coal in it; it's like a mud gutter where the air bubbles come out. But there is a rinsing tub for the men where they can wash off most of the scum; of course, there isn't one for the women. I asked my father why this is the case and he replied, 'It's because women are filthy to start out with anyway.' The poor, miserable women of Kyūshū!"

As he glanced quickly over at Nuiko, Tōru added, "It's not just in Kyūshū. There is at least some kind of bias separating men and women all over the country. In Japan, women as a whole are an oppressed class." He noticed that Nuiko was listening intently, holding her breath so as not to miss a word, so he added, "Well anyway, that's my take on it," and smiled shyly. "I think that the kind of oppressive jobs that women are forced to do actually created this kind of society. For example, meals; the food that you prepare over a span of one or two hours is finished in ten, twenty minutes, then there's nothing left except dirty dishes. The same goes for laundry and mending clothes. Women are hassled by exploitative nonpaying jobs like these the whole day. This drags down several million Japanese women daily. Knowing that it's these stupid, ridiculous causes that create oppressive conditions for women makes me really sad."

Nuiko didn't quite understand why, as a woman, she was a member of an oppressed class and she didn't particularly want to think about it any more at that point. Nevertheless, what Tōru called "exploitative nonwage" work really got her excited. From that evening straight through to the next, Nuiko reflected intensely on the discussion and, becoming overwhelmed with a desire to relate her thoughts to someone, she wrote a letter by lamplight. When she realized she had unconsciously addressed the letter directly to Tōru, she focused on the amazing changes she felt in her heart. She could feel herself physically lean in Tōru's direction, and by doing so, hoped that the action would relieve some of the pressure from what felt like a hole in her head, a head that suddenly seemed crammed with all kinds of things. She hoped that something fresh and new would flow into her brain from that depressurized hole, something that Nuiko hadn't been able to imagine before, and, further, that these new thoughts would all lead her into a different, more alive existence. Despite all that was going on in her head, she tried to keep the letter as simple as she could:

> . . . Yesterday, I believe that you sympathized with the women responsible for doing all the nonpaid work. If there were more people who thought the way you did, life would be brighter and happier for us. However, no matter how much you feel that these jobs are dull and unimportant, these kinds of jobs are often the only work available for some women. Because I think women have tendencies to do things driven only by emotions and feeling, this creates even more situations where women are left with unpaid jobs. For some reason, pleasant, happy thoughts were in my head today so I thought I should tell you; please forgive me. Please come visit again and teach me all kinds of things.

Even though she mailed the letter there were questions left unanswered in Nuiko's heart: Why must women be trampled on and treated disrespectfully just because they are responsible for the crucial, yet "nonwage" labor, like supporting their loved ones and raising children? Nuiko had been taught that women are walked all over not because of who they are, but because of the particular characteristics of men. She got these ideas in the first place from a woman teacher at the girls' school who treated Nuiko as her favorite student. She was a pretty young woman around twenty-five or twenty-six, whose complexion was so wan and beautiful it seemed that she'd had tuberculosis or something. In the spring of her fifth year, one year before graduation year, the teacher invited Nuiko to come join her for a chat in the garden of the school dormitory, underneath a lush group of blooming crabapple trees. "Miss Machida, come here, please; I want to share something," she said. She opened up a small book and showed it to Nuiko. Inside, there was something written in the teacher's own handwriting:

| teens | twenties | thirties | forties | fifties |
|---|---|---|---|---|
| Male— —beast— —madman— —failure— —manipulator— —criminal | | | | |
| Female— —angel— —Gretchen— —femme fatale— —sacred mother— —hag | | | | |

Nuiko looked up at the teacher and asked, "What does this all mean? I can understand the stuff about the women, but why are all the men . . . ?" The only response the teacher offered Nuiko was, "That's right, Miss Machida, this is why you shouldn't trust men and should not get married."

It was rumored that the teacher married a young philosophy student she met in a philosophy class at university, but he died suddenly after only three months, leaving her lungs infected with a grave disease at that. Whether she said these things to Nuiko out of bitterness from her own life experiences or had learned them in some philosophy book, Nuiko didn't know for sure. No matter what may have generated these thoughts, what the teacher said made a profound impression on Nuiko that couldn't be erased, and it happened around the same time she was first discovering her own feelings for boys. That evening after lights out, she looked out her dormitory window at the lights flickering over by the poplar trees and read, "Take this medicine and you'll cure your gonorrhea overnight — Riberu," absorbed in thinking about these new things in her life. But when she put these new ideas about men together with the reality of her *mother's* life, things started to make more sense and she felt the ideas had validity. Half of Mother's life was destroyed by the bad qualities of men illustrated in the chart. Father sure followed the men's trajectory to a letter: madman — failure — manipulator — criminal. And the brown rice bread boss, the drunken longshoremen who . . . and all the drunken men whoring around the red-light district; they all matched the chart perfectly. Nuiko saw the "beast" category in those teenage middle school boys who . . . her behind the classrooms when she was still just in grade school. She thought to herself, "If I'm going to be a hag when I'm in my fifties, I'd rather end up dead before I ever get there." She announced to her classmates that she'd never get married and she vowed repeatedly that she would spend her whole life as a working woman and fight against men. This kind of resolve had the effect of making Nuiko wary and timid around men; she wasn't at all interested in love and romance like so many of the other girls her age. If she did come across a potential romantic interest she made sure to avoid any contact with him; so it was natural that she never had to deal with any boy problems.

However, the situation was a little different with Tōru and he came to visit her the Sunday after she'd sent him the letter. It was spring and the apple blossoms were in full bloom. As they were walking through the orchard together Nuiko shrugged and wondered to herself, "Is this guy a beast and a madman, too?" As she asked herself this, she snuck a glance at him and tried to coldly appraise his tan, plain face and his cute round nose. As the sweet apple blossoms scattered above their heads and the two of them strolled shoulder to shoulder together, she thought of a scene from a movie she saw in Seoul called *The Wedding March* by Erich von Stroheim. The apple orchard in the outskirts of Vienna in that film was lusciously beautiful, but by contrast, here in colonial Korea she observed with disappointment that the apple trees were trimmed back to make the apples grow larger, and the bark, covered with pesticide, was gray and dry like an old man's bald head. Despite that regretful disappointment their conversation heated up excitedly. At one point Nuiko finally blurted out, "Why is it that women have to be looked down upon because their work is nonwaged? Isn't it because of male tyranny?" Tōru replied, "No, no; like I said before, it's the fault of the social system. There's a poem that the white-haired old sage Akita Ujaku[4] read when he returned to Japan from the Soviet Union, do you know it? It goes like this: 'Japanese women under the rising sun, why are you so dark and shadowy?' Anyway, when he writes that 'Japanese women under the rising sun are so dark,' what he's talking about is Japanese feudalism. But in the Soviet Union women and men live as equals, because the socialist system has liberated women. Women are able to join the productive workforce and are also able to enjoy the same economic independence as men. Furthermore, the legal system respects and protects women's bodies and work. If this 'nonwage labor' that you, Nuiko, just mentioned, happened in a more socialist structure, then it would be considered a productive, important job within the division of labor. The larger point I'm trying to make is: Japanese women suffer all kinds of misfortunes because they are trapped in patriarchal-controlled households without any economic, political, or legal rights."

Tōru recommended that Nuiko read Bebel's[5] *Theory of Women* and Nuiko devoured the book, attempting to understand further what Tōru was saying. The complicated theory left Nuiko completely overwhelmed after one and two readings, but started to make a little more sense after the third, fourth, and fifth time through the text. Her tenuous grasp of the book gradually expanded as Nuiko spent more time talking with Tōru about the things that perplexed her. While being engaged in this process all her worries and concerns seemed to get put in a neat order and the fog in her brain started to lift. Her heart bounced gleefully as she felt a totally different, new Nuiko grow inside her.

However, this happy interlude was suddenly interrupted by an unexpected event: one day Tōru suddenly stopped coming around to visit her. Even now, Nuiko holds onto the memory of their last day together with mixed feelings. She remembers going to Mother's forest with Tōru in the propeller boat to fish in a stream of the Han River. They caught a frisky carp that was struggling so hard to get away it almost broke their fishing line. Then they built a fire on the riverbank and threw the protesting fish into a pot of boiling soy sauce, which flavored the meat perfectly. They separated the meat from the bones and enjoyed the sweet, soy flavor; then they cooked rice to complete the feast. By this time the two had become much more comfortable with each other and were able to joke around lightly. On their way back home in the boat Tōru suddenly burst out with "Let's get married," and embraced Nuiko and kissed her firmly. Nuiko stiffened her body and tried to turn her face away from him. After being kissed, even though there was a sweet and pleasant aftertaste on her lips, her chest started to pound rapidly and painfully. Standing directly in front of Tōru, who was shocked to see such a painful look on Nuiko's face, bile worked its way into her mouth from her throat and she started to vomit. Nuiko thought to herself, "If I keep this up, Tōru might start to hate me." She tried to make herself stop vomiting, but a bitter flavor crawled uncontrollably up her throat and she kept throwing up. "Wow! Your body must really be weak if a little stimulation like that makes you puke. I don't know if you'll be able to handle life as a wife," Tōru laughed, as Nuiko leaned over the edge of the boat with her sickly, chalk-white face.

Tōru stopped visiting after that and Nuiko got really depressed; she felt he'd rejected her. Nuiko knew by the reaction she was having that she'd fallen head over heels in love with the irreplaceable Tōru. However, she found out later that Tōru had stopped visiting her for a completely different reason. Members of the left-wing study association of his school had been arrested and Tōru was one of them. Moreover, the left-wing students had approached some of the Korean tenant farmers who rented from Mother, which made the incident a much more serious one in the eyes of the authorities. Two or three months later, Tōru was taken by his father and repatriated back to Japan, without even being allowed to see Nuiko. Nuiko heard all this from her mother, who had gone to the police, but Tōru's actual whereabouts remained unknown, even after Mother said he'd been taken back to Japan.

Mother had a strong aversion to the idea of Nuiko getting intimate with Tōru and constantly tried to tear her away from him. Nuiko always felt the cold surveillance of Mother's eyes on her even when she met Tōru away from the farm for dates. As soon as Tōru disappeared, Mother pulled out photographs of a different man and asked Nuiko if she was interested in marrying him, as if she'd been long waiting for the chance to take Tōru out of the running for her daughter. Mother said that he was an assistant engineer for the colonial government's Agriculture and Forestry Bureau, who promised to take over responsibility for the farm and who would take good care of Nuiko. He looked feminine and delicate, with a small forehead and thin nose, features that disgusted Nuiko to the point where she wanted to run away and throw up. She firmly resisted the pressure to marry him and started to distance herself from Mother. Nuiko only wanted to stay shut up in her own room alone dreaming of Tōru's face, regardless of whether he was a "beast" or "madman." Autumn passed and winter arrived. Her horoscope in a magazine predicted: "Once the ice and snow have melted and the rosebuds start to bloom, you will be able to do what you've wanted to," and Nuiko started to feel that Tōru would magically appear and take her away somewhere once the roses came into season again. Even while she entertained these fantasies of escaping with Tōru, she still felt bad for Mother, who was clearly depressed that Nuiko was giving her the cold shoulder day in and day out. Then Nuiko heard from one of the maids that a Korean man who lived behind their orchard named Mr. Park was in fact Mother's most recent gigolo. Soon after this revelation an unattractive man with white, loose skin and sunken eyes began to come around and greet Nuiko with pleasantries. She wondered to herself, "How could Mother be sexually attracted to this ugly country bumpkin?" But then she started to strategize that if this man could comfort and be kind to Mother this might distract her, allowing Nuiko to escape from her suffocating attachments and head off toward her own liberated utopia.

Even though the rosebuds weren't in bloom yet, spring was just around the corner and the ice began to crack and float away on the Han River. By chance Nuiko got her hands on a letter from Tōru. It was in a stack with about ten other letters in the incoming mail that the mailman handed her in front of Mother's office one day and she picked it out of the pile. When she saw that it was the sixth letter in a series, she realized that Mother had disposed of the other five. The letter said that he was living under difficult circumstances in Tokyo. Although every day was a battle and he never knew what tomorrow would bring, he was still hopeful and full of energy. The letter also said that he'd made up his mind and wanted to know if her present situation would allow her to come to see him in Japan. When Nuiko read this she couldn't stand still. That evening, while Mother was away at some meeting, Nuiko begged the skipper of the propeller boat to help her. Free at last, she found herself racing down the still dangerously icy Han River at night with her heart filled with hope.

CHAPTER NINE

Nuiko searched everywhere in the back streets of Sugamo, but she just couldn't find Tōru's place. She finally located the confectionery store that rented cheap rooms in front, after she dismissed the cab driver that had driven her there. "There's no way you're gonna find him," the driver tossed off as he left. Although she'd left Tokyo station at nine in the morning, the neighborhood siren had already announced that it was noontime. When she entered the store she asked if "Mr. Kataoka" was residing there, using the false name he'd revealed to her in his letter. The friendly, plump landlady answered, "Yeah, he's here," and turned toward the second-floor stairs and yelled, "Mr. Kataoka, there's a visitor, a pretty visitor here to see you. . . . Still sleeping; ya know it's Saturday," the landlady told her, and said she should go right up. At this point Nuiko started climbing the stairs, making a squeaking sound as she climbed. When she reached the second floor she knocked on the door the landlady told her was Mr. Kataoka's. He was snoring so loudly that you could hear it from outside the sliding paper door to his room. When she finally opened the door, she found Tōru sleeping so soundly he was hugging his futon; the room was filled with a man's smell that went straight up her nostrils. With this smell, she now recollected vividly the lonely days on the farm after he left Korea for Japan; Nuiko wondered how many times she had put the kimono (the kimono that she wore the last day she went fishing with Tōru) to her face to breath in his smell, dreaming about her long-lost lover. Mixed in with the smell of tobacco that came off that kimono was something that called to mind the smell of Tōru's body. Nuiko cherished this kimono pattern of white chrysanthemums against a navy blue background, and chose to wear it on this first day of her reunion with Tōru. While she was looking down at Tōru's tired, sleeping face Nuiko felt reassured that her own reckless decision to leave home and come to Tokyo wasn't a mistake, even though she'd struggled hard trying to figure out how to communicate to him her resolve to share his life and political beliefs. Before long, Tōru woke up and he rubbed his bloodshot eyes over and over; then his voice exploded with surprise. He stared and stared at Nuiko as if to say, "You're really here; you came after all," then he grabbed her around the shoulders, exclaiming, "This isn't a dream, is it?" Nuiko replied, "You seem pretty casual; you weren't even expecting me. If it hadn't been me but a wicked person instead, you'd be in real trouble." The sarcastic remark flew out of her mouth even though this was clearly the point at which she'd determined to tell him her heroic decision to share his life. Tōru said with a laugh, "Last night was Saturday so I pulled an all-nighter editing the newspaper. All I could do after that was go right home and crash. That's because the guy named Mr. Kataoka Matsuo is supposed to be the epitome of a real bourgeois businessman." He laughs out loud as he says this. Suddenly, a feeling that they could rely on and be safe with each other rushed over them and nothing further had to be said. While Nuiko sat, her knees touching his body, she thought that this feeling they had of total trust was directly opposite to those situations where people have to swear oaths to each other; the fact that she was going to do that seemed ridiculous to her now. She asked him if he would let her live with him as his wife and coworker, who would live and die with him. Right there, right then Tōru embraced her. . . . All the sickness in her heart and any fear or doubts she'd had previously melted completely away. Much later, Tōru joked around by saying he should have forced Nuiko at knife point to swear to marry him, to test whether she was being sincere or not. Tōru told her a startling story that once the radical leader of a worker's party did just that when he was a member of . . . He added with a laugh, "But you know, when I saw the serious look on your face in that situation, I was really touched and realized that probably wasn't the correct approach."

On the day after her arrival she began her new life, a life that, as an ordinary businessman's housewife, seemed calm at a surface level. The landlady living downstairs would tease Nuiko, "I'm really jealous you two newlyweds are so lovey-dovey." Each morning, Tōru got dressed and would leave the house at eight carrying his briefcase, returning to their place every evening at six like a regular businessman. He left their house at 8 A.M. even after an all-nighter of political activities, claiming that he had to protect the safe house because . . .

Occasionally when he returned home late from some required engagement, Nuiko surmised from his ruddy cheeks that he had been drinking at some cheap bars along the way. At times like this, he would yell out an excuse at the entryway to the confectionary store, one that would be audible to everybody: "I had a party; sorry I'm late. Here's a present for my Nuiko." Then he'd hand Nuiko and the landlady small dishes of sushi.

Nuiko told Tōru that she'd learn how to type and went to the library and did research on topics and statistics for their group's newspaper. She also did all the labor necessary to keep their small household running smoothly. This involved frugally purchasing only one head of lettuce at a time and three-penny radishes, ignoring the frowning looks on the grocer's face. After shopping, she would wait at home making their humble dinner.

She also was responsible for delivering messages for their group. For this Tōru usually made Nuiko wait at a designated street corner at noon and three in the afternoon. When Tōru saw her at the location he'd invariably pretend he didn't know her and play his bourgeois gentleman role to the hilt, taking off his hat and saying, "Mrs. So and So, what is your noble destination today?" Nuiko would play along, bowing to him and saying, "Thank you for being so gracious," and bite her lip to try to keep from laughing.

One time when Nuiko saw Tōru off after one of these meetings, as he disappeared past the street corner, she had a scary feeling that they would never see each other again and desperately followed after him. Then, immediately after she set out in pursuit of him, Nuiko spied Tōru from the street corner dressed in his European-style clothing that made him look so heavyset—he was laughing out loud as he was being led along by three or four friends. If in fact he did notice Nuiko at this time he pretended not to have, so she started to think dark thoughts about him as he receded into the distance. That evening when he returned home, he was laughing as usual. Chuckling out loud he said, "You're being ridiculous." Then he elaborated: "At a time like today when you followed me, if there had been any communication at all between us it would have been extremely dangerous and most likely have exposed both of us. . . ."

One night while she was memorizing the whole map of Tokyo out of fear that she might make a mistake when they arranged secret meetings, Tōru asked Nuiko, "Do you know the name of the bus stop that has the biggest number in it?" After a painstaking search she replied that the Eighth block of Ginza is pretty small, so it seems that Kojimachi's Thirteenth block is the one with the biggest number. "There's still one more," Tōru teased her: "What about Senju-Ōhashi [the big bridge with a thousand houses]?" At this point, Nuiko finally realized that Tōru was teasing her with plays on words. So she replied with one of her own: "How about Mansei-bashi [the bridge of ten thousand generations]?" and leaped up from her seat with victorious delight. Tōru hugged Nuiko joyfully.

He pleaded, "Even when I'm completely beaten down and at wit's end, you need to encourage me to keep on with the struggle and remain my strong and supportive wife and comrade. If the time ever comes when I'm not around anymore, you'll have to take care of this whole game for me and take over all my responsibilities." The day after this speech, Tōru didn't return home. Only a little more than three months had passed since Nuiko had been in Tokyo. That day when Nuiko met Tōru at noon in the Ginza shopping district would be the last time she'd ever see him. Nuiko remembered the whole scene as being very festive and fun. They met in the toy department of a big store and as he handed her a prepared package he said, "How about buying a doll; there sure are some nice ones here." Tōru pointed to a doll called Okichi that was surrounded by French dolls and was wearing a price tag around its neck. "Thanks, but maybe next time, OK?" Nuiko responded kindly. Then Tōru, continuing to pretend to be a businessman, kicked in with "When I get my next bonus, I'll get you one . . ." and they giggled together.

But when it came time for their usual three o'clock meeting that same afternoon, Tōru didn't show up. Following the time on the big clock of the subway store at Sudachō, Nuiko waited there while watching the clock so intently it hurt her eyes. The second hand went around ten times and then twenty times, carrying its precise circle to the window of the second floor from its position above the first. She thought that something must have happened to him, so she returned home, trying to hope for the best. But once she got home she became increasingly certain that something bad did happen. While she was home the clock struck nine and then ten o'clock. Although it was in the middle of the hottest summer season, a shock of intense cold rushed to her head and ran all through her body. Midnight brought a strange calm to her and Nuiko (in preparation for a police raid on their place), as she had been instructed in the case of such an eventuality, brought all of Tōru's documents by taxi to a comrade's house in Hongô, traveling through the deserted midnight streets.

When she checked to see if he had returned the next morning, Tōru wasn't back. That day Nuiko greeted their suspicious land-lady with a detached "Thank you for your kindness," but as soon as she began folding and putting away Tōru's shirts and clothes, the tears started to flow down her cheeks. Nuiko knew that she had to move immediately from their place above the confectionary store to a safe house or the police would . . . at any time. Her heart was racing, but her physical movements were moving in the opposite direction, becoming slow and heavy. She wanted to preserve their house just as it was when they began their happy life together. Like

149

always, she yearned to be waiting for Tōru to return home to the food she'd laid out on the dinner table. If they had done him in she wanted to go down with him. Finally she got herself together. Before she even realized it, she had moved out of the confectionery store, trudging along pulling all their household possessions on a small bicycle trailer. That was the day Nuiko's arduous life of overwhelming, nomadic poverty began.

One corner of their chess game collapsed; when the knights attacked the king, many pawns had to be used to protect the king, leaving the queen pawnless and vulnerable to an attack. Nuiko's position on the chess game of life became vulnerable just like the queen's, and everything around her started to come apart.

Nuiko had obtained a position in Tōru's department at the left-wing newspaper, but her pay was so low she had to share a place with other women comrades in the movement. But one by one these women—like the pawn in the game of chess—were taken away by the police, so Nuiko had to change her whereabouts constantly and she ended up living with different women comrades all the time. Tōru and these women had lived with Nuiko and protected her while they dealt with all the usual political harassment. Nuiko thought that they protected her for the sole reason that they wanted her to be active in their group and this confirmed time and time again her resolution to . . .

When summer arrived once again this meant it had been one year since Tōru had vanished. Gradually she developed a bold confidence in her political commitments and could even express her principles in front of the senior men in the group. To get a story for their newspaper, Nuiko skillfully learned how to sneak into the railroad company's storage room and gain access to factories—places that were under strict police surveillance. Even with all the political repression surrounding her, she didn't feel particularly heroic. When she was walking on the glittery and festive Ginza, Nuiko no longer held her breath out of fear of being grabbed by the police at any moment, like she had before, when she was there with her lover. Instead, she remembered how Tōru carried himself by telling jokes with his signature "Ha, Ha" laugh as he handed over crucial secret documents. Nuiko learned to be subtle in dealing with problems and was therefore able to hide her real political activities.

Her political work was so complicated that as soon as she finished one street corner meeting she had to head to the next—and as she walked, she often found herself unable to recall whom she was supposed to meet next, or why. It was only when the next guy would appear in front of her that she'd remember who he was and what kind of political business she had with him.

To learn of operating conditions in other areas that were changing minute by minute, whenever she had a spare second Nuiko would dash off to the library. Every day she perused more than twenty local newspapers. The information that she garnered from these papers and the news going around in the group's information network was nothing like what she'd expected it to be when she was back on the farm in Korea—it was much more muddled, deadlocked, and opaque. Moreover, Nuiko realized that each incident from all this information could be explained through a single fundamental cause, similar to the way her difficult life with Mother shared the same underlying explanation as the lives of the poor people in Korea. On top of this, Nuiko realized that almost all lower-class women as one huge group are forced to follow the same miserable path; Mother wasn't the only one forced to deal with awful circumstances. She also learned from experience how best to determine what the most effective tactics were to smash through all the obstacles to liberation from the cruel destiny handed to women.

Nuiko was surprised and disappointed to discover that within the parameters of the class struggle itself—which was supposed to free women, too—lay actual obstacles to women's liberation. Among the men of Nuiko's left-wing group there were some who seemed to have a decent understanding of the gender discrimination against women, at least in their voiced opinions. But in their actual behavior, they were reactionary dinosaurs on the issue, even more backward than ordinary, nonpolitical young boys and bourgeois men in the city. To Nuiko the sexism of the older men was understandable given the transitional historical period that they were all living in; these men remained sexist simply because sexism itself was latent and deep-rooted in the nation-state system in Japan.

Something happened one evening while they were finishing important business at a coffee shop. Nuiko left the male comrades she was with and took the train to a bright, hilly block together with a woman who only a week before had been added to Nuiko's work detail. The woman was transferred to Tokyo after she'd shown lots of promise in her organizing activities at a large factory in Nagoya. She looked barely eighteen or nineteen years old and had a cute round face, with a typical girl's fresh, red cheeks. Even though it was already November she was wearing only a thin, delicate kimono. That night, Nuiko gave the girl her last warm, lined kimono wrapped in a *furoshiki* wrapping cloth.

While they were getting off at their stop, it was obvious that the young woman wanted to see what was in the wrapping cloth Nuiko had given her, so she stared at Nuiko and with a sweet voice said, "Is it OK if I take a look?" and immediately opened the cloth to check out what was inside. She held Nuiko's gift happily and said, "Wow, a kimono; fantastic! If I were still doing lousy factory work I would never own something like this. It's a special reward for my work, huh sister?" As she was saying this she jumped up in the air with glee and dared: "Starting tomorrow, we'll strut proudly down the Ginza with our heads high." She seemed so cute and childish. As they walked along the edge of a ditch Nuiko realized that she was trying to talk to her as a real sister and suggested, "If we get into any trouble, we'll give advice to each other, OK?"

The young woman took her up on this immediately: "Mr. Matsuda is being really nasty to me." Matsuda was the name of a high-ranking man in their political group who belonged to a different cell than Nuiko. According to the young woman's story, she had rented a room from him when she first came from Nagoya, and one night there, he had tried to force himself on her. When she resisted, he threatened her, saying, "Are you trying to put up a fight here? OK, go ahead and make a scene and call somebody for help; put me in jail right now, if you can . . . such betrayal against our political activities." Since it was the middle of the night, there was no chance for the young woman to escape, so after exhausting herself trying to resist, she ended up letting Matsuda do what he wanted. But even after the woman found a different place to live, he still pestered her. When she resisted, he tormented her with jeers like "Why don't you go back home! Girls who are worthless like you should go back to the sticks, because your brain's too damn weak to serve our cause." Finally the woman burst into tears, exclaiming, "It was my own boss . . . and until now there was nothing I could do." Nuiko thought this was terrible and decided to report the incident to the other comrades to banish the guy from the group. But before her appeal was put to the committee, it just so happened that Nuiko was transferred into Matsuda's cell; before long he approached Nuiko sexually as well, but she managed to escape his clutches. When Nuiko was returning home after having fled the sleazy Matsuda's place, her kimono belt was still all untied and her sleeve was ripped. Nuiko suddenly understood why her girls' school teacher in Korea cursed men and made her chart depicting their degenerate trajectory.

Very quickly, though, Matsuda was brought in for a criticism session by their political group's central committee, and the result of this was that he was demoted to the lowest possible rank. Although he was very capable and had lots of talent, because of his lapses as a political person and his weakness in taking advantage of his lower-ranking women comrades the group judged that this behavior was no different from that of a corrupt bourgeois politician; Matsuda was severely reprimanded by the central committee.

When winter arrived Nuiko came down with beriberi and her whole body was saddled with fever. Although she got sick at exactly the time when the group was looking for a house manager for an important officer, she applied for the position anyway. She accepted the cover role of "public wife" for this central committee member and spent many days working, keeping the group's documents and papers in order. Anytime something urgent came up that had to be dealt with and was stressful to her "public husband" she would make tea for him and sit with him sipping it. They were renting a small, cheap house in the suburbs and he would talk about the confusion in the central committee that day. He was responsible for straightening out the problems by the next day and he prepared to do so at the house in the suburbs. To calm his nerves, he would buy new paper for the sliding doors and carefully replace the old paper, gluing sheet by sheet in place—only then would he turn to the task at hand. He was very spiritual, a type Nuiko realized she had never seen before.

At first he loved Nuiko simply as a brother would love a sister; he never put one foot over that line. Two months passed, though, and Nuiko was surprised when she realized she was developing a crush on him. Despite the fact that they'd been sleeping in adjoining rooms for a while, Nuiko's new feelings made it increasingly difficult for her to fall asleep as she felt him breathing peacefully right beside her. Before long, though, Nuiko and this man were at different times arrested by the police in the streets. Coincidentally, Nuiko was grabbed at Sudachō subway store by a man with a thin mustache in the very same place where she had waited for Tōru for what turned out to be their last meeting, but for which he never showed up—he'd already been arrested. On the day Tōru disappeared Nuiko looked up at the big clock on the store building and as she waited tears welled up in her eyes. When she was taken by the police she looked up at that same clock and it said 7:28. Later, while she was under interrogation at a Tokyo police station, she tried real hard not to reveal any information about her public husband. She didn't know where he was being held, but she was told by the police what he had testified: "Nuiko is my wife; she's never been ordered by my group to be my housekeeper." Nuiko understood that her public husband's ultimate strategy was to get her released, so she decided to play along with his plan. Therefore, she went ahead and signed the *tenkō* statement claiming she had refused her left-wing beliefs. Even though she was out of jail, the period of time she would spend behind bars was bad physically for her, and put immense pressure on her psychologically. She had lots of back pain and she thought she might have pleurisy. Since the hottest part of the summer she'd been continually attacked by periods of intense, violent coughing. She looked up at the dark rainy sky from her jail cell's high window and she worried that, if she was defeated by this illness, she would also be defeated emotionally and wouldn't be able to fight political battles ever again.

## CHAPTER TEN

When she gets off the express train at Suwon, Nuiko transfers to a private train that is like a matchbox; this new train line had opened during the time she was in Tokyo. She's been riding on it for two hours straight when she gets off at the end of the line, and then she walks about three kilometers to her farmhouse. She walks about three hundred meters or so and rests; then she walks another five hundred meters and lies down in a meadow. She isn't sure if she has a fever or not, but something's burning all over her body and she desperately wants water. Despite the heat, at times she feels really cold and her legs are shivering. When she gets off at the last stop of the line, the sky is flooded with twilight; the sun has completely set while she was en route home. Relying on a light off in the distance to guide her (probably coming from inside the farmhouse's office), she walks up the slope completely lost in thought. On her way she's obsessed with the hope that Mother is still alive. "Mother sent fake telegrams to Tokyo only to make me return home and take her place as head of the farm," she hopes to herself but rehearsing this a few times makes Nuiko realize that it's in vain. Instead of that, she hopes that her mother is at least hanging on to life in critical condition, because if so, then Nuiko will at least be able to see her alive. Suddenly she feels really homesick for Mother. If Nuiko is able to make it home in time after all, she's sure that she'll throw herself at her mother's bosom and just bawl her eyes out. She hopes that this might bring her mother back to life, after which her condition could possibly improve. Before she realizes it, she's entering her mother's rice field. "Yeah, if I go a little farther there should be a stream coming down from the mountain." Nuiko scurries along, dragging her body. Just as she scoops up some water and drinks it, thinking, "Wow, it's sweet," she starts coughing violently. She's completely bent over by her hacking and coughing and something warm starts coming up from the bottom of her lungs. At the same time as something gets stuck in her mouth, some kind of fish smell goes up her nose. Nuiko panics, "Oh no! I'm spitting up blood," and she quickly tries to gulp it back down her throat. As she's trying to swallow the blood in her mouth, something else is forcing itself up insistently and flooding out her mouth. Even in the darkness, the thick drops of her red-black blood are visible in the mountain stream; Nuiko knows that the blood isn't going to stop.

Although she has no sense of how she's managed to physically walk the whole way and actually locate the house, somehow she makes it and is welcomed into the gathering party for her mother's wake. A casket has already been placed in the house with the boards removed at the top so the dead person's head can be seen. When Nuiko lifts up the covering cloth she immediately glimpses her mother's face—it looks like white wax. Her high nose looks particularly beautiful; she subconsciously feels that people become more beautiful after death. Up to this point she's thought of death for the most part as something awful, but right now it seems utterly gorgeous. Nuiko overhears parts of the conversation the workers' wives are having off to the side: "She had blood in her brain and died suddenly while she was apple picking; she was so worried about Nuiko." Nuiko has some sense that the others are saying "Go ahead and cry; it's time to close the coffin and say goodbye to your mother, so you better have a good cry. This is going to be the last time you'll see the woman who loved you so much." All these words are shooting straight through Nuiko's empty head. She thinks, "OK, OK. But should I cry? Do I want to cry?" But when she finally decides she *does* want to cry, the tears won't come. Even in sitting coffins, in such a tiny space as Mother has, the deceased is forced to sit with her legs all pulled up in a ball. Nuiko blurts out, "Can someone please fix the coffin! My poor mother must be miserable in that thing." Nuiko hears the cops from the station say, "It's already been three days since she's been in that coffin; we'll have to bring her to the crematorium now." Right then, for the first time, Nuiko notices a Korean man crying so hard and for so long that he seems to be shaking everything around her. Over on the opposite side of the coffin Mr. Park is kneeling down beside it and holding his hands together in supplication with his whole body writhing; he's weeping loudly. Someone says, "Wow, this pitiful small man is crying with such a huge, booming voice."

Before she realizes it, Nuiko finds herself walking behind the people carrying the coffin. On the side of the narrow road there are acacia trees lined up forming a kind of fence. A lullaby flows out of a house by the road. The face of a Korean woman with tightly pulled-back hair (who was trying to put her children to sleep on the porch) floats up like a white cloud in the shadow of the moon. Nuiko thinks that this lullaby is the same one she'd learned from the workers' wives and liked to sing to herself every once in a while:

Good little kid, don't cry; when your Mom comes the picked
   flower will be in her hair.
The brewed sake is in the pot and the mashed rice for cakes
   is in her hand.
Lots of chestnuts are in the bag there.
When the wings flap on the rooster drawn on the screen,
Mom will come back.
When the hairy dog boiling in the kettle begins to bark
Mom'll come back.

While Nuiko is listening to that song, she suddenly remembers how when she was a little kid in her house in Fukuoka her
mother held her and tried to make her sleep. Nuiko remembers
how happy she was in Japan when mother appeared while she
was waiting for her in the pampas grass field; Nuiko was so excited she jumped right up into her mother's arms. While having
these reveries Nuiko yells out loud: "Kakashama, Kakashama!"
The white coffin that holds her mother is now being carried by the
men and is shaking on the rocky, rough slope. All of a sudden, the
reality of her mother's death finally hits Nuiko. The coffin turns
the corner out of Nuiko's line of sight as it's carried alongside the
mud wall. When she sees this, she's overwhelmed by a sense of
being abandoned by her mother, and Nuiko calls out again, "Kakashama, Kakashama," and runs up ahead to keep pace with the coffin. While she's running intense emotions are pushing up into her
heart and a cry gushes out of her so loudly that she even surprises
herself. Then Nuiko finally gives herself up completely to her emotions and starts crawling on the ground with her hands and legs
flailing like when she was a small child. She cries and gnashes as
much as she physically can.

When she arrives at the crematorium that has been hastily
readied for her mother's coffin, it is already on the stone stand
to burn, and the people are waiting for Nuiko. Nuiko is handed a
bunch of straw that she sets on fire; then, as she's been instructed,
she uses that to ignite the straw that's already inside the bottom
of the coffin. Quickly, the fire starts to spread little by little. People
who are sitting around in a circle off in the distance drinking
booze invite her, "You've been out here a long time. It's so freezin'
out here; come over here and warm yourself." The fire starts to ig-

nite and crackle around the coffin. Nuiko stands up straight as a pole, completely obsessed with watching the fire. After a few minutes she sees something strange: the coffin is making noises—"Groan, Groan"—as the nailed wooden boards start to shake with the fire. Then the boards flip over backward, splinter into pieces and come crashing down. At the same time all this is happening, mother's leg becomes visible, sticking out of the coffin in the front of the fire. And after her leg sticks out, her arm, followed by her whole body juts out into the fire as if she's alive and just stretching out. The fire is shooting into and burning up Mother's hair; it's igniting with the fat that melts through her skin. When Nuiko sees her mother get up like that in the fire, she thinks she's coming back to life. Nuiko calls "Kakashama" and moves up close to the fire; her mother's eyes and mouth are open. It makes Nuiko think that she's trying to say something to her. Then, something like a shout emanates from her opened eyes, mouth, nose, fingertips, and the tips of her toes. At that point, the fire completely belches up from within her and roars all at once—she's clearly dead. Nuiko thinks that her mother's bones might have expanded because of the temperature of the fire; that's why Mother's body moved like that. Nuiko collapses into a squat on the ground. At last, she notices that the fire surrounds the whole body, which makes a blunt sound and rolls back into the coffin again.

This last visual impression of Mother hits Nuiko with full impact. The image of her as someone who had struggled and fought continually and who had just been incinerated by the flames comes together here at the end. Even after she stopped breathing, it appeared that she stood up in the fire and shouted out to Nuiko, who had also been defeated in political struggle, in life, and finally, defeated by her own body. Nuiko hallucinates that Mother is shouting, "Get up off the ground. Stand up!" Nuiko thinks weakly to herself, "I guess I have to stand up." So she tries to stretch out her legs and shake her hands, and finally forces herself to stand. It takes her a long time to eventually stand up completely erect, but when she does she fixes her gaze directly at the fire that is rising up in flames.

As she's staring at the flames, she's transfixed. The flames roar up violently toward her as if they're going to attack her as well and Nuiko thinks that the spirit alive in the fire is already her mother's.

This spirit is racing frantically from the center of her body trying to save Nuiko just as her mother's body is about to burn up into ashes; doesn't it look like the spirit is trying to ride the flames out to plant itself in Nuiko? Again and again that spirit reroutes the hungry flames toward Nuiko, continuing to attack her and to try to set her on fire. "Come closer; come and ignite me, too! Reignite the flames inside me and give me strength." Nuiko stands frozen right in front of the flames and, in one last attempt to mobilize her weak-kneed, tottering body, she opens her mouth as wide as she can, making a gesture that she's going to try to swallow the flames whole.

## Notes

1   I've translated the Sino-Japanese character compound *tenkō* first as "political conversion into patriotism for Japan" and second as "converted into loving Japan." See my introduction for an elaboration of the issues around this concept.

2   This ellipsis and others throughout the novel are in the original text, either censored by the government (Naimushō) censors or inserted by the author and/or publisher to avoid more drastic censorship by the Interior Ministry.

3   Saigō Takamori (1828–1877) was a legendary samurai leader from Satsuma who helped overthrow the Tokugawa rulers and restore the emperor. When Saigō's plan to invade Korea with decommissioned samurai was rejected by the new Meiji government, he responded by leading the Satsuma rebellion against the government.

4   Akita Ujaku (1883–1962) was a playwright and novelist. After he graduated from Waseda University he began a long life of socialist activism. He later became famous for his acting school.

5   August Bebel (1840–1913) was the founder of German social democracy and an ardent advocate of equal rights for women.

# Conclusion:

# Postcoloniality in Reverse

The massive size of Japanese aid [marked as compensation for Japan's colonial rule of Korea] relative to the North Korean economy . . . raises fears that it will help to sustain the Kim Jong Il regime and finance military modernization.
 —"Japan-North Korea Relations," *U.S. Congressional Report*,
    December 4, 2003

[Japanese colonial imperialism] never became a very important part of the national consciousness . . . [as] there were no Japanese Kiplings, there was little popular mystique about Japanese overlordship and relatively little national self-congratulation. . . . The passing of empire in Japan evokes little trauma and few regrets. It has in fact scarcely been discussed at all. In this a comparison would be drawn with the United States, whose imperialist era was, like that of Japan, a half a century in length, and the contrast would be with England. Like the Americans, and unlike the English, Japanese have not looked back.
 —Marius Jansen, *The Japanese Colonial Empire, 1895–1945*

I returned from three years of dissertation research and part-time language teaching in Tokyo in the summer of 1997 and obtained my first one-year academic appointment the following year at the University of Michigan. As I had been rushing to finish my dissertation on colonial imperialism, there was no spare time to prepare class readings, let alone syllabi. Nonetheless, I was excited about the chance to teach some of the things that were in my thesis, thematics that were inspired to a large extent by the rush of conferences and study groups that I had been fortunate to attend while in Japan. That period of 1994–1997 witnessed the cultural studies boom in Japan. This coincided with the heavily contested intellectual opening offered by the fiftieth anniversary of the end of World War II, an event whose temporality finally produced a body of exciting new work written in Japanese on colonialism and imperialism in East Asia. This new work was filling a huge hole in academic material treating Japan's imperial periphery in Asia,[1] and was also beginning to challenge the ways Japanese print and television media had narrowly framed imperial history through national concerns and Cold War and post–Cold War security interests.

My plan was to gather teaching materials for a class called "Colonial East Asia/Postcolonial Japan," scheduled for the spring term, as well as fiction treating Japan's colonialism and imperialism for "Survey of Modern Japanese Literature and Culture" in the fall. Although I had been warned not to expect to find much, I was confident in the excellent library at Michigan. In turn, colonial and postcolonial thematics were nearly hegemonic in Euro-American humanities departments, and I was sure the recent explosion in interest in East Asia around issues of Japanese colonialism and postcolonialism would have translated into such readings being available in English.

This book is the outcome of my fruitless search for those materials available in English on Japan's colonial imperialism. While the definitive work in English cited above, Mark Peattie and Ramon Meyer's edited *The Japanese Colonial Empire, 1895–1945*, accompanies several solid monographs in the fields of diplomatic history and international relations, texts in English that would thematize some of the ways subjectivity (and the ethnic, sex/gender, and class forms it takes) is produced in and through colonialism were nonexistent. I had stumbled upon something I began to configure as one of the X-files of modern Japanese studies. Like the theme of the popular late-1990s TV show about secret information concerning aliens and freaks hidden by intelligence agencies of the U.S. government, the field of Japanese studies in the English-speaking world had similarly repressed cultural narratives about Japan's colonialism. To rephrase this in terms of recent critical theory, the glaring absence of colonial texts pointed directly to a problem concerning the geopolitics of knowledge production about Japan. In a panic, the "Colonial East Asia/Postcolonial Japan" course was changed to "Topics in Globalization and Postcoloniality in East Asia: Pacific Rim Discourse." But owing equally to some insecurity about my knowledge of the topics covering postwar Japan and to an adamant refusal to reiterate the absence of texts on Japanese colonial imperialism in courses treating Japanese literature and culture, something drastic had to be done. So I spent my entire holiday break feverishly preparing a rough translation of the novel *Document of Flames* (aided in the first, second, and third chapters by Tōyama Sakura). Five weeks does not a complete or even coherent translation make, and I should apologize now to the students and grad students who had to wade through the sludge of typos and fractured clauses that were the testaments to that frantic translating holiday break of 1998. Three semesters later, while teaching in the International Division at Waseda University in Tokyo, I had time to finish a draft translation of *Kannani*, which, I had learned in the interim, was the best-known novel of Japanese colonialism.

Considering the fifty-year taboo against cultural-historical work on colonial imperialism done in Japanese and the absence of materials in English, the x-filing of the cultural studies of Japanese colonial imperialism had apparently occurred in nearly the same way in both Japan and the English-speaking world. There was a mutually reinforcing logic in play here. Embedded deep within the famous Japan-U.S. Security Treaty was a murkier, covert "cultural security" agreement. We know that the official Security Treaty was designed to establish Japan as a solid anticommunist presence for the United States during the Cold War. But who and what was this cultural security agreement protecting, and what was it guarding against? This had to be a very dangerous monster indeed given the fact that so much academic and intellectual energy was expended trying to keep it caged and hidden.

Given this state of affairs, it might be fruitful to ask why *The Japanese Colonial Empire, 1895–1945*, the definitive introduction in English to Japan's colonialism, did not stimulate more interest. It was published in 1984, simultaneous with the boom in colonial and postcolonial studies in Euro-American humanities departments. Surely, some of the wealth of issues and concerns embedded in Yuasa Katsuei's texts—diasporic migration, ethnic hybridity, erotic relations between colonizers and colonized, the violence and ambivalence surrounding instances of assimilation, transnational identifications and desires, the problems facing second-generation *nisei* Japanese living abroad, in short, many of the issues that have come to define a canon of sorts for postcolonial studies—could have found an early voice in *The Japanese Colonial Empire, 1895–1945.* We might also expect to find some rendering of the pluralist innovations in colonial governance that were a feature of Japan's imperialism until 1940, innovations that might be said to have preceded, or at least be usefully compared to, modes of governance in other multiethnic societies. At the very least, it seemed obvious to some younger scholars working in the field in the mid-1990s that to a great extent the multinational contours of Japan's colonial imperialism demanded that the claustrophobic, cultural-national focus on "Japaneseness" (Nihonshugi) that has characterized Japanese studies both in Japan and in the English-speaking world be suspended or even displaced by work on colonialism and postcolonialism. When I realized that my students in "Survey of Modern Japanese Literature and Culture" would need to consult it as an introduction to the assigned Yuasa novel *Document of Flames*, I was assuming many of these problematics would find a voice in *The Japanese Colonial Empire, 1895–1945.*

With the exception of Peter Duus's solid introduction to various economic aspects of Japan's colonialism, the first five essays (including the introduction and "Origins and Meanings of Japan's Colonial Empire") belong to only two authors, Marius Jansen and Mark Peattie, both powerful and important figures in U.S. East Asian studies for decades. Peattie's fifty-page introduction is without a doubt the most well-known and authoritative rendering of Japan's colonialism in any language. Cheered by the cheekiness of Hayden White (one of my professors at UC Santa Cruz), who often responded to questions about coverage of a certain text with, "Have I read it? Are you kidding? I haven't even *taught* it yet!," I assigned Peattie along with *Document of Flames* for the week of lectures I'd devoted to "Colonial Cultural Production." I found time only to read the introduction the weekend before. I was at first disappointed to find addressed there almost none of the issues and concerns of Japan's colonial imperialism I had planned to introduce to students. After a second, more nervously vigilant reading, I was stunned to register that it in fact contravened some of the themes I had scheduled for lecture and discussion.

The essay begins its central argument with a section titled "The Japanese Colonial Empire as an Anomaly." After casually dismissing Marxist/Leninist emphases on capital and social class as determinants of colonial imperialism, Peattie glosses the causal factors of Japan's advance into Asia in the following way: "In any event, after pondering the relative importance of the various drives and motivations which have been ascribed to the origins of the Japanese colonial empire, I am compelled to agree with the late William Lockwood when he wrote, over a quarter century ago: 'The quest for empire in East Asia was impelled by no single motive except as most Japanese were indoctrinated in varying degrees with a mystical faith in the Imperial Destiny'" (12). Peattie quickly expands on this surprising and totalizing reduction of the reasons for Japan's colonial imperialism as the culturally exceptionalist, irrational "indoctrination" of the emperor system. According to Peattie,

Historical circumstance and geographical location also had much to do with the inherently inconsistent Japanese attitudes toward empire in general and to their own in particular. On the one hand, the Japanese empire resembled its European counterparts in that its authority was based on an assumption of the superiority of the colonial rulers over their subject peoples. Yet, in part, this assumption also derived from credos that were uniquely Japanese. These included Japanese beliefs in the mythic origins of the Japanese race, the divine creation and inherent virtue of the Japanese Imperial House, and the mystical link between the emperor and his people. The relative isolation of the country throughout most of its history . . . had in centuries past prevented these beliefs of racial uniqueness from being transmogrified into a theory of racial supremacy. But a few decades of expanding dominion over neighboring Asian peoples, reinforced by notions of Social Darwinism, inevitably released the virus of racial assertiveness into the Japanese ideological bloodstream and quickened the Japanese sense of superiority to the rest of Asia. (13)

Mark Peattie is a serious scholar of modern Japanese history and is well read in Japanese colonial policy. Nevertheless, here he has trotted out as the central explanandum for Japanese colonialism the threadbare and racialized cliché of Japanese uniqueness and superiority, clichés that North Americans were "indoctrinated" with as World War II propaganda deployed against Japan. Unfortunately, these racialized codes from World War II have served other, more academic purposes, as this archive of wartime propaganda has been deftly transformed into "objective" history. Still, Peattie cannot just dismiss an issue that was ubiquitous in Japanese colonial discourse and was something that the majority of literate Japanese, Korean, Taiwanese, and Chinese believed up until the end of World War II: East Asians for the most part possess a shared ethnological and cultural history within the imperial Chinese regional sphere. It needs to be stated as emphatically as possible that this shared history was both scientifically accepted fact *and* something that was deployed (by officials who subscribed to the scientificity of it) instrumentally to advance the transforming operations of Japan's colonial imperialism. Peattie depicts this in the following way only *after* foregrounding the hoary clichés about Japanese premodern belief in the divinity of the emperor and Japanese uniqueness: "And yet, the Asian provenance of the empire meant that its two largest colonies, Taiwan and Korea, contained peoples not utterly alien to their conquerors in race and cultural tradition. It was the conflicting Japanese perceptions of this basic ambiguity which *clouded the purposes and policies* of Japan's social transformation of the empire" (39; my emphasis).

In other words, the basic ambiguity between the overwhelming sense of Japanese racial superiority on the one hand and the fact of racial and cultural similarity in East Asia on the other "clouded" "Japan's purposes and policies." And what were those? Well, Peattie has already claimed that the main cause of and purpose for Japanese colonialism was that gullible Japanese (along with Taiwanese, Koreans, Okinawans, and Manchurians) were to be indoctrinated and therefore duped by premodern irrationalities like the divinity of the emperor. And how about the policies? What would *real* history look like if the clouds were lifted from Japan's colonial-imperial policies and the masks forcibly removed from duplicitous and "two-faced" Japanese colonial policymakers? "This essay and others in this volume have stressed national interest and the modernizing experience of the metropole as central to the shaping of Japanese colonial policy" (35). In other words, Peattie states clearly that colonial-imperial policy was *really* about Japanese national interests and modernization imperatives. All the rest of it—Euro-American colonialism out of Asia, universal East-Asian civilization, and so on—were clouds that both shielded the insistent rising sun of Japanese uniqueness and rained on the parade of the modernizing dynamic of Japanese nationalism proper.

This narrow focus on Japanese nationalism filtered through the axiomatic laws of modernization theory (efficient state bureaucracies, capitalist markets and division of labor, homogeneous ethnoracial identity, monocultural nationalism, etc.) as the policy causality for imperialism impels Peattie in his next essay, "Attitudes towards Colonialism," to make several counterfactual claims. After introducing the important Japanese colonial-imperial program code borrowed from imperial China of *isshi dō-jin* (impartiality and equal favor), Peattie states the following:

> Despite the rhetoric of *isshi dōjin*, of course, the actual environment of Japanese colonialism was hostile to any true merger of the Japanese with their dependent peoples on the basis of familiarity or mutual respect. *Active Japanese discouragement of racial intermarriage and the isolation of colonial Japanese in their tight and exclusive urban communities hardly contributed to easy intercourse between the races.* Their feelings of superiority, their jealous grip on privilege and position, were insurmountable barriers . . . and mocked Japanese assertions of the historic capacity of their race to assimilate foreign peoples. (98; my emphasis)

Readers who have seen the popular 1987 film *The Last Emperor* and who will rewind to chapter 5 of *Kannani* (where Ryūji's school principal urges young Japanese men to be "heroes" and marry Koreans) and to my discussion of intermarriage between colonizers and colonized in the introduction to this book will notice a huge discrepancy between this information and what is claimed by Peattie as objective history. Moreover, Peattie's racialized cliché about snobbish colonial Japanese living in isolation "in their tight and exclusive urban communities" is contradicted in almost every chapter of *Kannani* and *Document of Flames*. What is astounding here is that Peattie, in a sincerely generous and expansive moment at the end of his introduction, when he suggests future research areas to be pursued in Japanese colonial imperialism, admits that he has no idea how colonizer Japanese lived and their daily life practices in any "actual environment." "The human dimension to Japanese colonialism will not be as easily traced as the other problems we have touched upon. As yet, it lies fragmented, we suspect in the biographical data provided in individual colonial surveys; in the files of such colonial newspapers as have survived the ravages of war. . . . Yet, in seeking it out, scholars might not only move beyond the limiting perspective of 'forces' in the evolution of Japanese colonialism, *but will abandon the stereotypical image of Japanese in the empire*" (52; my emphasis).

It is crucial to ask why a respected senior historian of modern Japan did not himself "abandon the stereotypical image." Instead of taking a serious, impartial look at significant parts of the historical record, Peattie chose to reproduce the stereotype, and in so doing brushed aside the abstract complex of determinations that need to be figured into a full understanding of this historical period.[2] The impression one is left with after reading Peattie's first two essays is that it does not matter much what the historical record says, as it is repeatedly overwritten by the racialized, wartime clichés about the deviousness of Japanese power and the "underdeveloped," weak minds of its collaborators—what I would call the propaganda archive. It also might not matter that old and new scholarship in Japan has taken seriously the contradiction first expressed in the 1950s between a Japanized emperor system and a pan-Asian collectivity. This is reiterated in the now standard colonial and postcolonial wisdom established by the mid-1990s as articulated by cultural and intellectual historians like Oguma Eiji and Naoki Sakai, which identifies a "double bind" of imperialism-nationalism as the formative contradiction of the period. Peattie's insistence is that the answer to all the questions and interrogations of Japan's colonial imperialism can only ever be One, with the inseparable flip sides of the same long-playing greatest hit record: renationalized history of Japanese modernization (A side) and snobbish Japanese uniqueness and ethnoracial homogeneity (B side).

I do not mean to blame Dr. Peattie as an individual. As I tried to foreground in the introduction, individuals themselves do not say anything; discourse and genre ideology alone speak. Nevertheless, every act of speech or writing transforms ever so slightly the discursive-ideological parameters within which we are positioned to express certain things and not others. This discussion would be incomplete if we did not ask why Peattie was incapable of granting importance to the double bind that was central to Japan's colonial imperialism, dismissing it instead as the mask and cloud camouflage behind which lay the "truth" of Japanese racial superiority and national modernization. The simple reason is that the genre of modernization historiography as produced in the United States in the 1950s through the 1980s thoroughly forbade this. That discourse of modernization posits cultural-national answers a priori to all questions about what was objectively a multinational and pluralist imperialism.

Student readers might draw on things they have learned in classes on race and ethnicity for some insights into the ways double binds or contradictions function in nominally pluralist power structures; there is nothing exceptional or "anomalous" about them at all. For example, it is obvious that a double bind analogous with Japan's imperialism-nationalism continues to generate privilege for white men within the ethnoracial hierarchy of U.S. pluralism, or similarly, generates universal authority to the United States within the nominally pluralist system of global governance in today's world.

As in the introduction, my intention here is to try to reconfigure questions so as to directly interrogate the conditions of knowledge production about Japan. Despite two excellent history books that feature an enviable erudition, Mark Peattie repressed questions like these in the name of particularizing and fixing Japan so as to mark it as deviant, exceptional, and particular with respect to the presupposed normative universality of the United States. This is what the discursive regulations of U.S. modernization theory—the overpowering lens through which Japan and other non-Euro-American sites have been visualized and appre-

hended in the humanities and social sciences after World War II—
"indoctrinates" and scripts for many analysts of Japan.

My argument here, which is channeling with a twist the axi-
oms of critical area studies, can be buffered by looking at what
Marius Jansen (one of the central figures of modernization history of Japan) claims about Japan's colonial imperialism in his contribution to *The Japanese Colonial Empire, 1895–1945* (my second
epigraph). Jansen's essay is structured by what rhetorical theory
calls a "metalepsis," which is normally understood as a reversal
of cause and effect. His justification for the lack of importance
given to Japan's colonial-imperial history is that since World War II
no one has paid any attention to it all: "The passing of empire in
Japan evokes little trauma and few regrets. It has in fact scarcely
been discussed at all" (76). Jansen's insistence that the "effects"
of Japan's colonial imperialism are absent in post–World War II
Japan impels him to claim that it could not have been important as
a "cause" for anything either. In fact, Jansen goes to some length
to explain that although no one was really in favor of colonial imperialism, no one was actively opposed to it either. *Truth* be told, it
wasn't much of a "national" concern. As this statement contradicts
much of leftist and liberal scholarship produced in Japan during
the first two decades after World War II, Jansen's opponents in this
essay appear right at the beginning, where he dismisses as mis-
guided and inappropriate the "postwar discussions of the origins
of Meiji imperialism . . . that are usually set in terms of condem-
nation and regret" (61). Against critical historians like Irokawa
Daikichi, Jansen proceeds to explain how colonial imperialism is
a natural—even biological—stage of any powerful modernizing
country. Therefore, why apologize for it? Or even try to historically
understand it?

Over and against the unnecessary hand-wringing vis-à-vis the
past, the fact that colonial imperialism largely disappeared as a
topic of serious public and academic debate in postwar Japan is
a commendable thing for Jansen: "Like the Americans, and unlike the English, Japanese have not looked back" (76). This is a
complicitous endorsement of the right-wing historical revisionism and denial of colonial imperialism that was taking place inside
Japan at the time that statement was made in the early 1980s. The
constant support and underwriting by U.S.-based, modernization-

inflected Japan scholars like Jansen and Peattie of right-wing nationalism inside Japan encouraged a new species of historical revisionism that surfaced in the mid-1990s in the form of the Society for History Textbook Reform. Not unlike the backlash against the Smithsonian *Enola Gay* exhibit in the United States, this neonationalism was a response to the provocative and exciting postcolonial "looking back" in the mid- to late 1990s. Here, in the early 1980s, Jansen applauds Japan for "not looking back" (at the two hundred thousand sex slaves/comfort women? at more than ten million East Asians killed in Japan's imperial wars?). Jansen sees the fact that historical debate on Japan's colonial-imperial past has subsided and historical memory has been repressed as an unequivocally positive contribution to the modernizing dynamo of post–World War II Japanese capitalism. "The even tenor of policy and growth in postwar Japan owes much to the absence of . . . sources for divisive arguments" (79). It is worth recalling that this is a professional *historian* and distinguished Princeton University professor who is downplaying the importance of or even need for historical reflection.

In their essays, Jansen and Peattie seem most anxious to demonstrate how "anomalous," exceptional, and particular colonialism was in East Asia—really just a temporary deviation from the proper path of homogeneous national culture and the modernizing State. Jansen's throwaway line that there were "no Japanese Kiplings" installs Europe as a universal standard represented by the English novelist Rudyard Kipling, against which Japan is judged as particular because it is "lacking" a similar figure. Peattie does something similar in his brief discussion of the deviant ways in which decolonization occurred in East Asia:

> The transfer of power from colonizer to colonized, unlike most Western de-colonization in the post-war era, came not as a gift bestowed by a gracefully departing colonial officialdom amid independence ceremonies marked by sentiments of mutual confidence and respect, but decreed by triumphant enemies of the colonial power . . . and received by peoples bitterly resentful of their recent colonial past. . . .
> [To the contrary] the ethos of Japanese colonialism bequeathed no legacy of cultural deference nor forged any bonds of mutual

affection. What did remain behind after the colonial rulers had departed were the standards of success set by Japan in meeting the challenge of modernity . . . provoking among its colonial peoples an appreciation . . . of Japanese organization, diligence, and competitiveness. (126–27)

I argue that what I am calling postcoloniality in reverse— the fabricated inversion assigned to East Asia of the normalized Euro-American trajectory of globalized multiculturalism—has been consolidated with reference to Japan's colonial imperialism through two mutually reinforcing logics. The first is the requirement for scholars in the United States to naturally position the United States as the site of universality, an achieved multicultural and multiracial society that contains the most enlightened contents of market capitalism and political pluralism: a new and utopian empire. The second is that, to muster evidence to demonstrate the uniqueness and superiority of the United States, all other places need to be shown to be lacking and deficient with respect to the presupposed universal model of the United States. In the case of Japan, this happens through an insistent repression and x-filing of the colonial-imperial and pluralist half of the double bind of East Asian history beginning in 1895 and consequent emphasis on only half the picture of cultural nationalism: Japaneseness.

Instead of an ethical interrogation of history, this production of postcoloniality in reverse denies any and all elements that interfere with a narrative of homogenized Japaneseness, like the pre– World War II facts of multiethnic policies, mixed marriages, and transnational and transcultural politics and poetics and the post– World War II facts of Korean residents of Japan and a postcolonial relation with North Korea.[3] To understand more fully how postcoloniality in reverse was consolidated, we have to shuttle back and forth between events in Japan and the United States, where the script for post–World War II empire was mainly written and where new regulations for what counts as universal and normative were pronounced.

The different meanings "postcoloniality" has taken on have expanded dramatically in the past two decades until it is almost

indistinguishable from "multiculturalism" itself.[4] In the introduction I offered a definition of postcoloniality as a historical
process that foregrounds the various movements of bodies and
codes from the decolonized peripheries into the pluralized and
hybridized imperial centers (London, Paris, New York; but *not*, in
most readings, Tokyo).[5] Postcoloniality is said to have transformed
the narrow national and monocultural spaces of the former imperial centers into transnational and transcultural ones, where
polyglot creolization is the new cultural dominant. Moreover, con-
comitant with the different modes of this creole hybridization
are new struggles for justice and equality around issues directly
concerning the material effects of postcoloniality: immigration
rights, citizenship for postcolonial peoples, justice for labor migration, and the whole panoply of antiracist and feminist politics.
Progressive postcolonial politics and poetics relentlessly critique
the self-congratulating "multiculturalism" of pluralist democra-
cies in the global North by pointing out that the ethnoracial hierarchies of these societies look very similar to the hierarchies characteristic of *colonial* discrimination and ethnoracial superiority.
In other words, postcolonial criticism often tries to demonstrate
how the violence of colonial domination is not something safely
confined to the past. Through the modalities in which colonialism was "overcome" by postcolonialism, colonial pasts are inserted into the matrix of contemporary social experience, carrying with them the whole structure of colonial domination as well
as anticolonial capacities for resistance and insubordination. It
should go without saying that this understanding of postcolonial politics and poetics as continuing a militant anticolonialism
on the new terrain of democratic pluralism is a long way indeed
from Mark Peattie's paternalistic understanding of postcolonial
freedom as a "gift" graciously bestowed from the white colonial
masters to the colonized slaves, a gift whose gentleman's agreement calls for the debt of "cultural deference." Cultural deference
is anathema to a postcolonial politics that understands that the
struggle for an ethical historical accounting of colonial imperialism's *past* violences is continuous with the struggle in the *present*
for justice against a plethora of ethnoracial, gender, national, and
class discriminations.

There are many elements we could introduce as constitutive

for the regime of postcoloniality in reverse,[6] for example, the various decisions made during the U.S. Occupation of Japan (including not to prosecute the Japanese emperor as a war criminal) that were intended to establish Japan as what Kang Sangjung calls the "junior partner" of the United States and capitalist "beachhead" against communism in Asia,[7] or the designation of Japan as an export platform to feed the voracious demands of the U.S. military during the decades of imperialist war in East and Southeast Asia. But I have chosen to look at three. The first addresses some of the ways Japanese culture was fetishized and fixed in the English-speaking world during the 1950s. The second is the controversy surrounding the production of a new history textbook for Japanese students in 2000 and 2001. The third briefly describes how postcoloniality in reverse operates in contemporary Hollywood depictions of modern Japanese history.

To get at the overdetermined structure of postcoloniality in reverse—how there are not just one or two causal factors but an abstract complex of them—I employ the metaphor of a screen, or framed event. "Screen" should be understood here as that which simultaneously projects something and "screens off" other things from a phenomenological field. Similar to the way television network news acts as a hypertext with several distinct screens containing different images within the same televisual frame, we can only approach the multicausality of postcoloniality in reverse while looking at several different historical screens at once. The first screen borrows a methodology from postcolonial literary criticism to show how the construction of the canon of Japanese literature through an exclusively cultural-national frame was one of the central catalysts leading to the deletion and forgetting of Japan's colonial imperialism.[8] This made it impossible for transnational writers based in Korea, such as Yuasa Katsuei, to be included, as the canon of Japanese literature functioned (and in many cases, still functions) as a policing mechanism that secured the homogenized borders of Japanese culture against hybrid and postcolonial contaminants.

In September 1955 one of the most influential scholars of Japanese literary culture, University of Michigan professor Edward Seidensticker, wrote a well-received article on Japanese literature and culture in a special supplement of the *Atlantic Monthly*.[9] This was the first major introduction of Japan to a high-brow English-reading audience in the United States and First World.[10] Seidensticker studied Japanese at the U.S. Navy Language School at UC Berkeley before serving in the U.S. military during the Pacific War, and his holistic image of Japan was formed and indoctrinated by the wartime needs of U.S. propaganda to construct the "Japanese enemy" as simplistically as possible.[11] He begins his essay with a sharp dismissal of many popular authors in Japan, accusing them of rejecting their cultural traditions and being obsessed with the "West."[12] As his essay is surrounded by those of left-wing Japanese critics and completely opposes them, he feels compelled to justify his stance: "The modern Japanese intellectual, however perceptive a critic he is, tends to be so dissatisfied with what is old-fashioned in his culture that he seems less interested in his literature as such than in attempts to change it, less interested in good authors than in good rebels" (168).

The Japanese writers Seidensticker proceeds to discuss and introduce to the world are Natsume Soseki, Nagai Kafū, Tanizaki Jun'ichirō, and Kawabata Yasunari, who are all recognized today as canonical modern Japanese writers, thanks in part to Seidensticker and modernization theory. All four are categorized as members of a "conservative tradition," authors who at one time were fascinated with the West but eventually returned to their own indigenous culture. Seidensticker's commentary is symptomatic of his modernization theory-inflected culturalism: "Natsume Soseki is deeply Oriental in his intellectual attitudes. Tanizaki is perhaps even more deeply Oriental, or more peculiarly Japanese, in his rejection of the intellect . . . he seldom allows an idea to trouble his novels . . . Kawabata, unlike the others, was never intoxicated with the West . . . but like Tanizaki, he is indifferent to the problems of the day" (169).

Seidensticker concludes his essay with the main criteria for "good" Japanese literature. First, the work must be isomorphic with and immanent to "Japanese tradition," understood here as an unbroken continuum lasting two thousand years and grounded by cultural and ethnoracial purity. Second, a good Japanese writer must refrain from intellectual thought tout court and, instead, should string together ephemeral, aestheticized images as if he (women are rarely mentioned by these U.S.-based Japanese literature scholars) were painting Zen landscapes. Although there are many things that could be said about this passage, what I want to highlight in this U.S. scholar's comments is what has been called a "boomerang effect" operating between the reconsolidated poles of the "Orient" (almost immediately represented by Japan) and the "West."[13] In other words, although the Japanese cultural nationalist writers were once in thrall to Western literary genres and techniques, their mimetic desire proved to be fruitless and they all eventually retreated into their "native" habitat. The strong implication is that their capacity to imitate modernist writers like James Joyce and Marcel Proust—what Gayatri Spivak calls "Euro-teleological"—was constrained and then doomed by their raciological identity as "deep Orientals."[14] The inevitable boomerang return to their proper racial determination brings with it the thorough rejection of rational, intellectual thought—presupposed by Seidensticker as Western—and the sense of artistic contentment that follows from the inevitable acceptance of their own raciocultural identities.

Within the historical parameters of the boomerang effect it is logical that the first two Japanese novels translated into English after World War II tell identical stories of two Japanese men who have discovered the peace and harmony of "traditional Japanese culture" after being first fascinated then disillusioned with Westernized Tokyo in Tanizaki's *Some Prefer Nettles* and in the case of a return from war in Osaragi Jirō's *Homecoming*.[15] The first English-language review of a Japanese novel published after World War II discussed *Homecoming* and was published in the *New York Times Book Review* on January 16, 1955. The review, called "The Past Is Nowhere," was written by scholar of Japan Dr. Seuss (more famous for his popular children's books, such as *The Cat in the Hat* and *How the Grinch Stole Christmas*). He boldly spells out the political stakes for the new reification of what he calls "Japanese cultural tradition" in both the United States and Japan: "On both sides of the Pacific, this simple event is being hailed as of real international importance, and political more than literary. The people praising the loudest are the groups of Americans and Japanese who have been working together, ever since the war, to promote a healthier exchange of ideas. They feel very strongly that unless we and the Japanese learn to see eye to eye the Japanese may learn to see eye to eye with the Russians."[16]

As both Seidensticker and Dr. Seuss confidently assume responsibility for the intellectual work of global reorganization (remember, Japanese male writers are better off not letting any intellectual ideas "trouble" their novels or interfere with the direct transcription of Japanese nature-culture) under the expressed sign of the Cold War, let us just pause and see what kind of ordering is called for in these texts. First, there is the recoding and reconfiguring of the common understanding of culture away from the previous understanding of it in the philosophical and anthropological modernity of Marx and Durkheim (i.e., that culture is that which must break away from nature and arrange nature intellectually and materially for the ends of an enlightened and rational society). The organicist notion of culture that became hegemonic in the United States in the Cold War humanities and modernization social sciences in the 1950s is actually conflated with nature. Following from this conflation of culture and nature is the raciologized metonymy, such as "Tanizaki is perhaps even more deeply Oriental, or more peculiarly Japanese," where the writer Tanizaki is asked to stand in first for the whole of the Orient, and then for a particularized Japaneseness. When we map this onto the ahistorical rendering of "Japanese tradition," it leaves us with the sense of a continuity of purified and homogenized cultural practices in the Japanese archipelago, curiously and conveniently severed from the Asian mainland. As most scholarship before this period had assumed a strong historicocultural movement and mixing of bodies and texts back and forth between China, Korea, Southeast Asia, and Japan, the way Asia is displaced in these texts is nothing but the software of U.S. Cold War ideology dutifully installed by its loyal modernization theory proponents. Intent on marginalizing communist China and emphasizing the unique *difference* of Japan from the Asian mainland, Seidensticker, Peattie, Jansen, and Dr. Seuss must be seen here as the modernization *Grinches*

*Who Stole Ethnicity* from these Japanese writers. In other words, rather than reading the different ethnicities within Japan (Ainu, Buraku, Okinawan, Korean, etc.) as constitutive of coloniality and postcoloniality, the Asian components of "Japanese" ethnicity are forgotten and violently displaced by the *racialization of ethnicity* that wants to place one newly racialized identity (Japaneseness) and culture neatly within the contours of a nation-state (Japan). A direct effect of this reverse postcolonial magic trick will be the massive disavowal and coerced forgetting of Japanese colonialism and militarism in Asia beginning just before the Korean War. Yet another violent effect of postcoloniality in reverse is the ubiquitous ethnic discrimination in Japan against anyone who does not fit the modernization-inspired ethnoracial profile and profiling of "the Japanese."[17]

## Screen Two

In June 2001 Japan's Ministry of Education approved for school districts a controversial junior high textbook on Japanese history. The culmination of the collective work of a group called the Japanese Society for History Textbook Reform (Atarashii Rekishi Kyōkasho o Tsukuru Kai), the text immediately created an international outcry, which itself compelled the Ministry of Education to ask the group to make cosmetic changes to the text.[18] After the changes the text was reapproved and has been available for purchase by local school districts, although by September 1, 2001, it had captured only 15 percent of the market for junior high history books, declining significantly since then.[19]

The Society for History Textbook Reform was organized in September 1996 in reaction against both the rush of historical reflection attendant upon the important fiftieth anniversary of Japan's surrender and the new postcolonial critiques that were gaining some acceptance in the media and academy.[20] The leaders include the notorious right-wing *manga* artist Kobayashi Yoshinori (honorary director), professor of Japanese history at the technical University of Electro-Communications Nishio Kanji, and professor of education at Tokyo University Fujioka Nobukatsu. The fiftieth anniversary of the end of World War II is crucial in configuring the emergence of this response. More particularly, the Japanese neo-nationalist center and right were incensed by a resolution sponsored by the powerful Liberal Democratic Party–led coalition (led temporarily by socialist Prime Minister Murayama Tomoichi) to apologize to "Asian victims of Japan's past aggression" on the anniversary of the war. After it passed in the House of Representatives in June 1995, this unprecedented public admission of some of the truths of Japan's violent colonial-imperial aggression in World War II was ultimately withdrawn. The withdrawal had much to do with the political shift to the neonationalist right, exacerbated by the weakness of Murayama himself, as prominent Cabinet members and influential LDP politicians—some of whom had opposed the resolution from the beginning—reiterated public claims that historical events like the Rape of Nanjing never occurred, that Japan's colonization of Korea was not so much colonization as a mere annexation or *heigō*, and that the comfort women never existed.

This public denial of wartime atrocities and even colonialism by the old and new right, whose public faces became Fujioka and Kobayashi, led to a noticeable turn to the right of the ideological contours of the Ministry of Education, the entity responsible for selecting the textbooks for junior and senior high school. Always eager to downplay Japan's wartime aggression and colonial history, the Ministry built on the hegemonic struggle waged by the right to actively intervene in the content of the history textbooks. The predicament of the comfort women was central here. The issue became unavoidable in the early 1990s when the Japanese government, then headed by Prime Minister Miyazawa, heard the testimonies of fifteen former comfort women in Seoul, which was followed by the surprising admission on August 4, 1993, by Chief Cabinet Secretary Kono Yohei that the Japanese military was "directly and indirectly involved in the establishment and administration of comfort facilities."[21] The most important effect of this was that authors and publishers of history textbooks could now reference this statement by Kono as support for the existence of the comfort women. Therefore, among the seven junior high history books approved in 1993 and 1994, all but one (a right-wing book designed by an LDP think tank) mentioned the comfort women.

By 1997 all seven made some reference to the issue. This led to the concerted backlash by politicians and neonationalist intellectuals and artists, which emboldened the Ministry to issue "guidelines for content" to publishers. By 2002 only one of the seven approved history books mentioned comfort women. Moreover, other controversial issues relating to Japan's colonial-imperial history have been erased as well. In other words, reverse postcolonialists in Japan had successfully responded to the first major attack against them.

This is the political background to the shift to approving the scandalously revisionist history textbook authored by the Society for History Textbook Reform. As six out of the seven other history textbooks had marginalized and deleted significant moments in Japan's colonial-imperial past and were in part revisionist history as well, the new textbook of the Society should not be seen as fundamentally opposed to them. The Society's aggressive media tactics were what singled them out from the other publishers and authors. Although most commentators have assumed that the Society has "lost" because its textbook has not done well commercially, its extreme position has made the other nationalist textbooks look moderate by contrast and has therefore discursively naturalized them as objective history. It is within these shifting ideological parameters and fluid political positions that the intervention of the Society must be configured.

In December 1996 the seven thousand–member group published their Declaration in Japanese newspapers and then, in 1998, globally circulated an English-language pamphlet in an attempt to drum up membership, money, and support.[22] The group's first line of attack in the Declaration consisted of identifying problems with the way Japan's history was represented in Japanese middle and high schools since the end of World War II:

> The problems of history education in this nation have been debated throughout the half-century following Japan's defeat in World War II. The debates notwithstanding, the problems have not been rectified. On the contrary, in recent years, inconsistencies have burgeoned, adding to the confusion surrounding history education. Particularly worthy of our attention are accounts of modern history in middle-school textbooks issued by

seven publishers that describe the years beginning with the Sino-Japanese War and ending with the Russo-Japanese War as an age of Japanese aggression in Asia. Furthermore, these textbooks depict the nation-state formed during the Meiji Restoration as an evil one, and condemn all of Japan's modern history, for that matter, as a succession of criminal acts. (1)

The chair of the Society, Nishio Kanji, has been the clearest about where these "problems" have originated. In a cover letter accompanying the pamphlet, Nishio writes, "Even now, in a world that has undergone dramatic changes such as the fall of the Soviet Union, Japanese history education has been violently distorted by historical views which *originated in foreign countries*, and Japan has not managed to recover the national identity which it lost with its defeat a half century ago. Our goal is to provide a clear spiritual path through the 21st century."[23] Nishio comes close to collapsing the supposed "succession of criminal acts" with the hijacking of the representational sovereignty of Japanese history by "foreign countries." But both in his own and the group's collective work there is the strong insistence that no criminal acts (again, the existence of comfort women and the occurrence of the Rape of Nanjing are the two issues that the Society most vociferously denies) were committed during the controversial period of what he sarcastically dismisses as "Japanese aggression in Asia." In the Declaration the controversial issue of the military comfort women is introduced first as evidentiary dismissal of the charges of criminal acts: "For instance, the widespread adoption of the irresponsible, unsubstantiated argument that the 'military comfort women' were forcibly transported to war zones can be traced to this same perverse, masochistic historical view. This is a prime example of the steady decline of national principles due to the loss of a national historical perception" (1).

Nishio does not stop to pursue this because the growing historical and political awareness of the military comfort women originated *inside* Japan in 1973 and became hegemonic in the early 1990s because of the transnational work of Japanese and Korean feminist activists and former military sex slaves themselves.[24] Nevertheless, similar to the impulse evident in U.S. modernization history, the desire to rehomogenize Japan by projecting all differences of politics and ethnicity outside of the policed boundaries of the homogeneous nation overwhelms any sense of history. The cultural-national vigilantes authoring the Declaration put this in no uncertain terms:

> During the postwar years, the Japanese have allowed two diametrically opposite perceptions of history, which divide the world in two (the United States and the former Soviet Union), to maintain an uneasy coexistence. Accounts in history textbooks are a prime example of the amalgam of these two perceptions. Two historical perceptions, those of nations that were victors in a war against Japan, each of which contradicts the other, and both of which discredit Japan's past history, have coalesced in the minds of Japan's postwar intellectuals. Consequently, Japan has been deprived of a proprietary historical perception. In light of circumstances in East Asia in the aftermath of the Cold War, we dare not allow this situation to continue. (31)

I want to pause here and look at the syntagmatic association of masochism with comfort women in the previous quotation, because this could be read with many other links in the Society's network. The most important of these would be Kobayashi Yoshinori's popular manga on Taiwan, called *A Statement on Taiwan (Taiwanron).*[25] Kobayashi's long illustrated novel narrates his visit to Taiwan in May 2000, when all the Taiwanese he meets love Japan, adore Japanese men like Kobayashi, and thank Japanese colonialists for establishing the modernizing infrastructure that enabled Taiwan to become the economic powerhouse that it is today. Kobayashi repeats the exact language deployed by Mark Peattie and Marius Jansen as justification for Japan's colonial rule —modernization (*kindaika*): the establishment of markets, bureaucracies, and national science and education—and attempts to argue that something implanted during the colonial period he calls the "Japanese spirit" is alive and well in contemporary Taiwan.[26] Furthermore, as he emphasizes in all his manga, postmodern Japanese would do well to revisit this pre–World War II sense of Japanese spirit. In completely whitewashing Japan's fifty-year history of colonial domination of Taiwan ("to liberate Korea, Japan went to war with China and ended up liberating Taiwan as well"; 77) he asks readers to believe that colonized Taiwanese were perfectly happy about being killed serving in Japan's military during World War II. Kobayashi blithely argues that Taiwanese were well aware that their death was fair recompense for the fact that Japan willingly "sacrificed" its own development to further development in Taiwan and Korea.

The astonishing historical revisionism and postcoloniality in reverse evidenced in *A Statement on Taiwan* features the Society's standard denial of Korean and Taiwanese comfort women/sex slaves. Parroting the distinction that the Society has fixated on, between "common prostitutes" and "young women" (*shōjo*), and claiming, infamously, that there were not any comfort women but "mere prostitutes" (*baishunfū*), Kobayashi manages to expand on this misogyny. He argues that it was "common sense" (*atarimae*) from "long ago" in Asia that "prostitutes" (*shōfu*) would go to war fronts because they "could make lots of money there" (108). For Kobayashi, it was just as commonsensical that modern sex workers in East Asia would want to serve the Japanese military because health and hygiene conditions insisted on by Japan were far superior to the conditions in brothels. According to Kobayashi's fallacious assertions, Japanese military policy insisted on perfect hygiene and condom use (109, 230), and prostitutes who worked at comfort stations were granted more "human rights" (*jinken*) than was normally the case; thus, East Asian women were grateful and eager to serve as sex slaves for the Japanese military: it was a "great step up in the world" (*daishusse*) and "success story" for them (231). As several Taiwanese women openly flirt with Kobayashi's character in this text—one hostess even suggesting that when she drinks she "ends up sleeping with Japanese men" (254) —and Japanese soldiers and colonizers are depicted as sexual and strong (not like the "feminized men who grew up in the Japan of post-war democracy"), this allows him to further naturalize the comfort women. In other words, because they were "just prostitutes" and, moreover, were all infatuated with Japanese men, they were actually competing with and stepping all over each other to be comfort women.

It is worth pausing here to decode this tortuous and conflicted logic. Kobayashi is arguing that (1) there were not any comfort women; (2) prostitutes were the only comfort women; and (3) because Taiwanese and Korean women were so obsessed with sexy

Japanese men, these colonized women could hardly wait to be comfort women.[27] As amazing as this is, it is logical when you witness the astonishment among members of the Society to discover that many Asians do not like Japan, and the subsequent disavowal of that dislike or distrust. This disavowal of the living trace of the historical antagonism (Asians do not like us) and what psychoanalytic theory calls a "retroversion" (they really do love us and want to be us!) is very similar to postimperial moments in England and the United States. In other words, "Why do Islamic fundamentalists hate us?" can never be answered with anything approaching historical truth about U.S. covert activity and military support for right-wing dictators worldwide. When it is bounded by cultural-national or "civilizational" determinants, the response must go something like this: They hate us (the performative that creates anew the national community) because they are envious of what we have. In other words, the response exposes the uncovered, ugly symptom of developmental teleology itself. They love us because they *lack* modernization, confident nationalism, human rights, democracy, and so on. It is so obvious that it barely needs to be commented on, but in the Lacanian psychoanalytic sense, this lack that originates in the self and the projection of it onto otherness is essential for self-constitution. The reason for pointing this out here is that I am intent on *not* particularizing and highlighting Japan's exceptional deviance in this formation, but on showing that there are similar moments in other postimperial histories. This is how that logic operates in the last paragraph of the Society for History Textbook Reform's Declaration:

> Each nation has its own perception of history, which differs from those of other nations. It's impossible for nations to share historical perceptions. *Japan has progressed far beyond the early stage of nationalism*, while our Asian neighbors are just arriving, and explosively so, at that point. If we are to make compromises with other Asian nations regarding our perception of history and vice versa, that would amount to an act of submission on the part of Japan. Such an act would only serve to aggravate the symptom that has already presented itself, i.e., the loss of a national history. We would like to reform the concepts that have prevailed throughout the 50 years since World War II by returning to

the basic principles, the true meaning, of history. (31; emphasis added)

Just as the U.S. media identified *jealousy* of U.S. progress on the part of terrorists and people in the global South as the answer to the post-9/11 question "Why do they hate us?" the Society for History Textbook Reform answers the question of why Asians do not like Japanese in a similar fashion: Asians are way behind us Japanese in terms of modern, sociotechnological development and they are jealous of us because of it. Here and in most of the Society's publications, there is always the foregrounding of the insistence that anti-Japanese sentiment has nothing to do with the historical past; Asians are simply envious of how great Japan is.

In basic object relations or Freudian terms, anxiety arises when the subject feels antagonism being directed against it from the outside, sometimes reaching the point where the subject feels that its imagined unity and self-possession are at stake. The subject has various mechanisms for displacing, repressing, or inverting these external antagonisms, such as the reversal of "They hate us" into "They secretly love us and want to become just like us." One of the most common ways of dealing with anxiety is to retreat further into the self and deny the interdependent relation with others in the world. Repressing an imperial-colonial relation with the world and then claiming that history has only been about maintaining sovereignty and homogeneity is something common to postimperial history writing in Japan, the United States, England, and France. A few months before the publication of their Declaration, the group published a "Statement of Founding Principles," which was appended to the Declaration. I finish this section with a quote from the Statement that demonstrates the erasure of colonial-imperial history through the centering of the dynamics of post-coloniality in reverse:

> Like all other nations, Japan has its own history. Since ancient times, our country has developed its own civilization and unique tradition. Throughout its history, Japan had made steady progress, keeping in stride with other advanced civilizations. During the age of imperialism, when Western powers sought to colonize and dominate East Asia, Japan made concerted efforts to maintain its independence, build a modern state, and to coexist har-

moniously with Western nations, drawing on its time-honored traditions. However, this period of history was fraught with difficulties that led to tension and strained relations between Japan and other nations.

For the secure, prosperous lifestyle we enjoy today, we are indebted to the untiring efforts of our ancestors. However, because of the way in which Japanese history has been taught since World War II, our citizens have been deprived of the opportunity to learn about their culture and traditions, and no longer take pride in being Japanese. This phenomenon is particularly evident in the teaching of modern and contemporary history: The Japanese are depicted as criminals on whose shoulders fate has placed the burden of atoning for their sins for generations to come. (32)

Screen Three

On June 29, 2001, there was a gala opening of the Walt Disney Co. film *Pearl Harbor* at the Tokyo Dome in front of thirty thousand screaming fans, most of whom had come to see the hunk Ben Affleck in person. At a press conference the next day called by the Disney Corporation, the director of the film, Michael Bay, producer Jerry Bruckheimer (*Top Gun, Coyote Ugly, Black Hawk Down*), and Affleck read from prepared statements and answered a few questions about the film through interpreters.

At least during the segments covered by Fuji TV, Affleck seemed to be the most garrulous. His introductory comments went like this:

It's an honor to be invited to Tokyo. I'd like to say how it's caused me to reflect on what a wonderful relationship our two countries have now in light of a movie about a war that was fought 60 years ago, in part between the U.S. and Japan. And I'd like to say that we certainly made every attempt to be fair and honest and accurate and to represent the Japanese soldiers and government as having been put in a position where war was inevitable, by the U.S. and the political realities of the time. We hope that the Japanese audience here feels respected and understood.[28]

During his introductory remarks, Bay preempted criticism by firmly stating: "The film wasn't supposed to be a history lesson. We gave the reason why the Japanese wanted to attack us—because we cut off their oil supply." This last line is lifted right from the film, where it is the second line spoken by Japanese military strategist Admiral Yamamoto Isoroku. Bay continued with the amazing statement that as director he wanted to demonstrate to the world "how courageous Japanese soldiers were, how dignified they were. I mean, they were doing something for their country." Bay went on to utter even more pablum directed entirely at stroking and seducing the Japanese domestic market, Hollywood's second largest after the United States.

We could resort to the most banal moral equivalents here by revealing a scenario where the German managers of the Nazi death camps were also "doing something for their country." Instead, as further evidence for postcoloniality in reverse, let us just register what elisions are produced by this scene of shameless salesmanship in Tokyo. The first and most obvious is that the statements from Affleck et al., to say nothing of the film itself, which is even more egregious in this regard, bilateralize the relation between Japan and the United States. The U.S. imperial imagination refuses to conceive of significant geopolitical situations where something is construed as lying outside of its influence and effective manipulation. In other words, the Japanese invasion of China in 1931 (the result of a forty-year interstate battle for regional hegemony) and the press-ganging of Korean, Taiwanese, and Okinawan colonial subjects is erased in the desire to bilateralize the historical relationship between Japan and the United States.

This deletion leads directly to a second. As I suggested in the introduction, among the multiple causes of World War II in Asia related to Japan's stunning string of victories against England, the United States, and Holland was the expressed purpose of ridding Asia of Euro-American colonial power. Although this was the idealistic political half of the mobilizing desire for the famous "advance south" of Japanese military strategy, the other half of the desire to chase out the Euro-American barbarians was the somewhat more cynical need to make Asia safe for Japanese profits and profiteering. This is, of course, very similar to the form in which Disney was trying to make Japan safe for Hollywood profiteering.

But, needless to say, neither of these equally "real" poles is addressed.

Here again, what was a multifaceted historical reality demanding a complex analysis is forcefully elided. But, Michael Bay warns us, *Pearl Harbor* is not a history lesson. Nevertheless, it is a lesson in the disavowal of history, a disavowal necessary to ground the United States serenely at the center of world history. One of the main supports of this grounding has been the need to imagine that no other colonial empire has presented a serious challenge to the United States at the level of pluralism, power, or productivity. Other histories of coloniality and postcoloniality must be reversed and rendered as "clouded" and "confused" stumbling blocks that some countries have regretfully experienced before assuming their proper role as junior partners to the United States and as "modernizing" capitalist states supported by homogenized cultural traditions and consensual political environments of the sort that Professor Jansen applauded in post–World War II Japan. But as readers noticed in the two colonial novels written by Yuasa Katsuei, the "real" history of Japanese colonial imperialism is unrecognizable from the images that both U.S.-based modernization scholars of Japan and right-wing historical revisionists based in Japan have offered. That complicit partnership has tried desperately to impose a narrow, modernization-inflected cultural-national frame onto a messily pluralist, transnational imperialism. This imposition has done plenty of damage in denying or marginalizing historical facts of Japan's colonial imperialism, such as the comfort women and the countless (because nobody with any authority was counting) dead Asians in Japan's imperial wars. But the reversal of the multiethnic and pluralist elements of Japan's colonialism has made invisible the postcolonial effects of Japan's colonialism, evident in the stubborn discrimination against "resident Koreans," Okinawans, and Chinese and Southeast Asian workers that is omnipresent in contemporary Japanese society.

The reversal of postcoloniality in reverse in the name of an enlightened transnational future must necessarily take on many forms and colors. The main impetus for spending several years on the translations in this volume is my conviction that one of the irreversible contributions to the overcoming of postcoloniality in reverse lies in an ethical interrogation of colonial-imperial history and culture. I hope students and scholars will be inspired either through support or hostile disagreement with what has appeared here to fracture and complicate these singular interrogations.

## Notes

1   Leo Ching reminded me that as late as 1993, the editor of the volume concerning cultural aspects of Japan's colonialism in the definitive eight-volume series on Japan's colonialism, *Kindai Nihon to shokuminchi* (Modern Japan and its colonies) (Iwanami, 1993), could state confidently that volume 7, *Bunka no naka shokuminchi* (Culture within colonialism), was "unique because the problematics treating Asia under Japan's colonialism and military occupation have not been investigated from the perspective of culture" (v). Although there had been the occasional work in Japanese treating cultural production within the parameters of colonial imperialism, it is fair to say that colonial imperialism was a structuring absence and taboo within the cultural-national obsession of the humanities in Japanese universities. It is symptomatic that this volume 7 of the Iwanami series on *Modern Japan and Its Colonies* had only one academic among its contributors, all the others being journalists and nonacademic writers. It is important to remember that Okinawa had also been off-limits until cultural anthropologist Tomiyama Ichirō's work established a whole new field inside Japan and out of Okinawa studies during the 1990s.

2   On page 36 he directs readers and students away from the abstractions of "specialized analytic methodology." One can surmise that this meant Marxism and structuralism at the time, but we can arguably assume that this would be updated to apply to postcolonial theory and world systems analyses of global capitalism today.

3   The colonial and postcolonial elements in the present situation with North Korea have been consistently marginalized in the media coverage of the nuclear standoff there. There may be no better place to understand how the erasure of colonial history on the part of Japanese nationalism and U.S. knowledge production of East Asia has contributed to a life-and-death situation. North Korea has been insistent that its defense concerns are directly related to the fact that Japan and the United States repressed its colonial history from 1910 until 1945, thereby denying it reparations as well. Japanese Prime Minister Koizumi went to North Korea for two weeks of negotiations in September 2002 and agreed to a reparations package in recognition of the violence

perpetrated by Japan's colonial imperialism. The package is currently on hold and, evidenced by my first epigraph, the U.S. State Department is strongly opposing it at the present moment—only the latest instance in a long series of post–World War II erasures in the United States of Japan's colonial imperialism in Asia. Japanese readers should consult the splendid "North Korea" issue of *Impaction*, no. 137 (September 2003).

4 See Slavoj Žižek, *Revolution at the Gates* (London: Verso, 2002) and Michael Hardt and Antonio Negri, *Empire* (Cambridge, Mass.: Harvard University Press, 2000).

5 Obviously this must also mean the less celebrated tendency as well, which is the postcolonial and postimperial movement of fixed, finance, and commodity capital from the imperial centers in the global North to the decolonized periphery. This used to be called neocolonialism, subimperialism, and the development of underdevelopment (Latin America, sub-Saharan Africa) and now signifies Empire, capitalist globalization, the neoliberal domination of the global South by the North, and so on.

6 Among the texts that have helped me conceptualize this conclusion, the most important are Komori Yoichi's *Posutokoroniaru* (Postcolonialism) (Iwanami Shoten, 2001); Kang Sangjung, *Futatsu no sengo to Nihon* (Japan and the two postwars) (Sanichi Shoten, 1995); and Kang's *Tōhoku Ajia kyōdō no ie o mesashite* (Locating familial community in northeast Asia) (Heibonsha, 2001).

7 Kang Sangjung, *Ajia no koji de ii no ka?* (Is it OK being the orphan of Asia?) (Wayts, 2003), 36.

8 There are several excellent essays that deal with this topic, including Edward Fowler's "Rendering Worlds, Traversing Cultures: On the Art and Politics of Translating Modern Japanese Fiction," *Journal of Japanese Studies* 18, no. 1 (1992); and Harrison S. Watson's "Ideological Transformation by Translation: *Izu no Odoriko*," *Comparative Literary Studies* 28, no. 3 (1991).

9 Edward Seidensticker, "The Conservative Tradition," *Perspective of Japan*, special supplement to *The Atlantic Monthly* 195 (1955): 168.

10 The year 1955 was also the year of the Bandung conference in Indonesia that installed the Third World as the tertiary and unaligned term in the Cold War recoding of the planet into First Word (represented by the United States) and Second World (represented by the Soviet Union).

11 For the best critical treatment of this process, see H. D. Harootunian, "America's Japan/Japan's America," in *Japan in the World*, ed. Masao Miyoshi and H. D. Harootunian (Durham: Duke University Press, 1993).

12 Along with denying that the Rape of Nanjing ever took place,

right-wing revisionist historians in Japan today often use the same phrasing of "obsession with Western ideas" as Seidensticker to dismiss Japan-based internationalists. See Nishio Kanji, *Kokumin no rekishi* (National history) (Fusōsha, 1999), 680–82.

13   Imagine scare quotes around such terms as "Japanese tradition" and the "West" because these are obviously not substantial entities that preexist their gathering in discourse. Rather, they are precisely structured in and through contemporary geopolitical discussions such as this one.

14   Gayatri Chakravorty Spivak, *A Critique of Postcolonial Reason: Toward a Critique of the Vanishing Present* (Cambridge, Mass.: Harvard University Press, 1999), 153. Paul Gilroy nominates raciology as the logic whereby racial phenotypes were mobilized as the sole explanation for all human endeavor. Raciology's operational matrix undergirded the "dangerous and destructive patterns that were established when the rational absurdity of 'race' was elevated into an essential concept and endowed with a unique power to both determine history and explain its selective unfolding." *Against Race: Imagining Political Culture beyond the Color Line* (Cambridge, Mass.: Harvard University Press, 2000), 14.

15   Tanizaki Jun'ichirō, *Tade kū mushi* (Some prefer nettles), trans. Edward Seidensticker (1929; Knopf, 1955); Osaragi Jirō, *Kikyō* (Homecoming), trans. Brewster Horowitz (1949; Knopf, 1955).

16   Dr. Seuss, "The Past Is Nowhere," *New York Times*, January 16, 1955, sec. 7, pp. 4, 33. Special thanks to Hoyt Long for bringing this piece to my attention. Theodor Seuss Geisel (Dr. Seuss) began his career in cartoons as the main illustrator for the magazine *PM* and gained popularity during World War II with his racialized depictions of Japanese and Germans. Like Ian Buruma and so many others who have come after him, he was militant in his belief that Japan needed to be forcefully instructed in the ways of Western reason and political responsibility. His famous children's cartoon *Horton Hears a Who* (1954) is about a friendly and wise elephant named Horton who hears a tiny, barely audible voice and realizes that the voice emanates from a speck of dust. Gradually, Horton (later, Dr. Seuss conceded that Horton was designed as an allegorical figure for the United States) learns that the speck of dust called a Who represents a whole civilization of tiny beings, what Seuss admitted was the allegorical coding of Japan. Even though the United States pursued an unprecedented strategy of killing civilians and destroying many of Japan's cities by dropping napalm and gas *before Hiroshima and Nagasaki*, Seuss had the temerity to have the mayor of Who-ville, representing "Japan," say this to their U.S. guardian Horton: " 'My friend,' came the voice, 'you're a very fine friend. You've saved all us folks on this dust speck no end. You've saved all our houses, our ceilings and floors. You've saved all our churches and grocery stores.' "

On Dr. Seuss's wartime and postwar cartoons, see the excellent text by Richard H. Minear, *Dr. Seuss Goes to War* (New York: New Press, 1999).

17  There are several excellent works in Japanese that make this point more concretely. See Iyotani Toshio and Sugihara Tōru, eds. *Nihon Shakai to Imin* (Japanese Society and immigration) (Meiseki Shoten, 1996).

18  There have been several controversial periods in post–World War II Japan concerning historical revisionism and censorship under the purview of Japan's Ministry of Education. The immediate predecessor to the recent history textbook controversy occurred in 1981–1982. See Tokutake Takeshi's *Kyōkasho no sengoshi* (The postwar history of textbooks) (Shinnihon Shuppansha, 1995).

19  *Japan Times*, September 3, 2001, 4.

20  In addition to Oguma Eiji's 1995 bestseller *Tanitsu minzoku shinwa no kigen* (The origin of the myth of the homogeneous nation), Tomiyama Ichirō's important *Senjō no Kioku* (Battlefield memories) appeared in 1995.

21  See the excellent essay by Yoshiko Nozaki, "Japanese Politics and the History Textbook Controversy, 1982–2001," *International Journal of Educational Research* 37, nos. 6–7 (2002): 603–22, and J. Victor Koschmann's "National Subjectivity and the Uses of Atonement in the Age of Recession," in *Millennial Japan*, special issue of *South Atlantic Quarterly* 99, no. 4 (fall 2000).

22  Society for History Textbook Reform, *The Restoration of National History: Why Was the Japanese Society for History Textbook Reform Established and What Are Its Goals* (Tokyo, 1998). Citations appear in the text.

23  Cover letter by Nishio Kanji accompanying ibid.; emphasis mine. There are several excellent texts criticizing the Society for History Textbook Reform. Two are Takahashi Testuya, *Rekishi/Shūseishugi* (History/revisionism) (Iwanami Shoten, 2001) and Oguma Eigi and Ueno Yōko, *Iyashi no nashonarizumu* (The cure for nationalism) (Keio Daigaku Shuppankai, 2003).

24  This culminated in the Women's International Tribunal Against Sex Crimes and War held in Tokyo in December 2000, where the Shōwa Emperor Hirohito was judged a war criminal by voice vote.

Women activists refer to the comfort women as "military sex slaves" —worth pointing out because Nishio and the Society are of the opinion that even "military comfort women" is too strong an admission; the Society's position is that the estimated 150,000 to 200,000 women were simply "common prostitutes." Both Nishio Kanji and Fujioka Nobukatsu used the phrase "typical prostitutes" (*futsū no baishunfu*) on the four-hour debate forum called *Asa made nama terebi* (Live, all-nighter TV) of May 25, 2001.

25  Kobayashi Yoshinori, *Taiwanron* (A statement on Taiwan) (Shōgakkan, 2000). For a series of fine readings of this text, see the collection

edited by the East Asian Network of Cultural Studies called *Kobayashi Yoshinori no "Taiwanron" o koete* (Sakuhinsha, 2001).

26  Unfortunately, Kobayashi is not exceptional in seeing himself (as Japanese) in other East and Southeast Asians formerly colonized or militarily occupied by Japan. Many writers and directors involved in the various "Asia booms" in Japanese mass culture during the last fifteen years or so follow the way Kobayashi sees "Japanese spirit" in contemporary Taiwanese and gaze melancholically at hardworking East Asians and—instead of perceiving any actual people in their alterity— see only themselves at an earlier stage of history. This inscription of postcoloniality in reverse is different both from "imperial nostalgia," whose mise-en-scène is the historical past, and from the so-called denial of coevalness depicted in Johannes Fabian's *Time and the Other*. The quality that distinguishes this as postcoloniality in reverse is that many Japanese colonizers by 1935 or so repressed the alterity of East Asians in exactly this way: instead of difference they saw all imperial subjects as real or potential Japanese. Iwai Shunji, the director of the popular 1996 film *Swallowtail Butterfly*, remarked that he wanted to show how the hardworking, hustling Asians trying to make a living in the means streets of Yen Town (Tokyo) in that film exemplified the determined, gritty qualities that formerly characterized Japanese people themselves. A similar dynamic is at work in the popular 1998 travelogue *Asia Road* by Kobayashi Kisei.

27  I have benefited from Song Yun Ok's analysis of Nishio Kanji's depiction of the comfort women at her presentation at the "Women, War, and Human Rights" annual conference at Waseda University on June 24, 2001. Marilyn Ivy uncovers a similar symptom in Kobayashi's *Sensōron*; see her "Revenge and Recapitation in Recessionary Japan," *Millennial Japan*, special issue of *South Atlantic Quarterly* (fall 2000): 819–40.

28  I am quoting and translating directly from my tape of the press conference as carried on the Japanese Fuji FTB station. Some of the comments from the press conference can also be found in *Japan Times*, July 11, 2001, 9.

Yuasa Katsuei (1910–1982)

was a novelist known for his politically controversial writings.

He was born in Japan but was raised in Korea, and in 1945

he repatriated to Japan. Many of his early novels depict

the relationship between Japan and

colonized Korea.


Mark Driscoll is an assistant professor of

Japanese and international studies at the University of

North Carolina, Chapel Hill.

Library of Congress Cataloging-in-Publication Data

Yuasa, Katsue, 1910–1982.

[Kannani. English]

Kannani ; and Document of flames : two Japanese colonial
novels / Yuasa Katsuei; translated and with an introduction
and critical afterword by Mark Driscoll.

p. cm.

Translation of Kannani and Homura no kiroku from Japanese.

Includes bibliographical references.

ISBN 0-8223-3505-0 (cloth : alk. paper)

ISBN 0-8223-3517-4 (pbk. : alk. paper)

1. Korea—History—Japanese occupation, 1910–1945
—Fiction. I. Driscoll, Mark W. (Mark William). II. Yuasa,
Katsue, 1910–1982. Homura no kiroku. English. III. Title:
Document of flames. IV. Title.

PL842.U23K35 2005

895.7′3—dc22      2004028256